A PLUME BOOK

LOST IN THE GARDEN

PHILIP BEARD, author of *Dear Zoe*, is a recovering attorney who still practices law part-time in Pittsburgh, where he lives with his wife and their three daughters. His first novel, *Dear Zoe*, was a Book Sense Pick, a Borders Original Voices Selection, and was chosen by Booklist as one of the ten best first novels of 2005.

Visit the author at www.philipbeard.net

Also by Philip Beard

Dear Zoe

Lost
in the
Garden

A NOVEL

Philip Beard

A PLUME BOOK

PLUME
Published by Penguin Group
Penguin Group (USA) Inc., 375 Hudson Street, New York, New York 10014, U.S.A.
Penguin Group (Canada), 90 Eglinton Avenue East, Suite 700, Toronto, Ontario, Canada M4P 2Y3 (a division of Pearson Penguin Canada Inc.)
Penguin Books Ltd., 80 Strand, London WC2R 0RL, England
Penguin Ireland, 25 St. Stephen's Green, Dublin 2, Ireland (a division of Penguin Books Ltd.)
Penguin Group (Australia), 250 Camberwell Road, Camberwell, Victoria 3124, Australia (a division of Pearson Australia Group Pty. Ltd.)
Penguin Books India Pvt. Ltd., 11 Community Centre, Panchsheel Park, New Delhi – 110 017, India
Penguin Group (NZ), 67 Apollo Drive, Rosedale, North Shore 0745, Auckland, New Zealand (a division of Pearson New Zealand Ltd.)
Penguin Books (South Africa) (Pty.) Ltd., 24 Sturdee Avenue, Rosebank, Johannesburg 2196, South Africa

Penguin Books Ltd., Registered Offices: 80 Strand, London WC2R 0RL, England

Published by Plume, a member of Penguin Group (USA) Inc. Previously published in a Viking edition.

First Plume Printing, June 2007
10 9 8 7 6 5 4 3 2 1

Page 232 constitutes an extension of this copyright page.

 REGISTERED TRADEMARK—MARCA REGISTRADA

CIP data is available.

ISBN 0-670-03759-1 (hc.)
ISBN 978-0-452-28842-3 (pbk.)

Printed in the United States of America

PUBLISHER'S NOTE
This is a work of fiction. Names, characters, places, and incidents are either the product of the author's imagination or are used fictitiously, and any resemblance to actual persons, living or dead, business establishments, events, or locales is entirely coincidental.

For Traci,
in humble recognition that
I totally over-chicked

Men are born for games. Nothing else. Every child knows that play is nobler than work. He knows too that the worth or merit of a game is not inherent in the game itself but rather in the value of that which is put at hazard.

—Cormac McCarthy

Prologue

If you choose books the way I do, you still have a chance to save yourself a few bucks. You are probably standing, feet comfortably spread, before the shelves of the Fiction section of your favorite bookstore. Having made a selection, you've settled onto your dominant side (for me, it is the left) to decide, based on the first page or two, whether this one is worth either the trouble or the cover price. You aren't looking for anything in particular. Even a single word can win you. You once bought a book because the word *macadam* appeared on the first page.

Maybe you picked this slim volume at random, even by mistake, Michael Benedict slipped inconspicuously between Saul Bellow and T. C. Boyle—two writers you already know to be worth your valuable time—and it was only after reading the summary text on the flaps that you realized you had just sat on the equivalent of a literary whoopee cushion. Very polite about it though, despite the momentary embarrassment, closing the book quietly, pulling the Boyle out first to make room for mine. Nice to have met you.

Perhaps, God forbid, the *cover* (and not the spine) was facing out, and you just couldn't help yourself—the bunny ears too illogical, too absurd to resist. I apologize for that. I tried to tell them that such a cover might serve to diminish the real crisis here: the crisis of a family that is, even more than most, on the verge of disintegration. One would think that an author would have at least a modicum of artistic input with regard to an issue as significant as jacket design. One would be wrong.

Let me save you some time. This is not a book that is meant to be bought; it's only a book that needed to be written. Although, to be fair, the fact that I am currently residing, at age forty-five, in my old bedroom at my parents' house has nothing to do with my "need" to record the events of the past months and everything to do with the fact that my wife, Kelly, packed my bag for me and placed it on the front seat of my car with an attitude that said, quite clearly, "Go *to your room.*"

I suppose if you have made it this far you may well have crossed (despite my warnings) that critical divide between browser and buyer, and for that you are entitled to a little personal background. If you are a regular reader of The Wall Street Journal, you may have originally paused upon seeing this book because you thought you recognized my name, a fact that would make my father (whose name you *really* recognized) angry enough to loosen his tie, if only briefly. My father, at age seventy, is still the head money manager of one of the largest offshore macro hedge funds in the world. If that means nothing to you, you are none the worse for it. For my purposes, you need only know he could make more money only by printing it himself, and even then the difference would be negligible. My recent decision to take up temporary residence in my old room, and my mother's decision to *let* me, coincided with my father beginning to introduce himself to others, quite pointedly, as

"Michael Benedict, *Senior*." This new introduction was his way of distancing himself from the son whose life seemed to be in an accelerated meltdown at an age when he himself had been beginning to reinvent the ways in which money is multiplied by those who already have it.

Or, at least, that's my take. My wife and I disagree on the source of my father's silence, his distance. I have always attributed it to disapproval. She insists otherwise. "Your father doesn't even talk to your *mother*, Michael. He's not a communicator. He's just a smart, gentle man living life the only way he knows how—by working *very* hard." But I am stubborn where my father's disfavor is concerned, despite the lack of supporting evidence, and I wear it alongside my love for him, regularly weighing one against the other.

To the unending astonishment of his Wall Street competitors and compatriots, my father has seldom left Pittsburgh since moving here to take his first job with Pittsburgh National Bank in 1957. My mother was a teller in the main downtown branch where the corporate offices were located, and when my father began cashing small checks at her window as if he were on a *per diem*, a great romance was born. He left PNB to open his own asset management firm in 1960, the year I was born, and my mother joined him as his office manager five years later. They still work together, and they still live in the same house that they bought in the tastefully upscale borough of Fox Run at the absolute *bottom* (of course) of the real estate market in 1967. In short, I was born into a world in which the only opportunity I lacked was that of becoming a self-made man, and somehow I have still managed to fuck it up.

Admittedly, being adrift is not a unique experience for me. In college, and even throughout law school, I wanted to be a writer. I spent those years stealing time to write eminently readable but thoroughly unpublishable short stories, several of which featured a troubled but ardent rich kid who was habitually trying to rescue beautiful young strippers and escorts from their sad lives of debauchery by inviting them out to a suburb strikingly similar to Fox Run for a home-cooked meal. Gradually, with the help of countless overly critical, underpublished professors, I convinced myself that writing required a kind of suffering from which my birthright would always protect me—a conclusion, thankfully, that has proved mostly true. "What is *at stake* here?" was my professors' consistent refrain. "Strippers," apparently, was not an acceptable answer.

The only other ambition I ever had was to become a professional golfer. I have been playing passionately since I was ten, and golf has always been the one area of my life where I possess at least a passing ability to live in the present tense. Any sports psychologist will tell you that there is no more important quality in an elite athlete than the ability to block out the past, especially the negative past, and focus solely on the shot, the pass, the pitch that is to be executed right *now*. The instinct to forget is one that I have had since the first time I felt that addicting *click* of the ball coming off the exact center of the clubface and rising, perfect white against perfect blue, into the evening sky. My father was there, having come home immediately after the four-thirty close of the market to begin teaching me the game he was just beginning to teach himself. I know he saw the look on my face because he told me about it years later. He said it was a look of sheer exhilaration that lasted precisely the amount of time it took my ball to travel a hundred yards or so down the fairway. Once it came to rest, he said the look disappeared completely, that I picked up my little junior bag (which still dragged along the grass when it was slung over my shoulder) and began marching purposefully forward, not even looking back at him for approval. It is an attribute that I inherited from him, the one that has made him rich, though he has never been able to move that ability to the golf course, and I have never been able to take it away from there.

I taught Kelly to play when we were dating. She's a more natural athlete than I am and developed a long, fluid swing that made her ponytail jump at impact in time with my own smitten heart. But the year our first daughter was born, she quit, and she has shown no interest in relearning. I had thought she loved it, that we'd play together forever.

"I learned because it was the only way to spend more time with you," she said once.

"What about now?"

"Now I already spend too much time with you."

"Ah."

But she did learn enough about the game to know what a good score is—what separates the pros from the good amateurs—so she was not unprepared to do battle when I went to her with my dream for the Middle Ages. I had been working up to it for months but didn't make my formal plea until immediately after an inspired, intimate celebration of my forty-fifth birthday in early March. I would begin (I proposed, in the irrational exuberance of post-coital flush) spending all of my free time working on my game with the goal of making the PGA Senior Tour when I turned fifty. We had accumulated a modest nest egg that would permit me (or so I argued) to scale back on my hours at the office and still spend plenty of time with our two girls (Megan, fourteen, and Hannah, eight). And besides, by the time I turned fifty, Megan would be in college and Hannah, like Megan now, wouldn't want anything to do with either of us. "Just think," I told her, sounding like a recruiting commercial for the armed services, "you could see the world while I do something I really enjoy for a change."

My wife is five years my junior and no less beautiful at forty than she was at twenty-five. She sat up on her elbow and regarded me with what appeared to be amusement, a reaction I hadn't expected after my command birthday performance.

"What's your best score ever?" is what she said.

What I said, reeling from the utter perfection of her question, was: "Ever?"

"Yeah. Ever. You know. Like from the beginning of time up until your forty-fifth birthday." She was sensing her advantage and let the sheet slide off her shoulder. She knows I can't concentrate when her clavicles are visible.

"I don't see the relevance," I ventured.

"You don't see the relevance of your best golf score to wanting to be a professional golfer." She said this in the monotone of a statement, rather than in the rising lilt of a question.

"No I don't."

"And you're sticking with that." Another statement.

"Look. The best performance of a once- or twice-a-week player is irrelevant to what that same player might accomplish if he really devoted himself to the game."

"Okay." She sat upright, making no effort to cover herself, moving in for the kill. "So what if a guy has been playing twice a week for twenty years and has never broken a hundred. Does he have the same chance as you of making the Senior Tour?"

"No."

"Why not?"

"Because there's a certain base level of aptitude for the game that he obviously—"

"So then his best score *is* relevant."

Jesus Christ. No wonder I hated being a lawyer. I couldn't even win an argument with a naked Girl Scout *den* mother.

"Okay. It's seventy. But I've done it five times."

"At Fox Run?"

"Yes. At Fox Run."

"Never anywhere else?"

"No."

"White tees or back tees?"

"Who *are* you?"

"What? You think I haven't learned anything in the last fifteen years living with Kenny frigging Venturi? White or blue?"

"White."

"Pardon?"

"*White.*"

Any thoughts of continuing the birthday celebration were withering quickly.

"Okay. Now correct me if I'm wrong" (she always says this when she is certain that she *isn't* wrong), "but don't even the old guys shoot in the sixties most of the time?"

"Only the winners. I don't think Chi Chi's broken seventy since the Reagan admin—"

"You don't want to win?"

"Of course I do. I'm just saying that . . ." But there was no longer any chance of recovery, so I turned away, pile-driving my head into my pillow like a jilted teenager. "Just forget it."

There was a rather long silence before she said, "You mean you're *serious?*"

I knew enough not to overplay my sulk, so I turned to face her.

"I think I am."

She looked at me hard. Then she said, "Jesus."

So we did what we always did—what any couple does who has come through seventeen years of marriage still surprised and thankful to see each other on the other side of the bed every morning. We negotiated a deal: I could play out my fantasy, but first I had to prove myself worthy. I had to shoot sixty-nine or better by the end of the season without giving up any part of my legal practice (the state courts are closed most of the summer anyway, so I pretended to be giving in on that issue in exchange for other concessions on her part), and it had to be from the back tees. (Okay, so there were no other concessions on her part.) We consummated the deal with a second round of spirited birthday festivities, something I don't think we'd done since my fortieth.

But that all seems like a very long time ago now. It's late October and I have a two-thirty tee time today to play, by myself, one of the last few rounds of the season. I haven't broken seventy yet, a fact rendered trivial by what I *have* done. You see, my current state of exile is well deserved. I have not only failed to prove myself worthy of this outlet for my midlife crisis, but have managed to prove myself *un*worthy of the mostly perfect woman who offered it to me like the gift I thought it was. Kelly is seven months pregnant with what we hope—this time—will be our third child, a product of the passionate, if somewhat irresponsible continuation of my birthday celebration. My reaction to the news was not the proper one, though that represents only the beginning of why I am here, sitting in front of a laptop in my childhood bedroom, trying to make sense out of the undeclared disaster area that has become our life . . . I almost said "together," but that is as yet unclear. For several months now I have, almost nightly, haunted the sidewalk outside the home where my wife and daughters are living without me, trying to piece together windowed snippets of their lives into something I can take hold of for sustenance. But part of the punishment seems to be that the images I'm able to grasp are far more fleeting than the pain they produce. Worse still, when I come back here and try to get it all down, try to tell the truth about myself to myself, I can still hear the authoritative voices from my past asking the same question, a question to which I should by now have a ready answer:

"What's *at stake* here?" they want to know.

Honestly? I'm still working on that part.

I

On the first tee, a golfer must expect only two things of himself: to have fun, and to focus his mind properly on every shot.

—Dr. Bob Rotella with Bob Cullen,
Golf Is Not a Game of Perfect

A fair percentage of the membership at the Fox Run Golf and Hunt Club suffer from creaky joints that don't operate properly in climates north of the Mason-Dixon after Labor Day. Most of the "younger" generation of men (of which I am still considered a member) actually work for a living, contrary to popular myth, and don't arrive at the Club on weekdays, if at all, until at least four o'clock. The women (who only just attained full membership status in 1998, following a battle that rivaled the one for women's suffrage in both acrimony and expense) are still not permitted to tee off between one and two-thirty on weekdays in deference to the after-lunch business golf "crowd" (usually two or three foursomes) and in recognition of the fact that most of them, even the young mothers, have all morning to play, nannies permitting. I am therefore very much alone on the putting green, and for as far as I can see around me for that matter, when Sal limps around the corner of the Club-house and starts down the hill with my bag.

I have one of those new lightweight, double-strap bags and, more often than not, I carry my own clubs. I like the exercise, and I am notoriously cheap. But dire situations call for drastic measures, and time is running out. I have shot seventy from the back tees twice this season, both before Memorial Day weekend. Since then, for reasons that I try hard not to dwell on out here, my best score is seventy-four. My confidence has faded and my mind, always my chief ally, is elsewhere. My quest to break seventy has lost any sense of mission and has become nothing more than an escape, my time out here time away from the reality of my forced exile from my home. The twelfth green at Fox Run stands elevated next to the practice green and is a struggling player's first easy opportunity to leave the course and trudge up the steep hill to the Clubhouse showers. When playing with friends the temptation of an early exit seldom outweighs the prospect of six more holes of competition and companionship, no matter how poorly played. But my rounds have increasingly been played alone, and of late I have exited nearly every round in which I had no chance of breaking seventy via the twelfth green.

But a good caddy can save even the best player a stroke or two per round, and Sal is the best we have. He carried bags here in the summer when he was a kid just so he could play the course on Mondays, then he showed up weekends for almost forty years, putting eight kids through college and taking early retirement from Wheeling Pittsburgh Steel just before it filed Chapter 11. He and my mother went to the local high school together—he claims to have taken her to a dance once; she will admit only that they were "friends"—and, at my mother's urging, my father offered to invest Sal's lump-sum retirement distribution for him. According to my father, Sal now has more money than half of the "irresponsible, third-generation" Fox Run members, but he's still out here every day, April to October. I've walked this golf course as many times with Sal as I have with my father, and some of my most vivid childhood memories are of rounds walked with both of them, Sal's constant chatter and encouragement the perfect antidote to my father's silent, dogged concentration. Sal just turned seventy-one and can't carry double anymore, but he's still a seeing-eye dog on these greens. There isn't a single putt to a single pin placement he hasn't seen a hundred times. He doesn't read putts so much as he remembers them. Had I had him with me on the two days I shot seventy, I might not be here today, still banging my head against that numerical wall. Hell, if I'd had him with me, I might still be sleeping with my wife. He's *that* good.

As always, he's smiling as he approaches, his thick, perfectly combed head of white hair looking so much like a toupee, I'm sure it's ready to spring straight up like a Three Stooges sight gag. His "uniform"—clean white T-shirt, blue pants and bright red suspenders—is such a constant that I sometimes don't recognize him right away when I see him off the grounds wearing anything else.

"Mr. B.," he says, extending his hand and looking from my face to the sky. "Looks like we got us a nice one." Despite my protests, and despite our history, he has insisted on calling me by my surname since the day I turned thirty.

I take his hand, which is a thick, curled gnarl of knuckles and nails, and return the strong grip that never fails to surprise me. Then I look up too, acknowledging the beauty of the afternoon, though I hadn't noticed until then. "Good thing, Sal. I need all the help I can get."

"Still tryin', are ya?"

"Come on. Don't you think you would've heard if I'd done it?"

"Oh I know you ain't *done* it. I just wasn't sure if you was still tryin'."

"Yeah, I'm not sure why, but I'm still at it."

"Glad to hear it. Never stop tryin', Mr. B. You stop tryin', you're halfway to dyin' is what I always say. You ready?"

"Yeah, let's go." Turning, I wait for one of the two questions that invariably accompany our walk to the first tee.

"How's that lovely mother of yours?" he wants to know, feigning only mild interest.

"The same. A royal pain in my ass."

"Glad to hear it. You tell her I said hello, would ya?"

"I'll do that. She already told me to do the same. Say hello to you, I mean."

"Did she now? Ain't that nice. You tell her Sal says hello."

It doesn't escape me that he knows not to ask the other question. Sal doesn't care for many Fox Run women, and his affection for the two in my life is a validation of the good fortune I have done my best to squander. He fell in love with Kelly shortly after I did, and while my mother is coyly noncommittal where Sal is concerned, Kelly's affection for him is unabashed. She lost her own father when she was thirteen, and my father and Sal, each in his own way, have helped to fill a void for her. The first time he caddied for Kelly and me, Sal pulled me aside as we walked off the eighteenth green and issued the following directive: "What a man gets for a mother is pure luck. What he gets for a wife is somethin' else again. But if you can manage to hang on to this one, Mikey, luck ain't gonna begin to describe it." Truthfully, my decision to carry my own bag all summer had less to do with my frugality and my current preference for solitude than with my desire to avoid Sal on the subject of my wife. Today, in the silence normally occupied with talk of Kelly Benedict, Sal sets my bag down and removes the head cover from my three-wood.

The first hole at Fox Run is a perfect opener: a 424-yard par-four, sand traps left and right of the fairway leading to a gentle, right-hand dogleg that's outlined on its inside corner by three huge pin oaks. My height and long arms allow me to hit the ball a long way, and a well-hit driver usually puts me through the dogleg and into the left rough here, which is why Sal is handing me the three-wood without a word.

When I'm playing well, I am thinking about nothing during the swing but my target (here, the left corner of the dogleg) and the shape of the shot: not my hand position, not how big my shoulder turn is, not releasing at impact, nothing. That's what practice time is for. Once you're out here, if you don't trust the swing you brought with you, you're dead. Today, at the top of my backswing, something happens that has been happening all too often lately. I suddenly remember the hard hook I hit here three weeks ago that almost put me out on Fox Run Road. Fighting that mental picture, my hands never release, sending the ball right of the right bunkers, right of the pin oaks, and almost into the narrow creek that separates the first hole from the eighteenth.

"Goddammit. Great start."

"Easy, slugger," Sal admonishes. "That won't hurt you none down there. That's the short way home. Let's go find 'er." I pull the broken tee out of the ground, snap it into the rough in disgust, then jog to catch up with Sal.

The Fox Run Golf and Hunt Club was established in 1921 and opened for play in 1924. The six founding members were headed by F. Porter Beason, a young man of twenty-five, who, in addition to descending from a Titusville, Pennsylvania oil family, had just managed to marry himself a Mellon. Well, she wasn't *exactly* a Mellon. Though her grandmother's maiden name had been Mellon, F. Porter's young bride, Fanny, had, through the vagaries of marriage, acquired the unfortunate last name of Bluster. But you didn't have to be "exactly" a Mellon to carry a pretty fair-size dowry, and the union of Fanny Bluster and F. Porter Beason was one of the most memorable events in Pittsburgh's social history. To make sure it stays that way, F. Porter's grandson ("F. III" or "Trip") generously donated three huge black-and-white framed photographs of the affair to be displayed prominently at the Club. His accountant reportedly valued them, for tax purposes, as if they were collectors' items.

Anyway, the founding members hired one of the hottest young golf-course architects in the country and instructed him to choose the most desirable land from the more than 3,700 acres of meadow and forest they had just acquired on the northern outskirts of Allegheny County. The rest of the land would be dedicated to fox hunting. Apparently, neither F. Porter nor any of his cohorts had ever actually hunted a fox, but the postwar euphoria and the parabolic rise of the stock market generated a lot of ideas that seem absurdly excessive in retrospect. They had to do *something* with all that money. As it turned out, the stock market crashed before many of the members had learned to distinguish a riding hat from a pith helmet, and the remaining acreage was sold to a group of monied Catholics who had been refused membership at Fox Run, and who proceeded to construct their own golf course close enough to thumb their collective nose at the Fox Run Protestants. Worse yet, the Catholics built an immense clubhouse on the highest point on the property, a woefully impractical spot but one that could be seen from just about anywhere on Fox Run. In fact, as Sal and I approach my errant tee shot (which, as Sal predicted, has a clear path to the green), the Pine Ridge clubhouse rises in the distance directly behind my target.

"Hit one at the Catholics," Sal says, handing me my nine-iron. This is a phrase that has somehow survived the intervening decades in which both clubs have admitted, sometimes even voluntarily, practitioners of nearly every major religion.

"I've still got close to a hundred and fifty yards, Sal. Give me the eight."

Sal doesn't look at me to show his disapproval but continues to look at the ball. "That's a flyer lie if I ever seen one, Mr. B. Look how pretty she's sittin' up. She's gonna take off like no one's business. Hit the nine. Right at the goddam Catholics."

I take the nine. I have grown stupid over the past few months, but not stupid enough to ignore Sal. Unfortunately, my subconscious doesn't trust the choice, and the extra distance I instinctively try to generate causes me to pull the shot left and long, into the bunker behind the green.

"God*dammit.*"

The club choice was perfect, and Sal knows it. "A flyer all right," he says as he hoists the bag back onto his shoulder and starts his gimpy trudge toward the green. "Let's go get 'er up and down," he calls back to me. But I am still thinking about the last shot (knowingly breaking my own cardinal rule a mere ten minutes into the round), and I'm taking a few practice swings to try to remedy the flaw. Of course, there is no "flaw" other than a lack of conviction, and I know it. But this constant rethinking and reworking has become my defense mechanism, and although I know it's ruining my golf game, it's better than the alternative, which is to spend my time out here thinking about what occupies my thoughts every *other* moment of the day. I take one last swipe at the grass and start to follow Sal.

So why is it still called Fox Run Golf *and Hunt* Club? Because the name should remain true to his grandfather's dream, says F. III, and there are enough members who like the idea of belonging to something that was *once* a hunt club, however briefly, that we're probably stuck with the name for good. Such unrestrained pomposity is not unprecedented in Pittsburgh. If one's money is old enough, and one has enough of it, one might be considered for membership at the original Pittsburgh Golf Club, which (no kidding) has no golf course.

As I approach, Sal is already shaking his head and miming a spatula-flipping motion with his right hand. This can mean only one thing. My ball has come to rest right in the center of the sand crater it created upon landing: a fried egg.

"Breakfast is served, Mr. B.," he says and hands me my sand wedge. "Just get it somewhere on the moss and let's get out of here with five."

But I don't. Despite the fact that there's not much you can do with this shot, no way to get it to spin and hold, I try to get it close for a shot at par rather than heeding Sal's wise advice. The result is that my ball lands on the hillside of the bunker, pauses there momentarily, then rolls back down into the trap. I have to do a little jig just to keep it from hitting my left foot. Red-faced, I don't even look at Sal, who has been, respectively, questioned and ignored on successive shots, and I take a thoughtless swat at the ball the instant it comes to rest. It lands and spins to a stop in the center of the green, at least twenty feet from the hole. This is the equivalent of a wasted shot and I know it, but suddenly I just don't care. It's a feeling I have never had on the first hole in my life, not even when I was a kid out here more for my father than myself. I take an indifferent look at the line of my first putt and hit it without a thought, even before Sal has finished raking the trap. I take the pin out myself as Sal climbs out of the bunker, and I rap in the two-footer that's left for my six one-handed. I toss the ball underhand across the green to Sal and jam the flagstick back in. As I pass him, walking quickly on my way to the second tee, Sal is working at the marks on the ball with the wet towel he keeps slung over one red suspender. He lifts his chin with a look that stops me.

"Mind if I ask you a question, Mr. B.?" he says, squinting. The look reminds me of the ones he used to give me when I was fifteen and still "Mikey" to him. He doesn't wait for my answer. "Why you botherin'?" He hands me the clean white ball, his rough fingertips scratching the soft center of my palm.

"I don't know."

"We ain't gonna be any closer to the Clubhouse than we are now until we hit twelve."

I look at him to see if he's serious. "You think we should just walk back?"

"What do *you* think? If you're gonna bother, then *bother*."

"Oh, I'm bothered all right, Sal. That's my problem. That and the fact I'm working real hard at not thinking about it."

"Why you doin' that?"

"Come on, Sal."

"No, no. That's not the why I mean. I mean why you tryin' not to think about it? What good's that gonna do you?"

"Because this is where I come to forget for a few hours. I'm just trying to stay focused."

"Workin' great so far." Sal smiles as he says this to make it clear that, despite our lifelong relationship, he's not crossing the demarcation between caddy and member, and it shocks me that I too am aware of this line. "Look," he says, "who ever told you that you needed to stay focused on nothing but golf for three or four hours?"

"My father used to make me tell him exactly what I was thinking about before I hit each shot. It's just habit now."

"What's your father's handicap?"

"I don't know. Twenty-eight, twenty-nine."

"I rest my case, counselor." Sal is now moving toward the crosswalk over Fox Run Road that leads to the second tee. He has made the decision for me but is kind enough to make sure that I have matched his pace before he has gone more than a few steps, so that, to anyone who might be watching, we look like we have made the turn together. "Look," he continues, "I owe your father almost as much as you do, and he knows a lot about lots of things, but golf ain't one of 'em. I never seen someone love somethin' so much and be so bad at it."

"Sal, this is one of the few places where we actually *talked*. Can you blame me for listening?"

"Nope. But now I'm tellin' you different. If you think I'm out here thinkin' every second about how I'm gonna suggest you play the next shot, you're nuts. You know what I'm thinkin'? I'm thinkin' how nice it's gonna be to see my daughters at Thanksgiving, even though every last one of 'em married assholes who don't know how good they got it. Or I'm thinkin' how not one of my sons appreciates the education they got that I never had, and that none of 'em would know an honest day's work if it slapped 'em. Or I'm thinkin' how if my wife had gone before me like they thought she was gonna for a while there, I might as well've jumped right in the hole with her for all the good I was gonna be." We're across the road now and rounding the shaded bend to the tee. "I start thinkin' about your next shot five paces before I get there. Shouldn't take *you* any longer. You oughta be gettin' more for all those dues you pay than sixty rounds a year and a few dips in the pool. I mean, look at this beautiful . . ." Sal catches my smile as he gestures to include everything that surrounds him. "Okay," he says, laughing. "All I'm sayin' is, I ain't out here for the lousy fifty bucks."

He hands me my driver and I'm puzzled for a moment. I always hit three-wood on this par-five. Sal holds up his hand. "I know. But you just made *six*, for chrissake. We're gonna hit this green in two."

You can choose whether to believe me or not, but the driver feels like nothing in my hands, like an extension of myself. When I draw it back I can already see the perfect arc of the shot starting left and cutting gently into the left center of the fairway, and when I look up, it's as if I'm seeing a continuation of the shot that began in my mind. It clears the pot bunker recently placed at the top of the hill to discourage long hitters—armed with ever-improving technology—from turning this par-five into a long par-four. But that's just what it will be for me today. I look at Sal (for approval? I don't know), but he has his eye on the spot where the ball has come to rest, and he has his hand out to receive the grip of my driver. I don't know what he's thinking, but it's got nothing to do with me.

2

"Silence, you perverts!" Ignatius cried. "Listen to me."

—John Kennedy Toole, *A Confederacy of Dunces*

I've certainly got more immediate problems, but they can almost all be traced back to the fact that I have been obsessed with the female body since I was six years old. My earliest sexual memory is of catching Jenny Teagle inside a Hula Hoop in my living room, dragging her into a closet, Spiderman flashlight in hand, and somehow convincing her that succeeding in this endeavor entitled me to pull her pants down. She agreed, as long as I did the same, and so we took turns lying on the floor of the closet "examining" each other. There was one important difference between us, though: she was merely curious; I was horny—a fact confirmed by the little nub of a hard-on bathed in the light of my flashlight.

"Why's it pointed up at the ceiling?" Jenny asked, wrinkling her brow but not taking her eyes off it.

"I don't know. It just does that sometimes."

"It looks silly that way."

"Shut *up*."

"Sorry." She bent down for a closer look. "Can you make it stop doing that?"

"No. It just does it when it wants to." (Just for the record, my early realization of this fact has done me no good since.)

"Hm." Jenny sat back up and pointed the flashlight at my face. "Can I touch it?"

"No! Just *look*."

She shined the light back on my little erection, leaned her shoulders left, then right, examining it carefully from both angles. Then she sat straight up. "Okay. I'm finished."

And that was it. For that day, anyway. At the time, my family lived in a residential plan of homes that just happened to house five six-year-old girls and only one six-year-old boy: me. And girls— even six-year-old girls—will talk, so that my penis became a popular topic of neighborhood conversation. The price of admission was clear. All you had to do was show Mikey Benedict yours and he'd show you his: *quid pro quo, pee-pee for pee-pee*. And if you were lucky, you would see it doing its little trick. I became the picture of the good country doctor, seeing patients in my home, making house calls, asking for little in return. The only difference was that each appointment ended with me taking my pants down to display the effects of the visit. And that's where the problem was: The effect was always the same, and my patients began to suspect that they weren't seeing a trick at all, but merely a freak of nature.

One day, Addie Crupp and I were locked in her parents' bathroom. She had just finished putting eight cartoon Band-Aids on my rear end (which was the only way I could get her to agree to another examination). Then she told me to turn over.

"I think it's just like that *all* the time," she posited, utterly nonplussed.

"It is *not*."

"Well, I see my brother's in the tub, and it's *never* like that."

In a clear violation of game rules, she then used her index finger to gently push the topic of her concern down between my legs, then let it spring back to its former position.

"Ouch!" I screamed, more out of fright than pain.

"Sorry," Addie said. "Maybe you should go to a *real* doctor."

I tugged my pants up, snapped and zipped them as fast as I could and ran home. Maybe Addie was right. Maybe there was something wrong with me. My mother confirmed as much for me later that night, finding the eight Band-Aids I'd forgotten about still stuck to my little white butt as she helped me into my pajamas.

"How did *these* get here, young man?"

"I don't know."

I have never been a particularly good liar.

"You don't *know?*" She turned me around to face her. "How stupid do you think I am?"

I at least knew enough not to answer that one.

"Did you put them on yourself?"

I shook my head.

"Then who *did?*" She spun me back around, pinched the edge of one of the Band-Aids between the fingernails of her thumb and index finger and ripped it off in one quick motion. I was driven to the truth by pain.

"*Ouch!* Addie did it!"

"Addie? Why in the world would you let Addie Crupp stick Band-Aids on your bare *bum?*" (Another *rip.*)

"I don't know," I lied softly, my eyes tearing. She was getting into a rhythm with the Band-Aids now.

"*What* on God's green *earth* is *wrong* with you, young man?" (*Rip, rip, rip, rip.*)

"I don't *knooowww!*" I wailed.

And I still don't know. What I do know is that whatever it is that's wrong with me hasn't changed much in the ensuing thirty-nine years. Whatever force that led me to allow Addie Crupp to play Pin the Band-Aid on the Ass in exchange for a brief viewing of her mostly boyish figure is the same force that has led to my current state of expatriation. But I can feel Sal pulling me back and, seeing that I am no more than five paces from where my drive on the second hole has come to rest, I shut off the memory, surprised at how easily I accomplish the transition. Sal is already pacing off the distance from the nearest sprinkler head as I assess my options.

Because my drive has cleared the top of the hill, the green is fully visible below. At least three fourths of its circumference is guarded by one continuous mound that grows out of the natural hillside left of the green. The effect is a bowl shape that is receptive to shots placed within its inside edges, but punishes anything outside. Left is out of bounds; right and long both drop precipitously down toward the number-three-tee boxes thirty feet below; in front of the green there is a huge sand trap that accentuates the height of the front wall of the bowl.

"Two-oh-eight to the front," Sal says. "One less club downhill. What're you smilin' about all of a sudden?"

"Nothing. Just enjoying the golf course for the first time in a while."

"Don't get too cocky, Mr. B. You've hit one good shot."

"Make up your mind, Sal. Should I relax or not?"

"Just stay with me when it's time. That's all I'm sayin'." Sal has a club halfway out of the bag already. "You want the four?"

"No. Give me five."

"Five's not enough unless you're gonna roll it through the opening."

"I'm going for the opening. I'd rather miss short here."

"I'll buy that." Sal lets the four-iron drop and fishes out the five.

The ball is slightly below my feet, so I aim left of the opening to let the shot take its natural left-to-right shape. It feels perfect as it leaves the clubface, but instead of starting left, it starts directly for the center of the opening and then fades a little right. It lands on the hillside that guards that side of the opening and kicks hard right into the center of the bunker.

"Okay, Mr. B. If you're not on the green, that's as good a place as any."

He doesn't have to tell me that.

· · ·

The place where my ball has come to rest is also the place where I first facilitated an orgasm that was not my own. It happened when I was nineteen and home from college for the summer, but the historic context of that sand trap, autobiographically speaking, dates all the way back to ninth-grade health class, *Chapter 17, Figure 3*.

The period of my life stretching between my brief kindergarten medical practice and my first productive orgasm (self-inflicted, of course) was, in a word, "dry." Not long after the sting of Addie Crupp's Band-Aids had subsided, my parents bought their current house in Fox Run. I wouldn't see another live vagina for more than ten years. My parents thought I would be pleased with the fact that most of the kids on our new street were boys. But they played with Matchbox cars, raced bikes, played tackle football and climbed up and down the slate rocks that formed the deep ravine in the woods that backed our dead-end street. None of the games I knew were applicable in this new life. Certainly, "doctor" was no longer an option. I had no Matchbox cars, couldn't catch a football and insisted on walking the footpath down to the ravine. In school, at recess, I avoided kickball in favor of playing chase with the girls, which, inexplicably, made me a "faggot." I remember asking my mother what that meant (the mere fact that she gave me a definition being proof that "politically correct" was not, in 1968, part of the cultural vernacular), then riding the bus to school the next day, armed with what I was sure was deadly information. I approached Dino Cardinale at recess. He greeted me as he always did:

"Hey faggot. Where's your purse?"

Dino and I were the same age, but I had to look straight up to speak to him. "Dino, did you know that a faggot is a boy who likes other boys better than girls?"

"Yeah? So what, faggot?"

End of conversation. How was I to deal with such perfect non-reasoning? And all of them seemed to be that way. By fifth grade, each boy had perfected a swagger learned from the athletes they admired, and they treated the rest of us as if we were autograph hounds to be waved off or admitted at their whim. And in a way we were. In 1970, I couldn't have named a Pittsburgh Pirate beyond Roberto Clemente and Willie Stargell, but I knew that Ricky Hufnagle was on the verge of becoming the first kickball player in my elementary school's history to put 100 balls over the playground's ten-foot chain-link fence in a single school year. (He finished the 1970–71 season with 104, a record that still stood when they tore the school down to build townhouses in 1976.)

Strangely, we boys who were (quite literally) on the outside of the fence looking in at these games never formed a group of our own. We confirmed the judgment of others by viewing one another as pitiful, and we wanted nothing to do with one another for one simple reason: A faggot didn't want to be seen with other faggots for fear he might be labeled a faggot. The frustrating truth is that the early instincts of our macho peers proved prophetic. I can name at least four boys from that playground who came out of the closet later in life, and, like me, they were all chasing little girls around the swing set with enthusiasm at age ten. It just happened that, despite all the outward signs (sensitivity, musicality and, yes, playing with girls), I was painfully straight.

As elementary school progressed, we all seemed to learn, without ever being told, that nudity was inappropriate, that "privates" were private. And while it never occurred to me to feel guilty about the things I had done with Jenny and Addie (and Cindy, Anna, Courtney and Adrienne), it also never occurred to me to break out the Hula Hoop and Spiderman flashlight when one of my fourth- or fifth-grade classmates came over for the afternoon. I was just completely, hopelessly, platonically in love with nearly all of them. Donna O'Connor's dimples made me weak; Laura Hilgers's electric blue eyes inspired my earliest poetry; the fine blond hair on Becky Kelhofer's bruised shins, crossed coyly under her desk, rendered long division incomprehensible. I could find something to stare at and make lovely in almost every one of them. Long fingers, long eyelashes, high cheekbones, big teeth. Knock-knees, skinned elbows, painted toenails, perfect ears for tucking hair behind. New glasses, new haircut, new clothes, new braces. All were tirelessly cataloged in the form of a carefully guarded, ever-changing top-ten wish list of female classmates who all thought of me as their best "little buddy." To think of Laura Hilgers and "erection" simultaneously would have been sacrilege. She and all of the others had my heart. Lust and love were not only different for me; they were mutually exclusive. Erections were no longer to be shared in closets with playmates but were reserved for women in magazines who looked out at you with eyes that seemed to say, well, "erection."

Those women became my other obsession. My early libido hadn't dissipated; it had just been redirected. Hugh Hefner was making pornography chic, and more than one of my friends had fathers who kept magazines, if not in plain view, then at least in a location that might be stumbled upon. The first gold mine I found was at Becky Kelhofer's house. She was one of the few girls who lived within walking distance of our new house, and we were home from school on a snow day, building an igloo in her backyard. My fingers were numb in my mittens, and I went inside to the bathroom to run warm water over them. When I went to dry them there wasn't a towel in sight, so I opened the cabinet under the sink. What I saw made my vision blur, and every pore in my body seemed to yawn open at once. Could these be *real*? Could they be *legal*? I had never seen a *Playboy* magazine before, but the covers alone, which appeared almost luminescent in the darkness of the cabinet, told me that I had just found my life's calling. The bathroom was suddenly sweltering, and I tore off my coat, locked the door and sat down to explore my find.

There were two neatly piled stacks, both the exact same height, and, as if they might be booby-trapped, I slid a magazine gently from the top of one of them. It seemed to magically fall open to a center page, where Miss January, 1970, unfolded before me. My God, there had never been a woman so beautiful and frightening as this. From the neck up she could have been my fifth-grade teacher. Her eyes were a soft brown, inviting, almost comforting. Her bleached-blond bouffant hairdo, topped with a paper New Year's party hat, could have been lifted and transplanted onto the heads of any one of my friends' mothers. And her perfect smile was right out of a hokey TV commercial: "Ladies. Is your man like a little boy? Does he bring home stubborn stains? . . ." But the rest of her body said, "Mikey, put one hand in your snow pants and *do* something with that little thing." So that's what I did. The only breasts I had ever seen before were my mother's. When I see pictures of her at that time, I realize that she was beautiful, and she was never modest when it came to nudity among family. But even for a little pervert like me, watching my mother wrestle topless with her panty hose in the morning did not qualify as a sexual event. Miss January was another matter entirely. Below her innocent, domestic face, she was cupping her impossibly large breasts in manicured hands and pointing them at me like a couple of bazookas. "Bang, bang, my little *buddy*." She was standing, leaning toward me from the waist, and her long legs, thank God, were modestly crossed at the knees. Despite the placid look on her face, her flat, almost concave stomach and protruding rib cage led me to believe that she must be holding her breath as she posed. It was nice to think of her as having this talent.

The addiction was instantaneous. I became frustrated by the deceptive thickness of these volumes. Surely no one *read* all this stuff. Soon, my Miss January was only one of a harem of women spread out on the floor before me. Blondes, brunettes, redheads. Tall and thin, short and buxom, sharp tan lines, no tan lines. Innocent, sultry, carefree, dangerous. It didn't matter. They were all painfully beautiful to me.

When Becky tapped lightly on the door, she might as well have been tripping an ejector seat in the floor.

"*Yeah!*" I yelled in midair.

"What're ya doin' in there?"

"I don't know." There were now at least ten magazines on the floor, and I was desperately trying to remember which had come from which pile. "I think I might be sick or something."

"Really? Did you throw up?"

"No, but I keep thinking I might. Which is why I've been in here so long. Have I been in here long?"

"No. Just like half an *hour.* I can't finish the igloo by myself. Are you gonna be able to help?"

"Geez, I don't think so." I was still shouting for some reason. "I think I'm going to have to get going."

"Really?"

"Yeah. Hey, could you go away for a minute? I really don't want you listening to me puking."

"Do you want me to get my mom?"

"*No!*" Whoa—that was way too loud. Easy, boy. "No. Don't do that. I'll be all right. Just leave me alone for a minute, okay?"

"Okay."

When I could no longer hear her footsteps, I began reconstructing her father's stacks as best I could. I remembered which ones had been on top of each, but beyond that the order was a complete crapshoot. Then I put on my coat, zipped it up and headed for the door. My hand was already on the knob when I realized I couldn't possibly leave empty-handed. I turned back, knelt down, opened the cabinet again and began sifting. Which had been my favorite? The trouble was, my favorite was always the one I had most recently opened. (Years later, one of my law school classmates, eyes half-mast after eight or ten beers at a local strip bar, would dub this the *New Girl Syndrome.* "You know," he explained groggily, "as soon as one girl's done getting naked, no matter how pretty she is, everyone's just waiting around to see the New Girl." Shortly thereafter, he was sound asleep face down on the bar, but his words were rendered no less true because of it.) So I pulled one from the bottom of the right-hand stack that I hadn't seen yet. I figured Becky's dad was bored with the ones on the bottom. I unzipped my coat, tucked the magazine partway into my snow pants for security and zipped back up. When I looked in the mirror, I thought I appeared perfectly normal, but a quick survey of Mr. Kelhofer's stash revealed a disequilibrium. *Jesus*, these things were thick. I'd have to take one from each stack. Afraid to add to my bulk in front, I managed to squeeze the second one down the back of my pants, then went back to the mirror. Not bad. Though when I watched myself walk, I looked a bit like someone in a full-body cast.

I had to pass through the kitchen to get out, and Becky was in there with her mother. She was one of those mothers who feels her kid's forehead every hour on the hour, and Becky must have been telling her about me because she headed for me like an E.R. nurse.

"Mikey, sweetheart! Are you okay?" She had a clammy hand on my forehead before I could even begin to protest. "You *are* warm. Here, take off this coat, and—"

"No!" In what must have appeared to Mrs. Kelhofer as an over-reaction that evidenced a mental as well as a physical malady, I locked my arms across my chest and bolted for the door.

"Michael Benedict! What has gotten into you?"

I had succeeded in securing the magazine in front with my arms, but my little sprint had loosened the elastic waistband of my snow pants, and I could feel the one in the back starting to slide down over my butt. I spun to face Mrs. Kelhofer, but that only hastened the descent.

"I'm sorry. I'm fine, really. You just scared me, that's all."

"Scared you? I was only trying to *help*."

"I know. And I appreciate that. I really do." The only thing supporting the magazine now was the crotch seam of my pants, and the weight of it was beginning to pull them down. "It's just that one time Laura Hilgers's mom pulled one of my baby teeth out before it was ready, and it really hurt like crazy, so now I try to just let my own mom take care of me."

Becky had been silent until now. "I never heard that." She was still pissed about the igloo and was in no mood to make my exit comfortable.

"I don't like to talk about it. That's why."

"Laura's my best friend and she never told me about it."

"I thought *I* was your best friend."

"Best *boy* friend," she clarified.

I can't tell you why this answer made me feel as if I had suddenly lost something, but it did.

"Anyway, I better get going." Although that wasn't going to be easy. I had gotten hold of the front of my waistband, but the full weight of the filler articles and advertising of the posterior *Playboy* had rendered me a reasonable facsimile of a Coppertone billboard from behind, except that instead of a little white rump I had Miss April, 1967, peeking out of my pants. I somehow managed to reach behind me and get the doorknob turned, though I must have looked about as natural as, well, a ten-year-old stealing pornography. I got the door open and backed out slowly, mumbling thank-yous and apologies, until I had pulled the door closed on their confused faces. Once outside, I resituated my cargo and headed for home. I knew Mrs. Kelhofer was already on the phone to my mother, so I took a path through the woods above the ravine that eventually brought me out onto our back patio, where I quickly lifted the heavy lid of the gas grill and tossed the magazines inside. Later that night, my father asleep on the couch, my mother folding laundry in the basement, I snuck them up to my room and slipped them under my mattress. Like some unbruisable Princess and the Pea, I slept fitfully on a mound of pornography for the next seven years.

. . .

I know I haven't gotten to orgasms yet, or even ninth-grade health class for that matter, but Sal is looking at me like he thinks he's lost me, and I need to hit this shot. He hands me my lob wedge.

"Just get 'er on the green, Mr. B., and give yourself a putt at it."

"Okay, chief."

As I dig my feet into the sand for support, I sense its weight and try to imagine the amount of the resistance my clubhead will meet when it strikes behind the ball. Even more than full shots, shots around the green must be executed with feel and imagination, not mechanics. Once I have a strong, sensual image, I don't waste any time overanalyzing it. Or at least I didn't used to. Sal's diagnosis would be that I have lately been overanalyzing everything out here in an effort to block out everything out *there*. Today, however, I haven't thought about this shot until the moment I step into the trap, when I see it perfectly. The heavy head strikes behind the ball with a sound like *pofff*, and the slice of sand I have cut lifts the ball gently up and out. I climb the bank in time to see it rolling, arcing right with the slope of the green, stopping no more than five feet from the hole.

"Looked good goin' up," Sal says. He has picked up a rake and has headed in behind me to clean up. I grab one from the hillside as well.

"Four or five feet," I let him know, waving him off as I descend into the bunker again. "Let me get this one."

"She's all yours."

Taking magazines from Mr. Kelhofer's bathroom (and, subsequently, from several other suburban locales) wasn't stealing, really. It was more like an alternative library program. I always returned the old material before checking out anything new, though, admittedly, the late fees would have broken me. Based on my sampling over the next few years, it seemed that nearly fifty percent of upper-middle-class homes contained accessible, transportable pornography. A stash revealed to me by Stewey Trammell, one of the boys from my street (and to this day my only close male friend) dwarfed Mr. Kelhofer's in both size and variety. Stewey was a meaty, slobbery kid whose taste in pornography was, depending on how you looked at it, either more base or more advanced than my own. He wanted to see (to put it more gently than Stewey ever did) the "inner workings" of the female anatomy, and his father's *Penthouse* collection provided plenty. None of the women in *Penthouse* magazine looked anything like my teacher, and the pained looks on their faces scared me a little. But the filler in *Penthouse* proved to be far more interesting than the movie reviews and college football All-American teams in *Playboy*. It was there that I learned about sex from the most unreliable of sources: the letters of "*Penthouse* Forum."

At the time, sex education in public schools was still controversial, and my junior-high administrators tried to allay parental fears by assigning the task to the teacher least likely to succeed in imparting any real knowledge about sex. The subject of human reproduction was covered once a year, for about a week, by a gym teacher who also taught driver's ed and who seemed to have been instructed to make the two topics as similar as possible: "Now we're not here to talk about religion or morals or any of that stuff. We're just talkin' about the general 'rules of the road' with a little plumbing thrown in" was Coach Johnson's annual, numbing introduction to the topic.

But in "*Penthouse* Forum," men *throbbed with desire* for women who were *wet with passion*. They met in offices and hotel bars, on ski slopes and exotic beaches. Sex almost never took place in homes or bedrooms, unless it was between two (or more) people who didn't both live there—husbands and nubile babysitters, wives and brawny pool boys, inexperienced daughters and fathers' best friends. Outside of these dangerous combinations, sex, to be any good, had to be in an elevator or a hot tub, on top of a pool table or under a crowded dining room table, on the roof of an Upper East

Side Manhattan apartment building or up against the wall of the church rectory. Preferably, the event should involve two (or more) people who have known each other for less than thirty minutes. "Penis" and "vagina," words we sniggered over as they fell from Coach Johnson's mouth, never appeared in the pages of *Penthouse*. Instead, these insatiable beings possessed reproductive organs that could be utilitarian (*rods, poles, pipes, tools, purses, banks* and *boxes*), edible (*baloney popsicles, beef bayonets, artichokes, muffins* and *cookies*), romantic (*love muscles* and *tunnels of love*), members of the animal kingdom (the always reliable *beavers, cocks* and *pussies*) or monuments to alliteration (*My one-eyed trouser troll sought her fleshy treasure trove*). To the unending delight of Stewey and me, many of the men even had *Johnsons*.

But we were freshmen now and thus deemed by the school board to be capable of handling the knowledge that sex could be pleasurable, even for a woman. I had an easy enough time imagining how it might be pleasurable for *me* (having been engaged since pre-school in an all-out effort to pound my own little pud to a pulp before sprouting my first pubic hair), but I had absolutely no idea how I might go about making a girl *wet with passion*. Despite all of my independent research on the female form, that part of a woman was still a mystery to me. The ugliness of the word *vagina* was not, in my estimation, misleading. Any part of a woman below the shoulders that had hair on it was better left unseen. I was a breast man; the rest of it intimidated me to the point of paralysis.

And it would continue to. Because although we were deemed capable of *knowing* about the pleasures of sex, we were apparently not capable of *talking* about them. Not on school-sponsored time anyway. Class time in ninth-grade health class was still all biology and plumbing. The "chemistry" part was to be read strictly on our own, and, in a transparent bit of strategy, we were told not to expect to see any of it on the test.

After I'd skimmed over the section on how the male is stimulated (What could possibly be simpler than that?), here's what I read in Chapter 17 of my ninth-grade health book about how I might reciprocate:

> Sex can be pleasurable for the woman as well [*that's a relief*], although women generally take longer to achieve orgasm than men [*that's okay—I've waited this long*], and some women have difficulty achieving orgasm at all [*great*]. The female counterpart to the male penis [*there's a counterpart?*] is the clitoris [*Jesus, can't they give anything a nice name?*]. Although many women experience pleasure through stimulation of the vaginal wall, most require direct stimulation of the clitoris to achieve orgasm. [*So where is it?*] The clitoris is located inside the vagina beneath several other layers of sensitive tissue. First, there are the outer labia, then the inner labia, then the clitoral hood, which hides and protects the clitoris until it is stimulated, then the clitoris itself. (See Fig. 3.)

Jesus Christ. Assuming I was ever lucky enough to meet a girl who would let me touch her there, it sounded like I was going to need a miner's helmet and a middle finger the length of a pushbroom handle just to find the goddam thing. And what was with the "hood"? Leave it to a girl to hide the one thing you need most to find. Maybe *Fig. 3* would help. Yep. There it was. But in that two-dimensional diagram, it looked to be hanging like a tiny epiglottis back in the furthest reaches of the "tunnel of love." I was doomed.

I dated sporadically in high school. Becky Kelhofer, Laura Hilgers, Donna O'Connor and countless others all became beautiful young women before my first shave. By the time my voice started to drop and my skinny bones started to stretch, they were all dating boy-men in letter jackets, and my status as best *boy* friend seemed immutable. I had "progressed" from kindergarten doctor to high school psychiatrist. They all came to me. Every unattainable female in my high school sought the wise counsel of Mikey Benedict because he was no threat, had no ulterior motives. What they didn't understand was that simply being in their company was my ulterior motive. I was the equivalent of the stereotypical gay confidant, except that I was in love with all of them. Laura's sad eyes looked pleadingly into mine every time Ricky Hufnagle so much as spoke to another girl. Becky's long, slender legs touched my own, sitting close on the bleachers, the day she was dumped (for the second time) by Dino Cardinale. My God, Donna changed her *shirt* right in front of me, in her bedroom, as if I had no eyes, the day she decided to accept Stewey Trammell's invitation to the senior prom. Stewey Trammell! Beefy, drooly Stewey had hardened in three short years into the anchor of both the offensive and defensive lines and was suddenly (or so he claimed) getting the kind of action we'd been reading about in his bathroom for years. I had my opportunities, of course, but never with the girl of my choice. I wish I could say that I was a better person then, but my eye had become more selective; every girl was *not* beautiful to me in high school. The gaps between the haves and have-nots had widened, and I had been spoiled by the company I kept. When someone as perfect as Donna O'Connor has stood before you in nothing but cut-off jeans and a powder-blue lace bra, even just for the purpose of asking which clean T-shirt you preferred, it was difficult (or so I told myself) to muster much desire for "lesser" girls. In retrospect, my attitude was pure defense mechanism. *Chapter 17, Figure 3* and its impossibly remote bundle of nerve endings still haunted me. And as long as I stayed in the company of women who wouldn't have me in that way, I was safe from failure.

My freshman year of college and the female students of a small upstate New York university introduced me to the cure for such defense mechanisms: the almost nightly consumption of alcohol and/or contraband. You couldn't throw a money clip on the pristine campus of my undergraduate institution without hitting a beautiful woman. You were also bound to hit either a keg or a bong. That combination of powder and fuse created a nightly explosion of sexual energy, especially among the newly liberated freshmen. Before September of 1978, I had never touched a postpubescent woman below the waist. By the time I went home for Christmas break, I had had my right arm halfway up the birth canals of six different coeds, none of whom, understandably, returned my calls thereafter. And because girls, especially freshman girls, will talk, my dance card second semester was barren.

Enter, the summer after my freshman year, Mrs. Heinrik (Dee Dee) Svenson. Dee Dee Svenson was the buxom bride of Heinrik (Henry) Svenson, one of the richest (and oldest) men at Fox Run. Had he not been both of those things, Dee Dee would have risked being the first wife ever refused spousal privileges at the Club. She was forty, looked thirty and acted eighteen. But Henry had been married for nearly fifty years to a mammoth battle-ax of a woman whose heart had eventually been consumed by the four eggs and six sausage links she'd been eating for breakfast every day of her life, and the years of accumulated sympathy and the size of Henry's bankroll combined as a compelling case for Dee Dee's admission. It should also be made clear that most of the rancor was issuing from the women, who, at the time, were not permitted to sit on the Admissions Committee anyway. The men found Dee Dee to be "charming," which was not surprising given her gift for looking at every man she met as if she wanted him to take his pants down right then and there. There were rumors that she and Henry had an "arrangement" as part of their prenuptial agreement. If she took care of his desires whenever he felt up to it, she could take care of her own in whatever ways she pleased, so long as she was discreet. If any of her private discretions became public indiscretions, the marriage would end, and she would get nothing. This rumor alone was enough to cause the wives of the Admissions Committee members to filibuster a late-evening meeting and threaten sexual reprisals of their own. But, in the end, the candidate's charms won out. There were no dissenting votes, and by the summer of 1979 Dee Dee

Svenson had been a wife in good standing at the Fox Run Golf and Hunt Club for nearly two years.

The circumstances that put me in the sand trap in front of the second green with Dee Dee Svenson in August of that summer are largely irrelevant: a late-night, post-tournament party for which I was parking cars, Henry having gone home hours earlier with his driver, Dee Dee weaving through the marbled foyer, Barbie Doll breasts spilling over silver sequins, spotting me, smiling, stopping to straighten my black tie for me, then saying something about giving me an extra ten if I'd run her out in a golf cart to retrieve a sand wedge she had left behind. You might find these details hard to believe, and, at the time, so did I. But I had grown nearly six inches since the day I graduated from high school, and I had joined a gym in an effort to add some muscle to my frail frame. No less an authority than my wife has seen pictures of me from that summer and pronounced me "not unhandsome." Still, the memory of the strange coolness in the humid August air rushing past us as we sped down the first fairway, Dee Dee Svenson's perfume trailing almost visibly behind us like the tail of a comet, seems utterly unreal to me now. She said nothing. She didn't press herself close to me on the seat or rub her palm over my thigh, though I am tempted to tell it that way. Instead, she sat on the front edge of the white vinyl seat, hands pressing for support on either side of her, leaning forward with something like expectation. If she was drunk, her face no longer showed it. She looked content, even a little nervous, fixing her gaze straight ahead. In the muted moonlight, she could have been my prom date, not a childless forty-year-old woman. We crossed over deserted Fox Run Road, and as we crested the hill of the second fairway and the bowl of the green came into view below, she pointed, still not looking at me. It was the perfect spot: concealed from the Clubhouse by the hill behind us and the sheer distance of more than a thousand yards, and shielded from the view of neighboring homes by the dense tree line and the steep front face of the bunker itself. She had come here before.

She made no pretense of looking for a lost club. She slipped off her shoes and set them on the floor of the cart, so I did the same, removing my socks as well. Then she stepped out, walked around to my side and held out her hand. I took it and followed her barefoot through the thick wetness of the grass onto the cool, dry sand. When we reached the center, she turned to me, took the lapels of my jacket and, in an almost motherly way, slid it off my shoulders. Then she spread it on the sand, sat down and lightly patted the empty space next to her. I sat.

"I love this spot." These were the first words she had spoken to me since asking me to bring her here.

"Do you come here often?" Excellent opener.

"Once in a while. Our house is just through those woods and up Quail Hollow Road. I usually take a walk after Henry goes to bed, and sometimes I end up sitting here for hours." With a well-manicured fingernail, she was absently tracing designs in the sand in front of us. "I guess you're probably wondering why I brought you along."

"Yeah, well, I think I know. I mean I *thought* I knew. Aren't you afraid of getting caught?"

"Not really."

"I mean everybody says . . . It's possible someone could see us and think—"

"That we were making love?"

"Yeah. They could think that." I was looking at her finger still sketching in the sand, trying to work up my courage. "Would they be right?"

She looked up at me from her drawing. "Maybe if they watch a little while longer." She laughed, and lines appeared at the corners of her eyes. Then she stood and, without a hint of self-consciousness, slid her panties down her legs, stepped out of them and sat back down. "You're nice to worry about me, but there is no *agreement*. I mean, there's an agreement, but it doesn't say what everyone says it says."

"Oh. Good."

Her panties were in the hand that was now resting on my knee, and it felt as if they might burn a hole in my pants.

"If you want to know the truth, I've been pretty faithful to him, all things considered."

Now she *was* rubbing her hand up and down my thigh, and all I could think about was the six women I had fumbled around inside during my first semester at school. I needed to stall for time.

"So why did you pick me?"

"I don't know. I've been watching you all summer, and you seemed so sweet." Boy, I'd heard *that* word enough from girls in my short lifetime. "You remind me of someone I knew when I was young. Someone I wasn't smart enough to fall in love with. You seemed easy to talk to like him."

"Yeah. That's what I hear. It's never done much for me in this department though."

"Be patient."

The rest is beyond my meager descriptive abilities, but there is one part I want to tell about, because it changed me forever. We undressed each other slowly, not like it was our first time, my first time, and made a small blanket with our clothes. She pulled me down beside her and kissed me before taking me in her hand. I knew this was my cue, but I didn't know what to do. Should I ask? Jesus. I could think of nothing less manly or less romantic than every permutation of the question ticking through my head—"Excuse me, Mrs. Svenson, but could you possibly show me the approximate location of your . . ." or "I know where it is on *most* women, technically, but just to make sure, could you show me where your . . ."—but I was numb with fear, shriveling in her grasp.

She said, "What's the matter?"

"Could you . . ." I gathered every ounce of daring I possessed. "Could you please show me where?"

She said, "Oh, you dear, sweet boy. *Always* ask." And then she took my hand, brought it to her face, took my middle finger into her mouth and rolled her tongue around it until I thought that my beating heart itself was inside that fingertip, and then she guided it right to the very center of *Chapter 17, Figure 3*.

"Right here, Michael."

(She had to be kidding me, right?)

"That's it. Yes. Slowly at first."

(Jesus H. Christ, Mary, Mother of God, she had to *frigging* be kidding me. Right *there*?)

"Now quick little flutters like . . . ahhh. Yes, that's it."

As Mrs. Svenson began to arch beneath my touch, I couldn't help but think about the six girls I had—what was the proper word?—*mutilated* last fall. It was right *there*, as prominent in its current state as the pop-up timer on a Butterball turkey. How could I ever make it up to them? But just then, Mrs. Svenson was giving me additional instructions.

I did everything she asked, her quickening breath validating instincts I never knew I had. And when she came, it was with a sound I will never forget, a sound that I thought surely had carried back to the main entrance, where my buddies were probably still retrieving expensive cars, and through the woods and up Quail Hollow Road into the room of the old man who could no longer make this happen. The power I felt was like a drug to which I knew I was instantly addicted, more so even than to that other drug, the one that was cultivated when she guided me inside her for the first time. To fulfill an urgent need of another human being in such an astonishing way was miraculous to me, and as Mrs. Svenson and I made love whenever and wherever we could during what little remained of that summer, I always started by asking.

Although it is unlikely that anyone else will be playing behind us today, I rake the center of the trap smooth, then pull the rake behind me to cover my footprints. By the time I come around the bank and onto the green, Sal already has the pin out.

"Inside right edge, firm," he says, handing me my putter. I step behind the ball and eye the line, not to check Sal's read, which I know to be perfect, but to picture the ball taking that line and rolling in. Then I step up and hit the putt, dead center, without a thought, for birdie.

"Good," Sal says. "We got one back. Let's keep 'er goin'."

This is why I am here: for the few passing moments like this one, when there is nothing but Sal and me and the game. Tonight, like most nights, I will be on the sidewalk outside my home, a prowler coveting what is inside, what used to be mine: Hannah twirling on the hardwood hallway floor, still in her leotard after dance class, her face and raised arms cut and prismed like a Picasso through the leaded glass of the entryway; Megan multitasking in the den, a new skill of her generation, toggling between homework and instant messages, downloading music and somehow talking on the phone at the same time, all with an enthusiasm that she hides as soon as any adult enters the room; Kelly, once the girls are in bed, settling on the couch with a bowl of canned peaches—just a habit now, but the only food she was ever able to keep down during any of her other, more difficult pregnancies—reading whatever her book club has chosen this month, just the same as if I were there. Once she is alone, it will be all I can do not to cross the yard, climb the steps and knock softly on the picture window, except that I know I won't be invited in. I suppose they are a form of self-flagellation, these visits—the pain present in the darkness so palpable, so solid in my chest, it feels as if it might be excised by a surgeon of a certain skill. But that's all later, which is why I'll take moments like this one, out here with Sal: not because I deserve them, but because I need them.

I take the ball from him. "Yeah. Let's keep 'er goin'."

3

The truth knocks on the door and you say, "Go away. I'm looking for the truth," and so it goes away. Puzzling.

—Robert M. Pirsig,
Zen and the Art of Motorcycle Maintenance

Until the time I graduated from law school in 1985, the land on the broad hillside across Valley Brook Road behind the third green was nothing but dense forest that every fall was transformed into a brilliant palette of colors. The only picture of Fox Run ever to appear in a major golf magazine is of this view, the lake in the foreground, a white flag in the center of the elevated green, the hillside serving as a vibrantly mottled backdrop. In 1986, however, F. III ran into some minor financial difficulties and sold that parcel of land to a developer who promised to construct, according to the contract, "no more than ten tasteful, residential structures" on the property. But F. III is no lawyer, and he didn't see the need to pay one to represent him in this small transaction, so it never occurred to him that "tasteful" was neither a defined legal term nor a term-of-art in the construction business. What now occupies the hillside, therefore, is a complex of no more than ten *monstrous* residential structures, ranging in size from 8,000 to 15,000 square feet of living space. The collection of red-brick Georgian homes resembles nothing so much as a small southern college campus and is now known at Fox Run, not so affectionately, as "F.U."

Although this par-three is 195 yards from the blue tees, the carry over the lake is only 150 yards from there, 100 from the whites, so that the water should only come into play for beginners. But for anyone who learned to play golf here, the image of the first time you managed to will your ball over to the far shore remains a vivid one, and a substantial portion of the doubt that sunk to the bottom of the lake with all of your failed attempts stays with you, so that memory always keeps the lake in play to some extent. F.U., despite its impending proximity, is not in play from the tee, unless it is Stag Night of the Men's Invitational weekend, post–cocktail hour, and you happen to have a driver in your hands.

"I'm thinkin' three-iron right at the East Wing of the Library," Sal is saying, as he releases a few blades of grass from his fingertips to check the breeze. ("The Library" is the given name of the largest building on the F.U. campus. It sits at the very base of the hill, just across Valley Brook Road from the green, and is occupied by a recently immigrated neurosurgeon and his wife. They have no children.)

I am done questioning Sal for the day, and I take the three without a word. Despite the fact that I was sulking like a six-year-old less than twenty minutes ago as we left the first green, I am now, as they say, "feelin' it," and the freedom of knowing I can trust Sal's choice implicitly only adds to my confidence. I have remembered how to forget, and Sal has sensed this. Aiming at the East Wing with more club than I need means he wants me to go right at it.

The swing feels balanced, powerful, effortless. I am pulling my tee from the ground and striding down off the tee box even before my ball has begun its descent. The shot is perfect. It lands on the gentle slope of the green fifteen feet left of the flag and feeds right, stopping no more than ten feet below the hole.

"Like candy from a baby, that putt, Mr. B.," Sal assures, pulling even with me.

"You're going to have to watch your references out here, Sal."

"Sorry? Oh . . . sorry," he offers, chastened, and I immediately regret that I have forced him to search for an awkward recovery. "How's she feelin'? Kelly."

"Better than with the last one. At least according to Megan. She's my double agent." In the past year, Sal's own wife has made a near-miraculous recovery from breast cancer. Kelly took nightly meals to him when his wife was in the hospital, and I ask about her now in an attempt to ease any discomfort I have caused.

"She's fine, thanks, Mr. B. She's stubborn, that one."

"We like the same kind of women, Sal."

He nods but is silent, doubting, I'm sure, even in his knowledge of Kelly, that there is another woman like his own.

We have reached the bridge that crosses over the narrow spillway on the west end of the lake, and I never cross it without thinking of my own stubborn wife. I was nearly two years out of law school, and Kelly and I had been dating for eight months when she figured out that she would see a lot more of me if she learned to play the game that so consumed me. It is a testament to my infatuation that I agreed. Because I am "overly focused," as Sal would say, I don't always pay attention to my playing partners, and I'm not much fun to play with. I had never risked dating on the golf course before. But the prospect of Kelly's endless legs in a short skirt striding down the fairway beside me overrode my usual misgivings.

To my relief, she was adamant that she wanted to work hard on the fundamentals before playing the golf course. "I'm already the mill-town girl around here. I'm not about to embarrass myself." And so we started spending much of our free evening time together at the driving range. She took a few lessons from the club pro to get started, and then I took over. She had a natural, athletic swing from the beginning, and her long, lithe body gave her a source of power off the tee. But she was used to being immediately good at any sport and could not accept that her abilities didn't translate to every aspect of this new game. As long as there were other members on the range, she held her temper. But whenever it was just the two of us, every mis-hit was followed by a profanity that seemed an impossible mismatch with the lovely mouth from which it emanated. "Fuck a *duck!*" she might say, as a ball ticked off the bottom of her club, or "Just *lick* me, why don'tcha," when a thick pelt of turf lopped over a red-striped Titleist. I heard her refer to herself, at one time or another, as "asswipe," "douchebag," "dick-bite," "prick-for-brains," and, inexplicably, "hairy moose cock." She tossed a pink visor into the stream that parallels the practice range and watched it float away. She broke my mother's old seven-iron.

I loved her more every evening.

When she finally proclaimed herself ready to play a few holes, she was hitting more good shots than bad and could hit her driver close to 150 yards. I warned her not to expect too much.

"It's not like the range," I told her. "You can't get into any kind of a rhythm. You're always changing clubs, the lie's always different—above you, below you, fairway, rough. Just try to stay positive."

"You're just afraid I might beat you on a hole or two," she said.

"Yeah. That's it."

"Come on, Arnie. Show me whatcha got."

So off we went. I asked Sal to go with us, not thinking until we reached the first tee that an extra spectator might make her nervous. But to her credit she ripped her first drive right in front of Sal and several members watching from the putting green. She gave the members a casual wave, picked her tee out of the ground and walked off ahead of me. No big deal. Sal looked at me and raised an eyebrow.

Amazingly, she continued to hit every shot solidly for the first two holes. "Nice one, missy!" Sal cheered with every swing, paying so little attention to me that I had to keep chasing him down for clubs. Kelly went so far as to proclaim it "easier" on the golf course, "because the grass is so much *nicer.*" She made a seven on the first hole and an eight on the par-five second, losing most of her shots on the green. "I'm used to windmills and kangaroo pouches," she quipped. She was actually smiling. Her muscular rear end twitched in her golf skirt, and she kept hip-checking me when we walked side by side. "This is *fun*," she said. I made two distracted sixes. Sal couldn't stop smiling.

When we reached the third tee, I thought about my own early failures there and tried to be encouraging.

"Don't even think about the water, Kel." Sal looked at me sharply.

"I wasn't," she said.

"It's only a hundred yards or so to clear it. You could probably even hit your five-wood and make the green."

"Okay." Sal handed her the five-wood and she started teeing up the brand-new Titleist she'd been playing with.

"Kel, I put some old balls in your bag if you want to use one of those instead."

"How come?"

"Well, just in case—"

"You don't think I can make it over, do you?"

"That's not it at all. Like I said, you can hit it plenty far enough. It's just, well, 'better safe than sorry,' you know?"

"You mean you're really going to be that sorry if I lose this stupid little ball? Am I hearing him correctly, Sal?"

"I couldn't tell you, missy." Sal pulled back behind me and did his best to disappear. In retrospect, this discussion could have served as a template for every argument we would have for the next eighteen years.

"Would you stop twisting everything I say?" I pleaded. "Of *course* I don't mean that."

"How much are these things?"

"About three bucks apiece, but—"

"I'll pay you back, Rockefeller."

"That's not the point . . ." It was useless. "Look, just hit whatever ball—"

"This is the one I've been playing well with, so this is the one I want to hit."

"Perfect."

She bent down to plug her tee into the ground, and her skirt hiked almost high enough to reveal what I knew to be white cotton panties. Good God, no wonder I was playing so badly. She took her stance, twitched her rear end a couple of times (I swear on purpose) and took a mighty swipe at the ball. I say "at" because she missed it entirely.

"That was practice," she said.

"Just like the driving range, Kel. Pretend the water's not even—"

"How can I do that if you keep reminding me?"

"Sorry. Nice and easy, that's all."

The next swing might have been even faster, but she got a piece of it. The ball ticked off the toe of the club and shot straight to the right before rolling down the bank and soundlessly into the lake.

I expected her to turn on me, to blame me, and I deserved it. In trying to head off disappointment, I had put doubt in her mind where none had existed. In golf, fears are not instinctual; they are learned. Kids, even beginners, are often better putters from close range than accomplished adults, because they haven't yet learned that three-footers are hard. They just step up and hit them. That's what Kelly was prepared to do before I opened my condescending yap. But, surprisingly, there was no profanity, directed at me or otherwise. She stood still for a while, and after the ripples in the surface of the lake had stretched and diffused to almost nothing, she turned, walked to where Sal was holding her bag, unzipped the pocket and pulled out one of the old balls I had put in there. She never looked at me.

"Want to hit another one, hon?" I asked lamely.

She caught a little bit more of the next one, but the only difference in the result was that the ball carried enough speed to skip once over the surface of the water before diving under for good. "Okay, Kel. Maybe next time. There's a drop area on the other side where you can . . ." She was already digging for another ball. "Okay. Maybe one more."

The third one looked like an instant replay of the second, as did the fourth, fifth and sixth. For variety's sake she threw in a pop-up for number seven that entered the water at a perfect ninety-degree angle with a sound like *pfloog*. Then she was back to the shanks. She was a machine now. She had it grooved. She was Iron Byron set on "chop." She had gone through all of the old balls. Eleven and twelve were the brand-new ones left from the sleeve I had bought for her in the pro shop. Finally, she looked at me.

She said, "Can you toss me one?"

"Hon, like I said, there's a drop area on the other side where you can—"

"Do you have any *fucking* balls?"

A short burst of air escaped Sal's lips.

"Yeah. But they're all brand new . . ." I caught myself. "Yeah."

Because I often carry my own bag, I never have many extra balls. All I had were the five pristine Titleists left from the two sleeves I had bought for myself. I got them all out and prepared to bid them farewell. She had no chance now. She had gone too far. Golf is the most mentally oriented of all sports, and the psyche of the beginner is most fragile. She was no longer capable of picturing a shot that cleared the lake and therefore was not capable of hitting one. I was not going to tell her this. I was also not going to tell her that on the next hole, with the water out of play, she was likely to be able to swing as if this had never happened. I said nothing. I was in damage-control mode now, already thinking about the rest of the evening. Any ill-advised commentary and there might as well be yellow police crime-scene tape in a three-foot radius around those white panties.

And then she did something amazing, something that proved both her status as a true athlete and mine as a pretender: she hit the last one over. And she did it *knowing* it was the last one. There was more pressure on that shot than on any of the previous ones, and yet there it was, number seventeen, sailing high and true. Kelly posed, holding her follow-through as if for the ESPN cameras, watching it land on the apron just short of the green and roll to within twenty-five feet of the flag. Once her ball (*my* ball, I suppose) had come to a stop, she turned to me and smiled.

"That's the one, missy!" Sal said. "Do you know how many years it took Mikey to do that?"

"Nice shot, hon," I said. "Ernst & Young is still tabulating the financial impact, but *nice* shot."

"There. I'm glad I got that out of the way." She was beaming. Where had I seen that look before? "You know, Sal, he's really cheap for a rich guy."

"I'm not rich. I'm spoiled. There's a difference."

"Aren't you going to hit?" she asked.

"With what?"

"Oh. Sorry."

"No problem. I think number fourteen got close enough to the far bank for me to retrieve it if I take my shoes and socks off."

"You were counting?"

"I *am* keeping score."

"What do I have so far?"

"Including penalties, you're putting for thirty-four. Though, if you were a member and you were going to turn this score in, the most you could take would be ten." We were crossing the bridge side by side now, Sal whistling behind us, and she was gently hip-checking me every few steps again. This was a good sign.

"You're kidding. Isn't that cheating?"

"No. It keeps handicaps from becoming inflated. It's telling the truth that's cheating."

"Only rich people could invent a system like that."

Another snort of suppressed laughter from Sal.

"Actually, it works pretty well," I assured her.

"How do I know if I'm getting better if I don't count them all?"

"You'll have balls left over."

"And you'll still be an ass." Hip check.

. . .

That's when I remembered where I had seen that look of perfect self-satisfaction on Kelly's face before. In the seven years since my initiation at the hands of the lovely Mrs. Svenson, I had never gone longer than a month between the end of one sexual relationship and the beginning of another. Not because *I* was irresistible by any measure, but because *sex* was irresistible to me. I was not on the lookout for life partners, just partners, and any woman of passable good looks and good humor who would have me, had me. Don't misunderstand; I was scrupulously faithful to all of them. But when one or the other of us decided it was time to move on, I moved quickly. Until Agnes, that is.

Agnes Humpstone was nineteen years old when I met her. Re-met her, actually. I had dated her older sister one summer during college, and Agnes was nothing more to me then than the skinny, gawky tenth grader who refused to go to bed and leave her sister and me alone. Three years later, after her freshman year at UNC Chapel Hill and my second year of law school, she ended up lifeguarding at the Fox Run swimming pool, and I ended up absurdly in love.

Little Agnes had grown up. A lot. She was nearly six feet tall, broad-shouldered from years of competitive swimming, and her face, with its prominent Roman nose, had taken on an almost haughty serenity that aged her. If she hadn't spoken to me, I never would have recognized her.

"Michael?" I was in the pool, squinting up at her voice, trying to figure out why one of the lifeguards was calling me by name. "Hey! It's me, Agnes."

"Excuse me?"

"Agnes Humpstone. Trudy's sister." I remember thinking when I was dating Trudy that no first name went well with "Humpstone," but that "Trudy" and "Agnes" could not have been unanimous family decisions.

"Agnes? My God." I had succeeded in getting to a spot below her chair from which I could see her clearly, and I was a little stunned. "You're so . . . big."

Ah, the seduction begins.

"Yeah. I guess I am."

I climbed out of the pool beside her chair and became instantly aware of my stomach muscles. I was looking up at her, but she was dutifully scanning the pool for heirs and heiresses in distress.

"I don't mean big like *big*. I just mean . . . well, the last time I saw you—"

"It's okay. You're at a bad angle."

I doubted there was such a thing.

She looked down briefly. "So what are you up to now?"

"I'm in law school. Actually, this summer I'm clerking for a judge, but I'll be starting my third year in September."

"That's cool."

Cool? She was tanned, wore Ray-Bans, a whistle around her neck and a braided leather thingamabob around her ankle. Standing there with my old-mannish trunks hanging on my bony hips, my dark brown face and limbs sprouting from my hospital-linen-white body, I felt the opposite of cool. Still, being an older man, practically a professional, had to count for something, so I decided to test the water, as it were.

"I'm done around nine," was her answer to the question I wasn't even sure I'd gotten out.

"Tonight?"

"Sure. Why not." She was smiling out at the pool. "You can help me clean up."

Let's be clear. I never went to the pool much before that summer. I stopped in occasionally on humid evenings after working up a good sweat on the practice range, but generally I avoided it. The pool was populated primarily by kept women and spoiled children, and while I had once been the latter and was likely someday to marry one of the former, the pool was no place for a bachelor in his prime hunting years. But by the end of that summer Fox Run might as well have had me on the payroll. Every evening that Agnes had the closing shift, I showed up to help take down the umbrella stands, move the tables and chairs off the lush grass and bus the dirty plastic dishes of my fellow members. For us, this qualified as foreplay. When the last employee was gone, we made frantic love in the pool, in the men's showers, in the women's showers, on the secluded playground or, on nights when we could wait long enough to get there, in the dense stand of pines left of the thirteenth fairway. And while Agnes has, in the grand scheme of things, become important only in the way that she helps to introduce and contextualize Kelly, there was a time when I thought she might eventually become my wife.

Our relationship lasted a year and a half, through the first semester of her junior year and my first four months of practice with a large downtown law firm. It seemed like more then, but my relationship with Agnes was based primarily on deciding where and when we could get together to have sex. We both still lived with our parents (she because she was still young enough), so that even when she was home from school, privacy was a commodity in short supply. Aside from our Fox Run haunts, we made love in cars (mine), on boats (her father's) and in other people's empty apartments (my friends'). We took late-night walks from our parents' homes and were typically horizontal in a neighbor's yard inside of ten minutes. And on nights when the weather didn't permit such daring, we did our muffled best in my parents' basement game room. It was all very "high school." But whether it was because of the thrill of all the planning, or some more significant connection between us that lay beneath the unabated physical attraction, I never tired of Agnes. To me, that seemed like love, and I found myself talking about her in the same terms of permanence that some of my friends had begun to use when speaking of their older mates. So when I called her on Valentine's Day of her junior year and she thanked me for the roses that I hadn't sent (apparently, there was no card, so sure was the sender that she would know his identity), I was utterly unprepared. She was caught, but she also had the perfect justification:

"Michael, I'm only twenty years old. You do know that, right?"

That was it, really. Agnes went from being the central focus of my life, even my future, to leaving an inconceivable hollow in the time frame of a single phone call. It had never occurred to me that she would be the one to break it off. I thought that the relationship was mine to maintain or dissolve as I pleased. I was the older man. She got to tell all of her friends she was dating a lawyer. That was *cool*, right?

This was my state when I met Kelly. Indeed, it had been my state for almost six months. I moved out of my parents' house so that I could revel in my own self-pity in isolation, away from my mother's well-meaning admonishments to "get on with it." I worked from 7:00 A.M. to 9:00 P.M. six days a week, looking straight ahead, plowing through discovery documents and preparing my senior partners for trial. I realized that I had few friends, that group always having consisted of Stewey Trammell (who was now married, inconceivably, to Donna O'Connor and the father of a baby girl), a few Fox Run playing buddies and whoever my current love interest was at the time. I went straight home after work, threw a Stouffer's frozen dinner in my counter-top microwave and fell asleep sitting upright on the couch I had pilfered from my parents' basement, watching reruns of shows I had watched as a kid: *The Brady Bunch, Leave It to Beaver, The Partridge Family*, for chrissake. I had cable TV and could have been surfing late-night Cinemax for a little pick-me-up, but even full-frontal nudity failed to cheer me. For the first time in my life, my penis was a disinterested appendage, a limp personal plumbing device, *bona non grata*.

And then I lost my secretary. Or so I was told. Truthfully, in a firm of two hundred attorneys, I had never been sure which one was mine. I dropped my filing and dictation in a box outside a corral of cubicles that housed all of the typists, and my finished work appeared, via office messenger, a few hours later. At any other point in my life, I would have been scouring that busy hive for a little honey, but they may as well have all looked like Miss Jane Hathaway from *The Beverly Hillbillies* for all I cared. I was asked to go to the main conference room to interview a candidate for one of two secretarial openings. The office manager would be assessing her skills. I was simply to determine whether I could get along with her as well as I had with my previous secretary. Apparently, our relationship had been exemplary.

Kelly Wisniewski was already in the main glassed-in conference room, which, from the fiftieth floor of the USX Tower, had a panoramic view of Pittsburgh's Golden Triangle and Three Rivers Stadium. Evidently, she was not expecting anyone so soon because, as I approached, I could see that she was standing at the center of the room-long window, on tiptoe, her forehead and the entire bridge of her nose pressed against the glass, as if she was trying to see straight down the full height of the building to the sidewalk below. I made myself invisible behind the heavy wooden door and knocked.

I have told you that my wife is beautiful, and she must have been that first day, but I didn't see it right away. She was wearing an ill-fitting gray skirt and blazer of a style more suited to someone twice her age, and the frilly white blouse under her jacket worked with the rest of the ensemble to remove any hint of her figure. She was tall—that much was clear, even in the orthopedic-looking gray pumps she wore on her feet. Her brown hair was up, though uncomfortably so, stapled in place by too many bobby pins, and two oversize, fake pearl earrings hung from her large ears. In short, she appeared to be a woman out of her element. But her face was warm and open, free of any detectable makeup, and she smiled easily when she saw me, the only hint of her pre-interview posture being the Texas Longhorns mark left by her nose and brow on the window behind her.

"Hi, I'm Michael Benedict." I extended my hand, and her long, thin fingers gripped mine. She shook hands like a man.

"Kelly Wisniewski. Nice to meet you."

"Long way up, aren't we?"

"Yeah. The firm I work for now is on the third floor of a little three-story building on the old First Side." She put her hand on my shoulder and had me sight along her other arm. "That one down there with the chaise lounge on the roof?"

"Got it."

"That's my lunchtime spot on sunny days." Her voice was my first clue that I was in trouble. It had the clear, resonant quality of a radio disc jockey with a little phone-sex operator thrown in.

"You know you're not likely to get any sun here."

"Yeah. But I figure my paycheck's not likely to depend on how good a month you have either." She said this without irony, as if she were sorry, in a way, to have to give that up.

"Have a seat."

"Thanks."

I sat at the head of the immense conference table, and she took the seat around the corner immediately to my left. She kept both feet flat on the ground, knees together, long fingers laced and resting on her lap. It was a posture straight from an interview training film. I tried to put her more at ease.

"Look, I've never done this before," I said.

"Me neither." She looked down at herself. "I wear jeans at my other job. I borrowed this awful suit from my mother. I guess we're both virgins."

Clue number two. I started again.

"I mean, I know there are things that I'm not allowed to ask, but I know nothing about employment law, so I don't know exactly what they are. I'm really just supposed to tell them whether I think I can work with you, when all they're going to do is bury you in a maze of cubicles a mile and a half away from my office anyway."

She smiled. "I won't stay buried."

"Excuse me?"

"I mean you don't have to worry about me getting lost here. If I work for you, you'll know it. I have a good ear for language, and I'll probably have suggestions on most everything you dictate."

Where had I gotten the idea that she needed to be put at ease?

"Look," she continued. "Let me save you some trouble. Here's what's not on my résumé, which I see you don't have anyway. I'm twenty-one years old. I went to Penn State for a couple of years on a partial basketball scholarship. It became clear pretty quickly that I was too skinny to compete with the big girls, but they let me keep my scholarship anyway. I showed my appreciation by getting pregnant the summer after my sophomore year by a guy I grew up with back here, a landscaper, sweet guy, and we decided to get married because it seemed like the thing to do. I didn't go back to school, lost the baby early in the first trimester and found myself married to a guy I had nothing but history in common with. I think we were both afraid of hurting each other, after the baby and all, so we stuck it out until it started to seem silly. I've been divorced for four months. I don't particularly want this job, I like it where I am, but I do need it. You have a kind face, and I think we *would* work well together."

At the time, I was shocked by her rambling candor, but knowing Kelly as I do now, as a woman of few, well-chosen words, I think she was, after all, a little nervous.

"I'm pretty sure you just answered every question I'm not allowed to ask."

She shrugged and smiled. "Too late."

"Anything else?"

"I'm also much prettier than I look in this rag."

"I'm beginning to see that."

"Are you allowed to say that?"

"Too late."

When we finished and shook hands again, there was a stirring I hadn't felt in a long time. It wasn't in the predictable place either. It was a sort of tingling warmth running from the space just behind my ears, down my neck and along the tops of my shoulders. Clue number three.

She got the job, of course, though not as my secretary. "Inappropriate relationships" were forbidden between attorneys and staff who reported directly to them. I convinced the office manager to hire Kelly for an opening with the new female associate. After all, I confessed, Kelly was attractive and might be a distraction to my work. I admitted that such distractions had occasionally occurred with my former secretary (I hoped that this was possible), and I didn't want any further drag on my efficiency. My request was honored, and my new secretary was a five-foot, one-inch, 140-pound lesbian named Henrietta, who went by "Hank."

I started courting her (Kelly, not Hank) over the cubicle walls almost immediately. I often find myself judging people's intelligence by whether or not they think I'm funny. Kelly appeared to be a genius. Wearing her own clothes now, her wavy hair in a simple ponytail, she was stunning in the way that tall, athletic women can be—as much in her presence and manner as in her looks. Hank was my ally, reporting back to me that "the skinny one with all the legs keeps talking about you." In a way, we were both on the rebound, and we rebounded into each other like a couple of oppositely charged ions. Kelly claims that, before me, she never slept with anyone before the fifth date, which is why we celebrate (or we did) August 23 as the anniversary of our first five dates. We went out for dinner. Briefly. We broke at least three traffic laws and could have been cited for more than one exposure violation on the reckless ride back to my apartment. By the time we tumbled to the floor together in front of my couch (the couch that had seen nothing racier in six months than Mr. Brady replacing his bookmark) we were already half naked. Her hands and mouth were everywhere, and the rest of our clothes were gone before I knew what had happened. I braced myself for what I was sure was going to be a wild ride. And then everything stopped.

Kelly gently pushed my shoulders until I rolled onto my back. Then she straddled me and, without once looking away from my face, slid me inside her and made love to me so slowly I thought I would stop breathing. She seemed weightless, but her look bore down on me, and I could feel movement that I couldn't see. Then her eyes rolled up and away and we came together, Kelly sitting utterly still on top of me.

When I felt I could speak, I said, "Jesus, where did you learn to do that?"

"I'm a natural."

When we started again, Dee Dee Svenson whispered in my ear. And so I asked. Kelly let out the same sigh of gratitude that Mrs. Svenson had seven years before, and she showed me exactly what she wanted. She wanted my tongue here, then here, then here. She wanted me slowly, slowly from behind. She wanted to be on her back, her arms pinned to the floor above her head. She wanted her breast in my mouth when she came.

I assumed that would be the end of the evening, except for the sleeping part, which I was more than ready for. Like most men, I think of myself as insatiable when I'm not having sex, but twice was already once more than my average. We had moved to the couch, my head on the armrest, hers on my chest, facing the television that bathed us in its own post-coital glow. We were paying no attention to David Letterman and his guest, but getting to know each other's bodies in these unhurried moments before sleep. When her hand strayed between my legs and lingered there, it was probably without intent, but I made the mistake of speaking.

I said, "There is no way."

She said, "Excuse me?"

I said, "There is absolutely no way."

She said, kissing her way down my chest and over my stomach, "Never challenge me like that, counselor." And when she had proved the possibility of what I had claimed impossible, she looked up at me with that expression of utter self-satisfaction—the one I would see again the following summer, when her last ball cleared the lake and bounced toward the flagstick. "Now you may go to sleep," she said.

We were married two years later. It took me that long only because of my natural aversion to the advice of my "loved ones," who were all clamoring for me to close the deal before Kelly realized her mistake. Sal was the first, but even my father, for whom advice was a form of communication and therefore parceled out only when disaster was imminent, asked what the hell I was waiting for. She was beautiful, she was smarter than most college graduates I knew, she was my best friend *and* she liked sleeping with me. What *was* I waiting for?

Partly, I think, history made me distrust my own good fortune. One night, in bed, I confided in her that I had spent my entire high school career as the harmless confidant of every woman who looked like her.

"I wouldn't have found you sexy in high school either," she said.

"You know, honesty is not always an admirable quality."

"No, really. Attractive girls are taught to be stupid about boys. As soon as the world sees you're going to be pretty, it starts teaching you to be insipid. 'Oh, *he's* cute. Why don't you go out with *him*.' You're supposed to go after the big, muscular jocks because you *can*. They're off limits to the others, so you think they must be special. It takes a while to realize that *attractive* and *attraction* are two very different things. Most of my high school friends still haven't figured it out." She paused, considering. "Look, I don't want to marry you because you're sexy. You're sexy because I want to marry you. Does that make any sense?"

I wasn't trying to make sense of what she said so much as I was trying to fill the immense space that the word *marry* now occupied between us.

"I would, you know," she said. "Marry you."

I'm slow, but I'm not stupid. I got out of the bed, knelt next to it and asked Kelly Wisniewski to be my wife. Since she'd really already said yes, what she said was, "Christ, it took you long enough," then pulled me back into bed, put her head on my chest and was asleep before my pulse had returned to normal.

Because Kelly and her mother could never have afforded the wedding, my father offered to pay for whatever Kelly wanted. If she wasn't already the daughter-in-law of his dreams, she was by the time she laid out our wedding plans. That she was not from Fox Run, or anyplace like it, headed a list of many things my father liked about Kelly Wisniewski. But when he gave her a blank check and she planned the equivalent of a blue-light special, she joined an elite order in my father's eyes, my mother being the only other living member.

We were married in my parents' backyard. In attendance were Stewey Trammell (best man) and his wife, my platonic junior-prom date, Donna; Elsa McGonagle (maid of honor), Kelly's best friend from high school, recently divorced from her own prom date; my parents and Kelly's mother; Sal (who gave the bride away wearing black suspenders); and my father's twelve-year-old golden retriever, Margin Call ("Marge"), who had been taught to bring the rings forward on a slightly dampened pillow, before retreating to a more distant location, where her chronic flatulence would disrupt only her own enjoyment of the proceedings. Kelly looked stunning and immune to superstition in Elsa's wedding dress (she would have worn her own again if moths hadn't gotten to it), and from the moment I slid the ring onto her finger until the moment she placed my overnight bag on the seat of my car, telling me to leave our home, it never occurred to me that I would spend one day of my life without her as my wife.

The window to the left of my desk overlooks my parents' front yard. It is the same desk that I sat hunched over for most of my adolescent life, trying to make sense of chemistry and calculus and Shakespeare with a number-two pencil and a yellow tablet. Now, I am simply trying to make sense of my own life by burning it onto a computer screen. In the artificial present tense I have created—of Sal and me approaching the third green—I make the straight, uphill birdie putt to get back to even par and somehow manage to find pleasure in that. But in the actual present tense, the here and now of Michael Benedict at his desk, I look out the same window through which I looked as a child and see my wife's 1996 Volvo station wagon pulling up the driveway. The connecting flagstone walkway splices empty flower beds, cleared for the coming winter, and leads to the stoop and the heavy front door directly below me. Megan and Hannah open opposite backseat doors, and Hannah leaps out with what I like to think of as glee: still, at eight, Daddy's little girl. Megan climbs out dutifully. She will be kind to me for the time she is here, as long as I let her spend half of it on the phone. But she is old enough to know that she hasn't been told everything, and the tension of no longer knowing quite what kind of person her father is, at a time when she doesn't know quite who she is, is too much for her and is almost visible in her posture. She wears an oversize hooded sweatshirt that hides every new curve, and she looks predeterminedly bored as she gives her mother a hand hoisting herself out of the front seat. It isn't possible to hide her mother's new curves. Kelly leans on Megan for a moment, letting the baby drop and settle away from her spine. I remember her leaning in to me that way, waiting for Megan to shift inside of her, to release her legs into movement, and the perfect symmetry of reality and memory constricts my throat as if around a stone I must swallow. And then another image approaches, the one that has returned with increasing frequency since the day Kelly announced the new life inside her. It is of Kelly, the last time she was pregnant, though not with Hannah, bearing down in a somber, cruelly named "delivery room" that seems to smell of everything but the pungence of new life, giving birth to a daughter we will name but never know. I have had to learn to push this image away in the name of functioning in the world, and that I can do so now, and replace it with nothing more significant than regret, is either a testament to human resilience or a condemnation of the same. I can never decide which.

This represents progress for us—her bringing them to me, even getting out of the car to say hello. Until recently, Kelly's official posture had been that I was not to see or speak to our girls. But even then she had been kind enough not to answer the phone (when the caller ID told her it was me) and not to question the girls, once September came, when they didn't arrive home on the school bus but rounded the corner a few minutes later, having emerged from the backseat of my car. Now Hannah is bolting around the far side of the wagon, brown pigtails bouncing against the light-blue shoulders of her Windbreaker as she passes her mother and sister, races up the walkway and disappears under the front door's overhang below me. The heavy brass knocker drops three times in quick succession. I sit a moment longer and watch Megan and Kelly make their way up the path. When they are just below me, still visible beyond the overhang, Megan kisses her mother dutifully on the cheek and pats her round tummy before leaving her alone below the stoop, hanging back like a mother waiting for her daughters trick-or-treating at a stranger's house. Kelly looks up and I wonder if she can see me, or at least a hint of me, in the window. Ironically, this pregnancy has been much easier than any of the others, with no hint of trouble, and she looks beautiful. For a brief moment, I think she is raising a hand in greeting, and I start to do the same. But she only brushes a stray wisp of hair from her forehead, then crosses her forearms over her abdomen. I push my chair back and blacken the screen, leaving behind one unfinished story for another.

4

But in fact, the serpent was already there, and our sports do not simulate, therefore, a constant state. Rather, between the days of work, sports or games only repeat and repeat our effort to go back, back to a freedom we cannot recall, save as a moment of play in some garden now lost.

—A. Bartlett Giamatti, *Take Time for Paradise*

C ell phones are contraband within the confines of the Fox Run Golf and Hunt Club. Only physicians and expectant fathers may carry them, and even then they must be pocketed and set on vibrate. God forbid incoming news of an organ donation in transit via chopper should disrupt a four-footer for bogey. Kelly and I haven't talked about whether or not she will call when it's time, but the thought that she might summon someone else, anyone else, when our child is ready to be born is too impossible to entertain. It's too early to expect her call. Not as early as last time, but too early just the same. Still, I have asked Sal to carry the phone in his pocket just to be safe, and when I see him fishing for it on our way to the fourth tee, my pulse instinctively quickens.

"Check the caller ID, Sal."

"Bet I know more about these things than you do."

"Sorry. Who is it?"

"Looks like your mother."

"Christ."

"Tell her I said hello," Sal instructs, handing me the phone. "I mean, since she told you to say hello to me." I swear he looks sixteen when he says this, and I am struck by the realization that, three years beyond their fiftieth reunion, my caddy still has a high school crush on my mother.

I love my mother too. Let me say that again for emphasis: *I love my mother.* But my mother the person and my mother the phone voice are two entirely different personalities. She is efficient to a fault, not only with her time and money, but with everyone else's as well. As a result, she has been using the phone as if there were per-second billing since roughly 1952. She always opens with what she believes to be the most essential piece of information she has to convey, so you have to mentally brace yourself. She once called me after my father had been in a minor car accident, and the first words out of her mouth were: "Your father's not dead." This, to my mother, was far more important than what actually *had* happened, which was that my father had sustained a cut on the bridge of his nose that required Neosporin and a Band-Aid. Over the years, I have learned to listen to her and to simultaneously supply for myself all of the cushioning details that a normal person might provide. Caller ID was invented to soften the impact of calls from people like my mother. Sal hands me the phone.

"Hey, Ma." (I say this like the harsh, northeastern "muh," not the softer, southern "maw.")

"Your father and I think you should seek professional help." My mother's voice is low, almost manly, with the added rasp of a former heavy smoker.

"Ma, I'm on the golf course."

"Goodness. Had I known you were *busy*, I never would have presumed—"

"Ma, I'm only supposed to use this phone for emergencies."

"Your life is a mess. What could be more of an emergency?"

Sal is motioning to me. "Oh. Sal says hello," I tell her.

"*That's* an emergency?"

"Look, Ma, we'll talk at home."

But that was the whole point of her call. We wouldn't talk at home. My parents are just as embarrassed to have me there as I am to be there, and so we all act as if I'm *not* there. I work in my room and delay my breakfast and shower until they leave for the office. If I'm not back in my room before they return, I try to stay out until they finish dinner and have retired to the den to read. That way, I can slip in through the kitchen door and back upstairs without any direct contact. Sometimes, my mother will leave a plate of food for me on the kitchen counter. If not, I slip downstairs for dinner and the late news once they've gone to bed. I'm sort of like Gregor Samsa with keys to the BMW, and although he had more severe outward problems, my parents are no less repulsed. The phone calls from my mother are her contribution to the ruse that I am otherwise unreachable.

"Don't you put me off for your silly game. Your father and I are giving you until the New Year, and then you're out."

"Ma—"

"There's nothing more to be said. We feel as though we've been forced to choose a side, and the wrong one at that. It's been almost three months, and you continue to be unconscionably unproductive. For all I know, you're even continuing to—"

"Ma, you know I've been writing."

"Which is only slightly less selfish than what you're doing at this very minute. You're still pipe-dreaming at a time when every ounce of your energy should be focused on those three lovely girls. That's all I have to say. Good-bye. I love you."

"Love you too, Ma."

She has a point, of course. But it's the same point that every woman has held over every man since Og first lurched out of the cave and created an implement that was to be used for something other than spearing or pummeling his food. Why am I out here doing this? What is it about men and their games that make them so inseparable? Why do we run to them, not just for the joy of playing them, but for solace as well? And don't try to tell me that women are no different, that their love for games has merely been suppressed by men through the ages. We are genetically different in this respect. I don't question that good female athletes love their sports with a fervor equal to that of their male counterparts. But there is no such thing as an obsessed *crummy* female athlete. If you ask, hypothetically, the twice-monthly male golfer who has never broken a hundred if he'd rather go play a quick nine before dark or make animal love to his paramour, he'll invariably pause and ask: "What will I shoot?"

So, I am here for love; I am here for solace. I am here because I can live for three hours entirely in the present tense without being frightened by what I see. And, yes, maybe I am here because I don't know quite what else to do. I hand the phone back to Sal.

"Everything okay?" he asks.

"Perfect," I assure us both.

The fourth hole at Fox Run is, in the judgment of the USGA handicappers, the most difficult hole on the golf course, and it's hard to argue with that appraisal. From the blue tees, it measures 485 yards, but unlike many other par-fours of that length, there's no part of it that's downhill. It is simply a straightaway, brutally long par-four that plays more like a reachable par-five. The only hint of slope in the fairway is right to left. Ten years ago I would play a draw here, using the natural right-to-left overspin of that shot to get an extra kick of distance off the sloping fairway. But the draw is too close a cousin to the snap hook, and after twenty-five years of taking penalty strokes out of the steep creek bed that lines the left side here, I have finally given up the draw for good.

Sal hands me the driver and reinforces what I'm already thinking. "Nothin' fancy, Mr. B. Just somethin' in the fairway. It's three shots to get there half the time anyway."

"Way ahead of you for once."

I press my hands forward at address to set the angle I will try to hold throughout the swing. Executed correctly, this helps to produce a boring power-fade, as opposed to the wristy, floating slice that most beginners battle. I take the club back slightly outside the normal line, reaching out and up, clubface square and wrists firm, then let it rip. The ball starts out low and left, headed toward the left rough, a path that would have scared me ten years ago, but then it starts to simultaneously rise and bend right, reaching its apex as it finds the center of the fairway. It drops gently, rolling only a yard or two.

Sal says nothing, only nodding his approval as he takes the driver from me. As we walk together off the tee, he is whistling an Italian aria that I recognize but cannot name. The sun isn't low, but it's already softening behind me in the October sky. Maudlin or no, it reminds me of myself. I'm not exactly sinking, but I am softening. It is hard to imagine that I will soon be responsible, am already responsible, for another new being who may someday walk with me over this very same ground. Is there anything we experience in this life that is not, ultimately, humbling?

Kelly told me about the pregnancy on a day that was much like today, but on the other side of summer, so the clear sky and cool air felt more like a promise. I was home early from the office, as had become my habit twice a week over the past six, and I had already shot seventy once, earlier in April, on the sheer adrenaline of the new possibilities that my deal with Kelly had opened. Even work felt less like drudgery. For years, it had meant nothing more to me than the dollars it generated. I typically billed just enough hours every year to support (by Fox Run standards anyway) a comfortable, modest lifestyle. We have no boats, no summer homes, we buy only used cars, and I pack a lunch to take to work every day. Our largest discretionary expense, by far, is Fox Run. Unlike most of the second-generation members here, I am no trust fund baby, but instead the product of a father who believes (probably now more than ever) that money should be given away to everyone *but* your children. As of the night of our deal, our college/retirement nest egg stood at approximately $250,000, all in government bonds, and while that is not a small amount of money, it occurred to me that, if I made the Senior Tour in five years, it would not be nearly enough to carry us through several years of questionable income. I had therefore begun to rededicate myself at the office. Instead of billing a leisurely five or six hours in a nine-hour day, I billed eight in an eight-hour day. Hank, who came with me as both secretary and office manager when I opened my own practice ten years ago, struggled to fill both roles now and said that she would need an assistant if I intended "to keep up this nonsense." Because of the connections I had through my father, I had never lacked for potential clients, and I stopped referring work to my friends in large law firms, keeping as much as possible for myself. I opened an online brokerage account with E*Trade, put half of our savings in it and began, with the advice of one of my father's best young analysts, to invest it aggressively in the stock market. For the first time since Megan and Hannah were toddlers, dependent on us for every joy and necessity, each day began for me with a distinct sense of purpose.

Before I tell about the rest of that day, about how Kelly followed me up the stairs for our accustomed debriefing of the day's events, about how she said, "I'm pregnant," as I loosened my tie, as easily as if she were saying, "I'm hungry," I want to tell about another day. And though it may be part of a different story, it feels to me like part of this one.

On this day, Kelly is not forty, but thirty-five years old. She is on her back and her feet are in the stirrups of a delivery bed at McGee Women's Hospital, though her abdomen scarcely rises beneath her gown. She is bearing down hard. Harder than with either Megan or Hannah, because her body doesn't understand why this is being made to happen now. It is only grudgingly obeying the Pitocin that has been dripping into her arm for the past two hours. No one could tell us when the baby's heart had stopped beating. The bleeding started just before Kelly was due for her six-month appointment, but it didn't seem severe enough to reschedule. We went together, both because of the bleeding and because I never tire of hearing the rapid fetal *fwoosh-fwoosh-fwoosh-fwoosh* through the monitor. We held hands as the doctor spread the cold, clear gel over the area she would check again and again, finding nothing. Thanks in no small part to the glut of malpractice lawsuits arising out of cesarean sections, Kelly would have to deliver.

The baby is breech. A common occurrence in early, induced labor. It is nothing to be concerned about, we are told. Unlike full-term deliveries, a breech presents few problems at six months because of the baby's small size. I am not holding Kelly's hand. She needs them both to grip the handlebars positioned at her side. With nothing else to do, I am watching my third daughter come backward into the world. And while the room is unnaturally quiet, the silence severed only by the doctor's gentle urgings and Kelly's constricted breath, I cannot stop the hope from welling from within when I see the feet. They look like Hannah's feet. Long and narrow, with toes skinny like fingers. The color is wrong, but that happens, doesn't it? Perhaps there had been a terrible mistake. A wonderful mistake. Her knees are Kelly's, her narrow hips and flat rump mine, her tummy is a healthy baby's tummy, the thick, veined lifeline still attached. Her chest narrows quickly to her long, elegant neck. But her face is quiet. And her arms come last in something like surrender.

We named her Jessica Elizabeth, after our two maternal grandmothers, and placed her in the as-yet-empty family plot my parents had bought in 1965. It says something about my life's good fortune that this is the closest thing to tragedy that I have had to endure. But that is also perhaps why it refuses to leave me. For the first year, Kelly and I marked together what would have been the events of Jessica's life: Now she would be smiling, now rolling over, now reaching to be held, now waving hello and good-bye. Our therapist said this was healthy. But after what would have been her first birthday, Kelly refused to participate anymore. It was time to move on, she said, and I supposed she was right. But I haven't been able to stop. I still say it to myself, and I suspect that Kelly does too: Now she would be going to preschool, now riding a bike with training wheels, now going to her first movie, sitting on Daddy's lap, eating popcorn in the dark.

If I might be so self-serving as to distinguish between explanation and excuse, then although Jessica's death doesn't excuse my reaction to the revelation of Kelly's pregnancy five years later, it does help to explain it. When she gave me the news—news that should have conveyed nothing but the possibility of new life—I heard only the possibility of another loss. And that, I believe, is why I asked the question that should never have been asked:

"What are we going to do about it?"

"Excuse me?"

My mind was such a blank slate of denial that I asked it again:

"What are we going to do about it?"

"You're serious?"

"You're forty, Kel. And with your—our—history—"

"Yes, Michael. With my *history*, this baby is a gift. No shots, no calendars, no thermometers. Just you and me, like we always hoped it would happen."

"But aren't you afraid?"

"Life is dangerous, Michael. You have a daughter who will be handed a driver's license in less than three years."

"Only if we teach her to drive."

"It's going to happen. And so are broken bones and broken hearts and car dates with boys who are pierced and tattooed. You can't protect them or me or *us* against everything. You should know that by now."

"What about me? Can't I protect myself? I could lose both of you."

She didn't say anything for a moment, and I thought maybe I had gotten to her. Then she shook her head.

"Michael, don't even try to pretend this will be harder for you than it will be for me."

"*Will?* Then you've decided?"

I will never forget the look on her face. It said that she had no idea who I was.

She said, "I'm sorry. I thought this was just an announcement."

And, of course, that's what it was. For us, there was no decision to be made. But I had succeeded in making her believe that for me there was. There was a certain amount of irreparable damage in that.

We moved carefully through the next few weeks, attending to all of the necessities of our life together with silent efficiency: Megan got to and from track practice and piano lessons; Hannah never missed her dance class. Bills were paid, meals were cooked, a school board meeting was attended and the grass got cut. The cats did not go hungry. I continued to practice or play twice during the week and on both Saturday and Sunday mornings. I was never told not to. We had a deal.

"We got a long way home, Mr. B. Hit this one."

What does it say about me that I am able to take the two-iron Sal is holding out and hit a perfect 215-yard rope to the center of the green, Kelly's voice still fresh in my memory? That I, someone who once lost one child and might now be losing a wife and three others, can lag the delicate, downhill twenty-five-foot birdie putt to within inches of the cup and find satisfaction, even significance, there? Is this quality that I share with so many men a genetic defect or attribute? It's not that we truly believe, I don't think, that our games are as important as love or birth or death. Their importance lies in the very fact that they are *not* those things. At least, that's what I tell myself.

5

There is no such thing as a golfer playing over his head.
A hot streak is simply a glimpse of a golfer's true potential.

—Dr. Bob Rotella with Bob Cullen,
Golf Is Not a Game of Perfect

B e honest. Have you looked forward to see if there are eighteen chapters? Four chapters, four holes so far. The impulse is natural. "Looked forward" might be presumptuous, though, since that phrase connotes a positive anticipation, when, in fact, you might be wishing right about now that you had heeded my first-page warnings. Or maybe you are like my wife's best friend who, when she can no longer handle the stress of not knowing the outcome of a plot or the fate of a favorite character, reads the last few pages. Never mind that the author has spent years at her desk creating the perfect crescendo to get there, neglecting her family, eating NoDoz as if it were a food group. Ruth needs to know whodunnit *now*. Well, you know whodunnit. I dunnit. You just don't know precisely what yet. I promise I'm getting there. It's just that it's so far from Fox Run and a perfect wife and two and a half beautiful children and the life my parents handed to me that I feel we need to take our time together. If we don't, you may find yourself perplexed, paging back to make sure my editor didn't inadvertently delete an enlightening chapter or two. Sure, you might be foreseeing another woman, which would be partially true. And it doesn't take Nostradamus to predict that my foray into online trading will cost me a few bucks. But neither of those happenstances is "book-worthy," even on my self-absorbed slice of the planet. I can promise only that it gets a lot worse for me, and thus better for you.

In return for your indulgence I'll quit with the one-chapter, one-hole bit. I admit that's where I was headed from the start. But my sense of pacing is telling me that if I continue favoring torpid over torrid, even those on my Christmas card list will be trading this in at their local used bookstore for Anne Tyler's seventeenth Baltimore novel. Besides, this is where the story starts to get a little weird and the golf downright spectacular, so they no longer match up particularly well. First things first.

You might consider two birdies in the first four holes a mini hot streak, but it didn't feel that way to me because I was still playing catch-up from the double bogey on one. But from the moment Sal hands me my three-iron on the tee of the short, par-four fifth hole, it's almost as if I'm on autopilot. Not "auto" in the mechanical sense, but in the sense that everything feels so easy, so natural, that I seem incapable of making a mistake. In the past, whenever a hint of this feeling would begin, I became consumed with analyzing just *why* I was playing so well, trying to store the secrets I thought I was learning for another day. Never mind what my experience told me—that there were no secrets, that you can never *own* a good swing but simply borrow it for few days, even a few holes at a time. But Sal's early advice that I let go of the game between shots has given me a kind of freedom from my overly analytical self. I am not trying to remember each previous good swing, just trusting the one I'm about to make.

I hit three-iron to one of the two flat spots on the fifth fairway, then nine-iron to eight feet. From there, the hole looks like a bucket and I knock it in for a birdie. On the tough par-three sixth, I tether a high, cutting four-iron to the back half of the elevated, kidney-shaped green, then burn the edge with what I thought was a perfect putt before tapping in for an easy par. On the short par-four seventh, Sal hands me the driver without even asking and I rip one 290 yards that almost rolls through the narrow opening in front of the green. I am left with an easy bump-and-run chip to a back pin that I nestle within two feet for another birdie. Sal and I are barely speaking. We are more like pitcher and catcher than caddy and golfer. He's putting down the signs, spotting the glove, and I'm hitting it in the center of the leather every time. I make an easy two-putt birdie on the short par-five eighth, and even the ninth, a daunting 450-yard par-four from the back tees, yields an easy two-putt par. Sal and I make the turn in thirty-three. Three under par.

After a drive that splits the fairway on the 415-yard par-four tenth hole, we would ordinarily stop at the halfway shack for a drink and a brief rest. But this late in the season, this late in the day, the shelter is shut up as if condemned, so we keep moving. Sal peels off as we come down off the tee and holds up my phone as a way of asking if he can make a quick call. It strikes me as odd, but I figure he's calling his wife to let her know we're making good time. He'll be home early for dinner. I nod toward the fairway to say I'll meet him out there, and I slow down to give him time.

It's no later than four o'clock, but the sun is already more orange than yellow, and its angle is making the cart tracks and footprints of the few others who have played before us today visible in the fairway. In the morning, the grounds crew will erase all evidence of our passing with hulking, sharp-bladed machinery. It will take close to twenty men to prepare the course for the twenty or so who will play it tomorrow.

Sal catches up at a limping jog just as I reach my ball.

"Easy," I tell him.

"You too," he says. "Seven-iron. Middle of the green. Nothin' fancy."

But it is better than that. It is perfect. And not because it lands in the center of the green, fifteen feet left of the hole, just where Sal wants it. But because of the way the evening is already coming on, the way the sun is behind us, setting the ball on fire in the sky, hot white against cool blue, no different from that first airborne shot with my father more than thirty-five years ago.

When we reach the green, Sal pulls the pin and silently points the base of it to the line he sees, six inches outside-right. The stroke I put on the putt is so pure I barely feel the impact of club-face and ball, and it rolls along Sal's line and into the hole as if tracked by some gravitational pull. My God, this game can be beautiful. I can't help smiling as it drops, briefly losing my game face, and I see that Sal does the same. He never looks at me, though. His pitcher still has a no-hitter going.

When I see where the pin is on the short par-three eleventh, the birdie on ten feels even better. The eleventh is the easiest hole on the course, except when the hole is cut in the back right corner, where it is today. There's no way to place a tee shot on that little shelf, even when you're dialed-in like I am now.

"Not worth it," Sal says, making sure, as he hands me eight-iron.

I put one in the center of the green, two putt for par, and feel lucky.

The twelfth is another matter. It is ripe for a birdie attempt, and Sal and I both see it at the same time. I let loose a little extra adrenaline on the drive and fly the pot bunker on the right side of the fairway 270 yards away. It kicks forward another twenty, leaving only sixty yards to the hole, which today is cut on the flattest part of this green, right up front. I have spent countless hours practicing, calibrating these short shots, and I know that sixty yards is a choked-down, three-quarter sand wedge. I see the shot so clearly as I approach that it's almost as if I have already hit it. When I nip it perfectly off the fairway, hear the *ffzzzz* of the backspin as it leaves the club and watch it land just beyond the flagstick, I am seeing an instant replay. It bounces once, then jolts back toward the hole. The pin looks to be splitting the ball in two, and I start to run up the apron because, for a moment, I think it might go in. It is, in fact, sitting no more than three inches behind the back lip. Not waiting for Sal, I pull the pin with one hand and tap in for birdie with the blade of my sand wedge in the other. The twelfth is the hole that returns to the Clubhouse, just behind me now on the hill. The putting green, where I stood waiting for Sal two hours ago, lies below. I am standing on the very green from which I have exited this golf course in disgust innumerable times over the past four months, and I am five under par. *I am five under par.* I replace the flag and take long strides across the green to the steep railroad-tie stairs up to the thirteenth tee, and I take them two at a time.

The thought comes at me from nowhere and manifests before I can stop it. It comes before I have even reached the top of the stairs. It comes despite my knowledge that it is my enemy. And it comes despite the fact that I know I am heading into the toughest six-hole stretch on the golf course:

It will be a cakewalk from here, is what the evil spirit says.

I battle it the whole way up, trying to counteract it with every clichéd bit of wisdom I can dredge up: *Take it one shot at a time, don't count your chickens, it ain't over till . . .* But there it is again:

"I can go three over par over the next six holes and still shoot sixty- . . ."

No. Don't even *think* it. Thou shalt neither speak nor contemplate the love number until it's in the books.

This silence is killing me. Where's Sal? Here he comes. A little slow up the stairs. He has no idea what has just happened to his pitcher. Who was that Pirate? The hero of the '71 World Series? By '73, he couldn't do anything but skip the ball in front of home plate. Steve Blass. The color guy now. Literally could not get the ball to the catcher, even though his arm was as strong as ever. Oh, this thought process is helping a lot. You're a mental giant, Michael. Your father barely yawned when the crashing April 2000 NASDAQ took a billion dollars out of his clients' paper pockets, but you can't handle a hot streak at the country club. What are you going to do when Hale Irwin is staring you down? Maybe by then they'll have developed a line of Depends that won't inhibit your hip turn. I need to hear a human voice that's not inside my own head, though I don't mean to yell.

"Hey, Sal!"

He has just reached the top of the stairs and looks at me like I just farted in church.

"Whatja think of that little pitch shot?"

"You okay?"

6

Strippers love to eat. I don't know why this is true, but if you stay more than an hour at almost any club, you are bound to see a pack of them gathered around a pizza like hyenas around a kill. At upscale, resort-town clubs, they generally do you the favor of re-donning their sequined evening gowns. But in the average Pittsburgh-area adult-entertainment establishment, at least half of the talent is likely to be gorging in the buff. In one of my favorite *Seinfeld* episodes, Jerry makes a fine distinction between "good naked" and "bad naked." Big-haired, well-fed western Pennsylvania women chewing cheese like cud and licking pepperoni grease off their wrists is in a dead heat with my mother pulling on her panty hose for the bad-naked blue ribbon. Which is why, during my third year of law school, when thoughts of the faraway Agnes Humpstone otherwise drove me to seek visible skin wherever I might find it, I decided to boycott every strip bar in town but Melvin's.

This was in 1985, before seaside institutions like the Crazy Horse and Thee Doll House became national franchises, popping up like little turquoise-and-pink oases, even in the Rust Belt. The proprietor of Melvin's (whose name, inexplicably, was Frank) was somehow able to lure beach-quality dancers to his quaint little bar in the Oakland section of Pittsburgh, within blocks of both the university's business school (where Stewey Trammell was enrolled) and the law school. Frank protected his girls like daughters and enforced a strict no-touch policy. Patrons were not permitted to so much as slip a tip under a dancer's garter. Dollar bills were to be handed to them with courtesy, and they would make the deposit themselves. A first violation carried a one-month ban. A second brought permanent exile and might be accompanied by violence at the hands of Frank, who had fists like rib racks.

My decision vexed Stewey, for whom there was no bad naked. The worse the naked, the better. I broke the news over a Roy Rogers greaseburger between classes.

"Geez, Mikey. There's no nasty factor in that place." Stewey is just the kind of guy who, at age twenty-four, could be a strip-club connoisseur and still use the word *geez*.

"I'm not looking for nasty, Stewey. I'm looking for beauty."

"Bullshit, Mr. Hefner. You're looking for friction just like the rest of us."

"I'm not interested in full-body contact with someone who's got a racing stripe on her diaphragm."

The high school transformation of Stewey Trammell from beefy to brawny had, by this time, begun to reverse itself. Our thrice-weekly lunches were not helping. He shook his big head at me.

"Do you know what you are?" he said.

"No. But I'm sure you're going to enlighten me."

"You, my friend, are a titty snob."

"Excuse me?"

"You heard me."

"Your new bride would be so proud of you right now."

"Donna knows it too."

"Your wife thinks I'm a titty snob?"

"She knows you always liked being seen with her when we were in high school, even though you weren't getting any." He knew he had hit an old wound, so he held my gaze for emphasis and no-look-dipped a fry in the lake of ketchup on his tray.

"So how Donna looked in her cheerleading sweater had no influence over you."

Stewey finished chewing his fry and pointed the next one at me. "You know Donna's mother, right?"

"I introduced you to her."

"Does she, or does she not, have hips like the Fort Pitt Tunnels?"

"So what?"

"So that's what Donna will look like after three or four kids, but we're *still* gonna be yumpin' like bunnies, because *I'm* no titty snob."

"You better hope she's not either. You're working on a nice set there yourself."

A giant, fry-wielding paw clipped the side of my head. "Look, Mikey. All I'm trying to say is, assuming you ever grow up enough to get married, there will always be someone more beautiful than your wife."

"I can't believe I'm being lectured to on this topic by someone whose weekly goal is to leave the Pink Pony with stinky-finger."

"Hey, I don't do that anymore."

"Since when?"

"Since the wedding day." Stewey began crumpling what little food was left into his empty foil burger wrapper. "Forget it," he said. "Go to Melvin's. Ogle your airbrushed beauties. Take another one home for dinner, why don't you? What was her name?"

"Amethyst."

"Ah, yes. Real name, or stage?"

"Very funny."

"What did you tell your mother about her?"

"That she was a fellow law student."

"Brilliant cover. And did you get anywhere with her?"

"Nope. Didn't even try. I'm attached, remember?"

"How could I forget. Agnes. Is she driving yet?"

"Fuck you."

"No, seriously. Donna and I will be in the market for babysitters by next year, and we'll be looking for someone reliable who can—"

"Agnes happens to be extremely mature for her age."

"Then maybe she's too old for you."

"Jesus Christ. Did you get a bad piece of bacon? How did a conversation that began with you trying to convince me to go to sleazier strip bars lead to you questioning *my* maturity?"

"I just think your decision is symptomatic."

"Of what? My superior taste?"

"No. Of your need to please beautiful women."

"Tell me, *herr doktor*. How am I pleasing the women at Melvin's?"

"By handing them money. By taking them home for *dinner*, for chrissake. By treating them like they mean something to you, when you mean nothing to them. At least I know no one at the Pink Pony thinks I'm a great guy."

I didn't see Stewey's point then. And the vindication of marrying Kelly four years later, who, by Stewey's own admission, was too good for me, obliterated this conversation from my memory. It was only the events of this past spring and a recommendation from Stewey himself that made me recall it.

It says something about the elemental nature of men, or at least the elemental nature of *this* man, that the argument between Kelly and me about the new life inside of her eventually became an argument about sex. Pregnancy has never been easy for Kelly, at any stage. It took us more than two years to conceive Megan; six more years and two very early miscarriages preceded Hannah. With Jessica, we ended up seeing a fertility specialist. Kelly endured painful intramuscular injections, and something resembling a turkey baster replaced me as the mode of delivery. All of this made the loss of Jessica late in the sixth month that much more difficult, and made even more inexcusable my reaction to what was really the miracle of Kelly's current pregnancy. But it was impossible for me to put out of my mind the process of living through the pregnancies themselves, which were horrendous experiences (even Kelly would admit) for both of us. She had difficulty gaining weight and subsisted almost solely on Saltines, rice and canned peaches. The sex leading to these pregnancies was all very scheduled, very scientific. I was instructed not to "relieve myself" during the four days prior to the appointed date and time, so that I could deliver a full compliment of strong swimmers. Just in case they weren't so strong, Kelly was advised to make sure they had gravity on their side by keeping her legs in the air for thirty minutes afterward. Bad naked.

Once "success" was achieved, the nausea came on as if it were being caused by the first cell division. There was never any need for a pregnancy test. Kelly knew. I knew too. Because in addition to dealing with the nausea, Kelly was transformed by the hormonal imbalance into a post-possession version of Linda Blair. Her head never did a complete revolution, but she did once stab me over a shopping list:

"Where are the peaches?" She was digging frantically through each of the fifteen grocery bags I had just lugged in from the car.

"Peaches?"

The look I got in response to this question was maniacal. This was her first pregnancy, with Megan, and she hadn't yet gotten the hang of recognizing and heading off irrationality. Come to think of it, she never really got the hang of that.

"Yeah, *peaches*. You remember. Those things that grow on trees in tropical places you've never taken me to but that are available here in the great gray North in cans filled with heavy syrup?" She was moving closer to me with big steps through the minefield of brown paper bags. "Those things I've been eating next to you on the couch every night for five months while you watch *SportsCenter*? The item at the very *top* of the list in capital letters that Joe *Paterno* could read without his glasses?"

"Ah," I said. "The list."

Together, we both looked across the kitchen at the crowded corkboard. Sure enough. I could read PEACHES from where I stood.

"You forgot the list?"

"I know it seems that way, but—"

"No. It doesn't *seem* that way! It's hanging right in front of your face! That list has never seen the outside world! That is a *cloistered* list! A *virgin* list!"

Something *I* had not yet gotten the hang of was saying either "Yes, dear" or "I'm sorry, hon," without thought or discrimination, in response to every communication from my pregnant wife. So what I said, instead, was: "I never meant to take the list."

I am here to tell you that spontaneous human combustion is no myth.

"You *what*?" She was now as close to me as her abdomen would permit. "How can you go *fucking* shopping without taking the fucking *list*?" This last word splashed against my face.

"I never take the list."

There's a lot about my part in this conversation I would change now.

"Ex*cuse* me?"

"I never take the list. I don't know where anything is, so the list just confuses me."

"Lists don't *confuse*, Michael. They tell. They explain. They *list*!" Splash.

"I disagree." I was trying to talk as slowly and softly as possible, portraying myself as the reasonable one. Another strategy I would now know enough to abandon. "When I have the list, I go up and down every aisle six times looking for what's on the list. When I don't have the list, I take one slow pass through the entire store and pick up everything we need."

"No, Michael. You *don't*! That's the whole point! We need peaches! *I* need peaches! No. It's more than that. I *require* them. Peaches are like *air* to me. Yet you can go cruising past that huge display of green-and-yellow Del Monte cans—God, I can see them! Row six, on the left if you're facing the back of the store, right across from the soups!—you can just *stroll* past them without even *thinking* of me. How is that possible?"

"I'll go back."

"Of *course* you'll go back. I'm so glad to see that the obvious does not *always* escape you." She began to stride with purpose (and without regard for the scattering groceries) across the kitchen to the corkboard. "You'll go back. And you'll take the list."

"Hon, that's ridiculous. All we need are—"

"*Shut up!*" She pulled the tack from the corkboard and the list came off with it. "I can't bear to watch you go out that door again and know that you don't have the list. You *obviously* need practice." The path she had already made through the groceries hastened her return trip. "So you might as well start *now*." She had grabbed my hand, and with the word "*now*" plunged the tack and its impaled list into the center of my palm.

The searing pain was instantaneous but subsided almost as quickly, like the first prick of a doctor's needle, only ten gauges thicker. "*Ow! Fuck!* Are you crazy?" The answer to that question, at least temporarily, was clear. There was a look of unmitigated terror on Kelly's face. My instinct was to shake my hand frenetically, but that only brought back the pain. The list stayed put. So I turned my palm up, between Kelly and me, the huge PEACHES just below the red shaft of the tack, and I pulled it free.

As soon as the blood began to flow, Kelly was transformed. Her head, figuratively speaking, spun fully back the other direction, and she was suddenly horrified at herself.

"Oh, my God! Michael! Oh, my God! What have I done to you!"

"Don't worry, hon. I don't think it's as bad as it looks. We'll just clean it up and—"

"Pressure! Apply pressure!" She was crying hysterically now. "Jesus Christ, I'm a lunatic! I could have killed you!"

"Don't be silly, Kel. You couldn't have hurt me any worse with this thing than you did." I made a fist to slow the bleeding and held the tack up to her with my other hand.

"No. I mean I wasn't even thinking! What if there had been a knife nearby? Or a gun! I wanted to hurt you!"

She collapsed into me, as much as a woman approaching her third trimester can. It was sort of a full-lean embrace.

"No you didn't, sweetie," I said. "It's okay." She cried like a child and I rubbed her back, one hand fisted, one hand flat, until she stopped. We cleaned the tiny hole as best we could (Kelly kissing it over and over, as she would a scrape on Megan's knee years later) and applied iodine, antibiotic and a Band-Aid. Then we put the groceries away and went back to the store to get peaches, together.

In one of her more lucid moments, sitting on the couch with me eating a bowl of peaches, Kelly explained the phenomenon of her Mr. Hyde this way:

"When I wake up in the morning, I feel like *me*. I do. I feel like myself. But as soon as I sit up—Jesus, maybe I should stay prone all day—as soon as I'm vertical, it's like this other person comes out of my ass and points across the bed at you and says, *"Come on! Let's go fuck up his day!"*

In addition to my deeper fears, it was the specter of this personage, this *anti-wife*, that began to haunt me as soon as the words "I'm pregnant" fell from Kelly's beautiful lips. As the kids were getting older, Kelly and I were starting to discover each other again. We "dated" every Saturday night, usually catching an early movie followed by a leisurely dinner. We lingered over a bottle of wine until we thought the kids would be in bed, never mind that they remained the primary topic of conversation. Then we went home to make love. It was a kind of planned spontaneity. Sex, now that it was off the biological clock, was just for fun again, and it was better than ever. We were too old to be shocked anymore, too comfortable with each other to be shy. I got back into the habit of asking, and she was giving me new answers. "Oil" was one. "Toys" another. My shopping destinations expanded to two: Hackers Helper and Condom Nation. We were like a couple of aging, once-a-week porn stars disguised as June and Ward Cleaver. We even put the video camera on a tripod one night:

"Are you sure you want to do this?"

I remember saying this as part of a boxer-clad jog around the room, checking the camera angle, lighting candles, then back to the viewfinder. Neither of us cared for sex with the lights on, but the camera needed light, so there were enough candles aflame around the room that we probably needed some kind of permit.

"You've been after me to do this for, what, ten years? And now you're inviting second thoughts?" Kelly was already naked, sitting back against a propped pillow, alone in our king-size bed, the sheet pulled up and tucked under both underarms, like Alice without Bob, Carol or Ted.

"Sorry."

"Watch the curtains!"

"Sorry!"

"Should we just call the fire department now and have them wait out in the street?"

"Can you say that again? I want to check the sound."

"Michael, it's not going to matter much what we're saying, is it?" I zoomed in on her face as she said this, and her sly, crooked smile stirred something below the elastic equator.

"I was hoping maybe you'd be inspired by the camera." I kept looking at her through the viewfinder.

"To what?"

"You know. Talk."

"Like dirty talk?"

"Yeah. Exactly like that."

"I'm too shy." But she was still smiling, looking sideways at the camera, and a piece of the sheet found its way between her teeth.

"The face I'm seeing in here? This is not a shy face."

She looked right at the camera: "I'm not a porn star. But I play one on TV."

"Wait. Don't do anything good yet."

"Come on. I'm getting lonely over here. And cold." As I widened the angle in the shot to take in the rest of her, Kelly let the sheet drop just enough to expose one erect nipple—"See?"—then tucked the sheet back under her arm.

"Okay. I think I'm ready."

"I'll be the judge of that. Come *here*."

"On my way."

I hit RECORD, slid my boxer shorts off and prepared to make an entrance. That was my first mistake. My second was trying to make it from anywhere but one of the two *sides* of the bed, opting instead for an Edwin Moses improv. The toes of my left foot caught the footboard mid-hurdle, and my right knee came down on it with a sound like a home-run ball off a major-leaguer's bat.

"OW—FUCK!"

"Sweetie! Oooh! Are you okay?"

"FUCK-fucka-fucka-fucka-fucka-fucka-FUCK!"

"Oooh, rub it, honey! Rub it quick!"

"Awwwwgh."

"Here, let me see. Move your hands and let me see."

"Brrrrrrrrk."

"You have to move your hands, sweetie. That's it. Oooh, I think it's swelling already, hon. I think maybe you should see someone. I think we should . . . I'll wake Megan and tell her that we're going to the—"

"*No.*" I still remember the pain and the way it pulsed, the swelling stretching at my skin. But it *had* taken me ten years to get the camera into our bedroom, and I wasn't about to turn it off for something as relatively insignificant as a shattered kneecap. "Just lie with me here for a minute—*FUCK!*—I'll be fine."

"Are you sure?"

"I'm sure."

I was not sure. My knee felt as if it had been injected with a half-gallon of kerosene and then lit from the inside. The rest of my body had the shivers, so I turned onto my back and pulled the covers up around me. Kelly curled in, the side of her face tucked in to my neck, a hand on my chest.

"Mm. This is okay too," she said.

"Yeah." I couldn't straighten my leg so I let it flop to the side. "Auugh."

"Do you want me to get you some ice?"

"I'm now thinking that might be a good idea."

Kelly climbed out of bed and went downstairs. I could hear her pulling ice from the freezer, then was perplexed to hear the microwave come on. When she came back up she paused in the doorway, still naked, holding a Ziploc freezer bag of ice in one hand, a basket of popcorn in the other, and a beer tucked under either arm. She kicked a hip out and posed.

"My dreamgirl."

"*Man*, these things are cold." She took quick steps to the bed, flapped her elbows up and let both beers drop. I managed to work my way to a sitting position, twisted the cap off one of the bottles and took a long drag.

"Ah."

She came around to my side and pulled the sheet back. "Here. Let me see." My knee looked like a blood orange. "Oh, hon, we need to get someone to look at this."

"We're both looking at it."

"You know what I mean."

"Come back to bed. It's date night. We'll see what the ice does. I'll go in the morning if it's not better."

Kelly went around to her side, climbed in and scooted over until we were touching. She set the popcorn down, half on her thigh, half on mine, and popped her beer. "Cheers."

"Cheers." The ice was already dulling the pain, and the beer wasn't going to hurt either.

"It's still on, you know," I told her.

"What?"

I pointed the top of my bottle at the camera. "Can you go turn it off?"

"Why? This is nice." She tossed a piece of popcorn in the air and caught it in her mouth, a trick she had been trying, without much success, to teach Hannah.

"Not very watchable, though, is it?"

"But think about it. This is sort of a momentous event."

"How do you figure?"

"When the girls were little the sound of you crashing into the bed like it was a tackling dummy would've brought two sets of scampering feet and meant *four* of us in the bed. End of date night."

"True enough."

"Welcome to your new, grown-up life, Michael Benedict."

"Thank you."

We clicked bottles, then were quiet.

"It feels weird, though. Don't you think?" I said finally. "Like we're being watched."

"You wanted to record us having *sex*, and you think *this* feels weird?"

"I see your point. But yes."

Kelly wedged her beer between us and squared her shoulders to me.

"Kiss me."

"What?"

"We've got seventy-two hours of tape of the kids doing everything imaginable, including wiping their little bottoms, and I bet there isn't even five seconds of us kissing."

"But we do now have excellent footage of me setting the new gold standard in bad naked."

"Which we will watch later in slow motion."

"You are both cruel and unusual."

"Come on. Kiss me."

I kissed her.

"Not that kind of kiss. A *real* one." She suddenly had an anxious, ardent look on her face. "One that we can show at our fiftieth wedding anniversary and make everybody in attendance jealous of our whole lives together. One that would make everyone who *didn't* marry one of us wish they did."

I must have looked stricken by the pressure.

"I'm sorry," she said. "I'm not being fair. Here." She took her beer bottle from where it still stood between us and held it like a microphone. "Let me set the mood, and you'll do fine." She patted my thigh and then turned to the camera.

Here's how that section of the tape now plays. We have watched it every year since, on our anniversary:

"*Ladies and gentlemen, you are about to witness a re-enactment of the first kiss of Kelly Wisniewski and Michael Benedict.*"

"*Whoa. No pressure there.*"

"*The actor who just spoke off-script will be playing the part of Michael. I, of course, will be playing Kelly. Just a few weeks ago, Michael interviewed Kelly for a job—which, of course, she got . . .*"

"*You're telling it wrong already. Hank got that job. You got—*"

"*—and they have been eyeing each other over the tops of the office cubicles ever since. He finally got around to asking her out—he was understandably intimidated by her considerable beauty—and they have just had a lovely dinner together that included a bottle of cabernet that would have made the Reverend Mother feel romantic.*"

Here Kelly begins to slow down and is no longer playful.

"*Neither remembers much of what they talked about at dinner—he remembers the curve of her bare shoulders, she the way he used his hands when he talked—and they laugh once in a while, nervously, during the silent ride back to his apartment.*"

She is speaking more quietly now and has turned to look at me. This is no melodrama. She is tender and earnest and beautiful.

"Although unspoken, they both know what is about to happen. He is going to see and touch every part of her for the first time. She is going to put her hands on the broad expanse of his back and pull him to her. But something has to start it. Something has to get them there, and that is what they are both thinking about most. That first kiss: the one that—if this is the right person, the one finally worth loving—they'll remember and talk about forever because it started their life together."

She puts the bottle down and brings her hands to my face.

"Ready?" she whispers.

I nod into her hands and her fingers go to my ears.

She whispers again: *"Still want me to turn the camera off?"*

"No. Keep it rolling."

Kelly's announcement last spring brought this idyllic period in our relationship to an immediate and abrupt halt. It was almost as if it all *had* been a movie. Ironically, though, this time it was not Kelly's evil pregnancy twin that came between us. It was me and my massive muzzle. Kelly felt fine. Wonderful, in fact. She *looked* spectacular. Her breasts swelled before the rest of her, and there was a healthy ruddiness to her face that gave her a summer look in April. I had heard about the pregnancy "glow," but I had never seen it on my own wife. I was transfixed. I was also cut off. I had entered the month as John Holmes. I was leaving it as Barney Fife.

"Don't even think about it."

I had slowly slid my hand across the cool of the mattress between us, and it was now resting on her hip.

"I'm not thinking about anything. Though, come to think of it—"

"Look, Michael. Sex sometimes has consequences. Since you are not someone willing to live with those consequences, you are—"

"I said I was *sorry*. How many times do I have to say it before you believe me? I'm *excited* about the baby. I really am."

"No you're not. You're excited about my tits."

How is it that I don't know her as well as she knows me?

"Well, can't a guy be excited about two things at once?"

"You are. My tits. Both of them."

This was the way it started out. She was serious, but she was also playful, with a certain fierceness, in the way she held me off. But she never let up. And, gradually, all of the play went out of both of us. There is something that my mother told me more than thirty years ago that has always stayed with me. She said it when she caught me bent close, one evening, over my ninth-grade health book, *Chapter 17, Figure 3*.

"Always remember, Michael," she said. "Men and women are terribly mismatched. Women require intimacy to enjoy sex. Men require sex to enjoy intimacy. If you are ever fortunate enough to find a woman with whom you can solve that conundrum, you will be a lucky man."

I thought Kelly and I had solved it. But the things I had said to her, especially that first thing—"What are we going to do about it?"—discredited me, maybe forever, and undermined the intimacy that had allowed her absolute freedom from her inhibitions when she was with me. At the same time, her utter refusal to make love to me, however justified, made me feel increasingly distant. We were now, ourselves, a conundrum. To me, this was different from before. When Kelly was struggling through her pregnancies with Megan, then Hannah, then Jessica, sex was almost a physical impossibility. This time, it was by choice. Her choice. And that was debilitating to me.

Fortunately, or so I thought, I still had Stewey Trammell looking out for me.

As much as I had always appreciated—even revered—tasteful, gratuitous nudity, my obsession had never sunk to what I considered to be the seedier depths. Liberty Avenue, which was at one time Pittsburgh's red-light district and leads right to the doorstep of the renovated train station that houses my office, never held any interest for me. All that remains of that stretch of once-lowly vibrance, after hundreds of millions of redevelopment dollars and two decades of legal battles over eminent domain and the constitutional rights of pornographers, are a couple of "upscale" (if there is such a thing) adult book/novelty stores, a Melvin's-like strip club that serves a businessman's lunch buffet, and a single basement massage parlor. The streetwalkers are gone, one of the old Turkish baths has been converted into an exclusive health club and most of the strip bars have moved to the suburbs. Even the old "Art Cinema," with its cement floors like flypaper, has been restored and now shows *actual* art films. For their perseverance, the sex-industry participants that still remain all got a facelift at the expense of the city taxpayers, the better to blend in with the new neighborhood. Condom Nation shares a new granite façade with Brookstone. One-stop shopping.

The *Shan Gri La* Health Spa did not get a facelift. But in exchange for moving its sign below street level, the elaborate wrought-iron railing that led down to the single, windowless door was wire-brushed and given a fresh coat of Rust-Oleum, and the top two stairs were refashioned from cobblestones to match the new surrounding sidewalk. That the sign could no longer be read by passersby was of no consequence. The *Shan Gri La* had never relied on walk-ups or curb appeal but on word-of-mouth, the Yellow Pages and the sports section.

In my almost daily travels down Liberty Avenue toward Market Square for lunch or the City Office Building for an administrative hearing, I would see well-dressed men, some of whom I recognized, descend those stairs, quickly, when they thought they were unobserved. I often wondered what would drive an otherwise successful male to such a place. I wondered, that is, until Kelly's bedroom strike had entered its eighth week, and previously reliable methods of dealing with my sorry state were becoming increasingly difficult to execute. I lived with three women; each had the nose and ears of a bloodhound. The days of having the luxury of fast-forwarding through a full-length feature of *Ordinary Peep-Hole (A Real Jerker)* with a box of tissues at my side were long gone. At the office, Hank habitually knocked on the bathroom door to inform me of every quasi-important phone call. Let me tell you, there is nothing that will snap a good fantasy back to reality faster than a short, squat lesbian knuckle-rapping three feet from your ear and yelling, "Mr. Benedict! It's Mr. Phelps regarding the sewer treatment plant!" I was a man with no outlet for his output, and suddenly the stairs down to the *Shan Gri La* looked enticing.

I also began to understand (for the first time, really) how it is that married men are capable of rationalizing almost anything in the name of sex. As with any good rationalization, there is a natural progression that permits a ludicrous conclusion from a fairly reasonable start: Magazines and movies are just looking; strip bars are just magazines come to life; lap-dances are acceptable, because one or both parties are still wearing some form of clothing; a sensual massage is just sort of a naked lap-dance; oral sex isn't really sex and therefore does not constitute infidelity; sex for pay is not infidelity; sex without love is not infidelity. No less authority than the highest man in the land had sought removal of the loveless blowjob from beneath the sexual umbrella. Like everyone, I professed to be appalled by our president's behavior, and yet here I was, one administration later, calling the *Shan Gri La* Health Spa for rates while Hank was out on her lunch break.

Rates for *what*, I didn't know. I was pitifully naïve, as I would later learn, about what services were offered in such a place. The *Shan Gri La* had occupied its current residence for as long as I could remember. Surely, everything was in at least *technical* compliance with the relevant statutes; otherwise they would have been shut down years ago, right? Certainly, I expected some bending of the rules. Sort of like strippers who wore pasties and G-strings not being considered "nude" by the Pennsylvania Liquor Control Board. I expected *that* kind of spirited compliance.

For the fourth day in a row I was sitting at my desk, sports pages open, punching in the number. I had not yet succeeded in contacting anyone, though the day before I had managed to let it ring three times before slamming the phone down. How did guys do this? I had talked myself around the fact that it was "wrong" by way of my own flawless rationalizaton. I needed it. Like Kelly needed peaches. She didn't want to give it to me. I was *required* to go elsewhere. What I was having more trouble with was the humiliation factor. What would I say? What would I ask for? I knew what I *didn't* want. I didn't want a hooker. At least not in the sense that I had always thought of a hooker. The word was dirty and so was my mental picture of what went with it. I wanted what I had always wanted. I wanted beauty. What was in my lecherous but idealistic mind as I sat at my desk, nervously listening to my phone reaching out to the *Shan Gri La,* was lying face down on a comfortable table, a beautiful woman standing over me, touching me all over, saying all the right things in something just above a whisper. She would take her time, and she would take pleasure in pleasing me. A full-contact Melvin's with no nasty factor. Stewey would have thought me pitiful. Who knew? Maybe this woman and I would even become friends. I would be her favorite customer, the one bright spot in her otherwise desultory day. She would share her dreams with me. She would break the rules and kiss me on the lips when we parted. She would—

"Yah?"

Jesus, someone had answered the phone.

"Uh . . . hello . . . my name is . . . No . . . what I mean to say is . . ."

"You want appointment?"

Was that voice female?

"Well, it's funny you should ask that." It is? "I'm not exactly sure. You see, I've never really been to a place like this. . . . By that I don't mean in any way to imply . . . It's just that I'm not exactly sure . . ."

"Fifty dollah, half-owah. Ninety dollah, owah."

"Well, that seems . . . And what all does that . . . ?"

"Nice massage. You rike."

"I'm sure I would. Now, there aren't any extra charges, are there?

I mean, I don't want to pay the fifty dollars, or the ninety dollars for that matter, and then find out that there are hidden—"

"You talk to guhl."

"Well. All right. Put her on."

"When you *get* heah, stoopid."

"Ma'am. Is it ma'am? There's no call for—"

"Bye-bye."

Any person in a normal state of mind would have been dissuaded by this initial contact. But there in my lap was the newspaper ad, still beckoning me with the curvaceous silhouette of a long-haired, long-armed beauty. The woman I had spoken to was the practical, protective "madam." Behind her, the premises were filled with enthusiastic cheerleader types and demure geishas. The phone call was actually a *good* sign. They ran a tight ship at the *Shan Gri La*. The call also had the effect of placing me into their world. I had crossed over. Why not stop by and take a look?

I had walked down this street thousands of times, but never before with the feeling that every person I passed was staring at me and sensed exactly where I was headed. I detected knowing looks, real or imagined, from business types, street vendors, shoppers, the homeless, the toothless and the feckless. Even the nutty woman with the wild hair and lipstick up to her nostrils, who stopped me once a week to tell me that the world was coming to an end, shook her head and stepped aside, as if *I* were the one to be avoided today. Hester Prynne had attracted less attention from her Puritan towns-folk than I was getting from my fellow lowlifes in the big city. There was a neon, scarlet letter M plugged into my lapel, and I hadn't yet had so much as a deltoid rubbed.

When the shiny black railing came into view, I tried not to look at it. Maybe if everyone saw me not looking at it, saw me walk right on by without so much as a curious glance, they would leave me alone. So that's what I did. I ignored that railing. I snubbed it. Then I turned with purpose into a card store five doors down.

That's where he was headed all the time, folks. Nothing to see here. Go on about your business.

I made myself appear busy in the card store until I could see that the lunch rush outside had begun to subside. Pittsburghers don't shop during their lunch hour. Most of the city had reached its dining destination, and the streets would be quiet again until the mass exodus an hour or so from now. I set down the package of gold-leaf thank-you cards I had been examining with rapt interest and pushed back out onto the street. My stride was long, confident, my eyes locked far ahead. But I kept the railing in my peripheral vision, and when I was precisely parallel with it, I did what could only be described as an abrupt side-step free-fall, as if through a trap door, down the stairs.

When I reached the bottom, I felt as though I were in an observation pit, a reptile trapped in a cement-walled, open-topped terrarium. Though uncrowded by urban standards, Liberty Avenue at 12:30 P.M. was not exactly the Appalachian Trail, and everyone who walked by the railing could, if they were so inclined, look directly down on my thinning vertex. I had a fleeting thought of turning and bolting back up the stairs, but that threatened to be even more revealing. Arousal had brought me here, but now I wanted in for protection. There was a lighted doorbell to the left of the steel door, and I jammed my finger into it as if trying to push it through the concrete. I could hear the buzzer reverberating inside, but no one answered. I was as close to the door as I could get, trying to shield myself from the view of all of the morally superior passersby above, so close that I could hardly read the sign that had been moved down from street level as part of the redevelopment deal. I read it now in the hope that the passing seconds would feel less like hours:

Shan Gri La Health Spa
Japanese Massage, Sauna, Body Shampoo,
Private Rooms, Exercise Equipment.
Mon–Sat 12 P.M.–2 A.M.
"Come in for some relax!"

Still no one. I hit the buzzer again. Glaciers moved perceptibly. Generations of fruit flies came and went, leaving behind family trees like giant sequoias, and still the door did not open. I contemplated my choices from the sign. At least now I knew where to come if I ever needed to work out at 1:00 A.M. Body shampoo. That sounded nice. And clean. Maybe I'd just get one of those. Yes, I'd ask for one of those. If anyone would ever answer the *fucking* door. Now I began pressing the buzzer in a steady rhythm, like a car alarm, and decided I would keep at it until someone got annoyed enough to respond. After fifteen or twenty pulses, I heard a crackling near my chest.

"Yah?" *Click.*

I hadn't noticed the intercom box beside the doorbell. Jesus, now I had to *talk* down here?

I switched my finger to the intercom button and, trying not to let my voice carry to the street, I spoke toward the box.

"Yes," I almost whispered. "I called earlier." *Click.*

"What?" *Click.*

I crouched down and touched my lips to the colandered metal. "I called earlier. About your rates?" *Click.* I suspected that my voice now had a Darth Vader quality to it coming through on the other side that might be a little unsettling.

"You have appointment?" *Click.*

I tried not to sound too menacing. "Do I *need* an appointment?" Luke, I am your *fah-tha. Click.*

"No. I let you in." *Click.* With that I heard two deadbolts slide and the door opened on the *Shan Gri La.*

The outer room was gigantic, encompassing the basement of one of the buildings next door. Paint was peeling off the white cinderblock walls, except for the right-hand wall, which was mirrored. Against the mirrors leaned a few pieces of ancient fitness equipment that hadn't been used in decades, and probably never in this room. This was apparently the *Shan Gri La*'s feeble attempt at a cover.

An elderly Asian woman, barely four feet tall, appeared from behind the open door, then closed it behind me. Across the room from where I stood, the wall was bisected by the entrance to a narrow, dark hallway. She began shuffling toward it and motioned for me to follow.

"You heah befo?" she asked, not turning to face me.

"No. I actually pass by here almost every day, but this is the first time—"

"Come." She said this with a sort of impatient disdain that encompassed me and all of the other rookies she had led this way. I suspect most of them had been a few years younger than I.

"You know, I'm thinking I'll just use the sauna this time. I think that would do the trick for what—"

"Sauna no wok. *Come.*"

Funny as it sounds, and as much as I now wanted to turn and run, I could not disobey her. She was a strangely irresistible little force. I followed her down the hallway, past four narrow, curtained doorways, two on either side. There was a fifth on the right side, and she drew the curtain back to reveal a cramped, dark, bunkerlike room.

"You sit heah," she said, gesturing toward the massage table I could only just make out in the corner. "I bring guhl."

"Look, I'm really not sure—"

"You rike huh. Sit."

"How many girls . . . I mean, can I at least choose—"

"I *say*, you *rike* huh. *Sit!*"

I sat.

The curtain closed and it took a moment for my eyes to adjust to my surroundings. There wasn't much to see. There was a small nightstand in the corner opposite the massage table, and on it stood a small lamp with a potbellied porcelain base. The lamp was perched and centered on a little lace doily, and it held a dim red lightbulb, further veiled by a thick shade. Next to the lamp were bottles of what I supposed to be massage oil, though the lamp didn't throw off enough light for me to read the labels. Next to the nightstand, on the floor, were a pile of cloth towels, a roll of paper towels and a transistor radio already tuned to an easy-listening station. On the wall across from me were two clothes hooks. That was it.

When the curtain was drawn back again, what I had formerly perceived as dim light in the hallway blinded me. The black, back-lit figure of a woman entered, and the curtain dropped again.

"Hi," she said.

"Hi."

"Half-owah, oh owah?"

"Just a half, I think."

"You change you mine, you say so, okay?" My eyes were readjusting and I could see that she was smiling. "That fifty, okay?"

"Sure." I took the bills out of my wallet, then stood and hung my suit jacket on one of the hooks. By the time I handed her the money, my eyes were once again accustomed to the darkness. The lighting disguised her age—she could have been twenty-five, or she could have been my age—but I could see that she was quite pretty. She wore her hair in a very traditional, short, blunt cut, and she had on a modest, one-piece bathing suit that revealed a nice figure. She was sort of a sexy version of Mrs. Livingston, the housekeeper from *The Courtship of Eddie's Father*.

"What you name?" she asked.

"Eddie," I said.

"I am Mika," she said, putting her hand to her chest. "You get comftable on table, Eddie. I be back." She smiled again and touched her palm to my cheek. Then she disappeared through the curtain.

I assumed that I was supposed to take off my clothes, even if a massage was all I was getting, so that's what I did. I left my boxers on, though, so as not to seem presumptuous. It's hard for me to describe the mood surrounding the few moments that I lay, face down on the table, waiting for Mika's return. I felt apprehensive, guilty, even a little stupid. I had come here in search of a sexually charged atmosphere, but what dominated was an air of inevitability. I had started something I didn't want to finish, but I was both too curious and too proud to bail.

My eyes were closed but I felt the room become light, then dark again. Then I heard Mika laugh.

"Eddie. You so *funny*. You leave *shots* on!"

"Yeah. I wasn't sure."

"I get them." She whisked my boxers off in one motion, like an experienced mother removing a diaper. Then I could hear her walk over toward the nightstand. She turned the radio up a little. (Christ. Is it only in Pittsburgh that you can still hear Juice Newton asking you to just call her angel of the morning?) Then she must have picked up a bottle of the massage oil and removed her bathing suit, because the next thing I knew, she was sitting naked astride my rear end, kneading my shoulders and humming along with Juice.

Hey. This was okay. A guy could get used to this. It felt like Mika had ten fingers on each hand, sliding over, around and through muscle groups I didn't know I had.

"You so tight," she said. "Mika fix you."

Whatever else Mika might have been, she was also a trained masseuse. She worked her way from my shoulders to my lower back to my rump and down both legs. She made no effort to arouse me. She was on a mission to loosen old Eddie up first. Now she hummed with Anne Murray, who was crooning about one of the many men who had dumped her whiny ass.

"My God, this is incredible. Do you make house calls?"

"Onry fo you!"

"What kind of massage is this?"

"It's Japanese. Shiatsu."

"God bless you."

"You so *funny*, Eddie!"

My kind of girl.

"Best part to come." I thought I knew what she meant by this, but I was soon to learn otherwise.

When she finished with my toes I felt as if I had been poured onto the table. I had never been so relaxed in my entire life. I was Gumby in the tropics. I was Snoop Dogg after twelve bong hits.

The next sensation I had was of the head of a baseball bat being ground into my left shoulder blade like a giant pestle.

"Ahhgh!"

"Sorry, I should warn you." Now the other shoulder blade.

"AHHGH!"

"This acupressure. Good, yes?"

Oh, yeah. If you like the sensation of F.D.R. walking around on your back with his wrist crutches.

"Ye-*ahhgh*. Guh-*hood*," I managed. Somehow, Mika seemed to be exerting no effort at all. In fact, she was singing. As I fought for air, her voice mourned along with Paul McCartney's.

"The rong and rinding road. Tha-aa-at reads, to yo doe."

"Are . . . you . . . walk . . . ing . . . on . . . your . . . *knees* . . . up . . . there?"

"You so *funny*, Eddie."

When she was finished I felt like a plucked chicken released from a hydraulic press. I was certain there were multiple fractures. Would this kind of injury be covered? What would I tell my primary care physician?

Mika had gotten down off the table and bent to whisper in my ear. "Time foh otha side!" she sang.

"I'm not sure I can turn over."

"Mika hep you." Together, we got me onto my back. My entire body was limp, most notably the part that I figured was her next target. "Now. What I do foh you?"

"Look, I really don't think—"

"You no rike Mika?"

All right. Nine chances out of ten, it was an act. But her pretty face looked crestfallen. What the hell. I had made it (barely) this far.

"Okay," I said. Mika perked up. "You can probably tell I've never done this before, so I'm going to have to ask you about my choices."

"I give you nice massage *heah*." She touched me to show me where. No immediate response. "Nutha fifty dollah."

"*What*? I was *specifically* told . . ."

Then I remembered: No, I wasn't.

"I put you *heah*," she said, indicating her mouth and licking her own finger with apparent relish (maybe she didn't look like Mrs. Livingston), "nutha hunded dolla. I put you *heah*" (three guesses), "nutha hunded-fifty dollah."

Have I mentioned that for the son of a multimillionaire, I'm tight with a buck?

"It's all very tempting, really. But I'll have to settle for the massage this time. I don't have much more money with me."

"That okay. Next time, you stay owah. Bring moh money."

"Yes, I'll have to do that."

I have come to believe that there are many things men start in response to their libidos and then, realizing their mistake, finish out of chivalry. I didn't want to disappoint Mika. It was as simple as that. Fortunately, she was tender, and she was skilled. I could never have made it otherwise. And when I finished, it was with a supreme sense of relief, though in a much different way than I had anticipated when I had picked up the phone an hour before. I was relieved to be putting my suit back on. Relieved to be leaving the *Shan Gri La*. Relieved to have this behind me, my stupidity having cost me nothing more than a hundred bucks and a few bruised vertebrae.

But, as I said, Stewey Trammell was looking out for me, and he had other ideas.

During the first ten years or so after graduating from business school, Stewey had toiled in relative obscurity for a number of small businesses. Not surprisingly, he didn't interview well, and prospective employers took his oafish, unkempt appearance as an indication of professional lethargy, which, in fact, could not have been further from the truth. As is often the case with people who make a poor first impression, Stewey was driven to prove himself. In 1992, he joined Pittsburgh's fledgling High Tech Council, was later asked to serve on its board and parlayed his contacts there into a CFO position with one of the fastest-growing software companies in the city. He had reached the modest pinnacle of his career and he knew it. Stewey wasn't a "big picture" guy; he was a grinder who had managed to grind his way to a six-figure income and a house in Fox Run. But neither his success nor what I still considered to be Donna O'Connor's confounding decision to marry him had, as far as I could tell, checked his zest for prurient pleasures. We still had lunch together once a week, and he ridiculed me when I shared the details of my recent misadventure at the *Shan Gri La*.

"Christ, Mikey. You can't just open the Yellow Pages and *plunk* your finger down. You need to do some *research*. The internet is like the booty Library of *Congress*, for chrissake." He shook his now-even-bigger head. "Why didn't you come to me *first*, my son?"

"Forgive me, Father, for I have sinned."

"Look. Next week, I'm going to bring you a little something."

"What?"

"It's a surprise. A late birthday present."

"I don't need another one of those."

"Trust me."

Okay. Have I ever said it wasn't my own stupid fault?

7

BOOGIE *(to a beautiful* GIRL *on horseback)*: What's your name?
GIRL: Jane Chisholm. As in the Chisholm Trail. (*She gallops away.*)
BOOGIE (over the roof of his car to FENWICK): What fuckin' Chisholm Trail?
FENWICK: You get the feeling there's something going on that we don't know about?

—Barry Levinson, *Diner*

All men come equipped with a hair trigger. If the list of things capable of arousing our mates might fit on a sparse, well-chosen dinner menu, the same list applicable to us would need to be alphabetized in something roughly the size of the Sears catalog. In fact, catalogs themselves are dangerous. Pottery Barn, Lillian Vernon and their ilk are wasted forestry to us. But any publication containing even the most conservative bathing-suit or lingerie section is worth a quick perusal. "This would look good on you, hon," is our gender-wide cover. Show me a house where the Victoria's Secret catalog has just been delivered, and I'll show you a woman under siege.

But it goes beyond the tactile, corporeal world. Men are capable of working themselves into a state of pleasant titillation, with no outside stimulation whatsoever, just to pass the time. Out of sheer boredom. We discover this technique (I hesitate to call it a "talent") at an early age, usually in high school, to keep from falling asleep in class. Later, we use it to stay awake on long drives and in movies chosen by our wives and adapted from Jane Austen novels.

About a week after Stewey bestowed upon me my "birthday present," I found myself in the front row at a continuing legal-education seminar on ethics being given by a retired Third-Circuit judge. "Found myself" isn't accurate, I suppose. I *placed* myself in the front row with the mistaken assumption that it would be the one spot in the room where I would be unable to fall asleep. Many of my colleagues bring newspapers and sit in the back of these compulsory sessions (the irony of two rows of dark-suited attorneys, finance sections raised against the foe—*ethics*—apparently escaping them). I have never had the chutzpah to behave so obviously, but I recognize that my motivation is no different. We are all trying to stay vertical in order to get the required credits. Unfortunately, I had grossly underestimated the somnolent powers of the venerable Judge Fagenbaum and, after less than forty minutes, I was doing head-bobs that threatened to put me in a neck brace.

Judge Fagenbaum's method of "teaching" ethics was to read from the ABA Model Rules, word for word, in a wheezing monotone. He had been on the drafting committee and therefore deemed the Model Rules "self-explanatory to anyone who takes the time to read them." Judge Fagenbaum took the time. He sat, hunched over an open rule book, his bony shoulders barely even with the top of the table that had been placed on the dais, and directed his voice (or what was left of it) downward at the text in front of him. Periodically, one of the ABA education coordinators would try to reposition the microphone, but it was useless. He sounded like the teacher in the *Peanuts* cartoons. "Mwah mwah mwah *mwah*-mwah mwah." At first, I was able to amuse myself by watching the string of white mucousy material that magically stayed attached to both his upper and lower lips like a cobweb. But when he yawned and it still failed to retract either up or down, I began to feel ill and had to look away. Then he started in with the name-dropping. Judge Fagenbaum was famous for this. Oddly, he never mentioned legal or political heavyweights, though he knew many. It was always sports and entertainment figures. The prevailing theory was that he had been such an outcast for the majority of his early life that he couldn't resist the temptation to reinvent himself before death. Nearly everyone he mentioned was already dead, or close, so there was no real way of checking the accuracy of his stories.

The one advantage of these digressions was that they were *audible*, because he actually looked up from the Rule Book to deliver them. On this particular day, he followed his electrifying rendition of Model Rule 1 with a riveting tale about the "Splendid Splinter."

"You know, I once had the good fortune of sitting next to a gentleman by the name of Ted Williams on a flight from Boston to Miami. You might have heard of him."

Yes. And thanks to cryogenics, Ted was still in better shape than the judge, despite his death three years earlier.

"I'm sure you all know that he was the last man to bat .400. But did you know he hit .388 when he was *forty* years old?"

The judge panned the room (during what was supposed to be a dramatic pause) to see if any heads were nodding. They were, though not voluntarily.

"And that was against the likes of Bob Feller and Whitey Ford. Before expansion *ruined* baseball."

Most everything, for Judge Fagenbaum, had been "ruined" by no later than 1970.

"You know, Williams hit a home run in his very last at-bat in Fenway Park? The fans were going ber*serk*, but he re*fused* to come out of the dugout to tip his cap in acknowledgment. I asked him about that. On the plane. He said, 'Judge'—he insisted on calling me that—he said, 'Judge, I'd hit five hundred and twenty home runs before that and never tipped my cap. I didn't see why that one was any different.'" Dramatic pause. Pan the room. Next rule. "Mwah-*wah*-wah, mwah mwah *mwah* . . ."

Desperate for something to occupy my attention, I opened my Rule Book and tried to follow along with where I thought he might be. But the combination of the ponderous legalese and the drone of the judge's muffled voice was like a barbiturate. I was beginning to lose consciousness. Thank God for another story after Rule 2. At least it was loud.

"I once had the good fortune of sharing a limousine with a gentleman by the name of Frank Sinatra. You might have heard of him."

Have you ever tried to speak after exhaling *all* of your available breath? That's how every word from the judge sounded.

"Frank—he insisted that I call him that—Frank was in Las Vegas entertaining the Association of Trial Lawyers of America, of which I was then president . . ."

Christ, I'd heard this one before. Old Blue Eyes and Old Mucous Lips engage in an enlightened discussion on race relations, concluding that it was a crime the way "a gentleman by the name of Sammy Davis, Junior" was treated early in his career. I suppose this was his attempt at an ethics connection.

At the end of this inspirational yarn, someone from the Bar Association placed a note in front of the judge. He read it and frowned. "It seems that we are running behind schedule," he said, with apparent disdain for anyone who would impose a time limit on the sharing of his wisdom. "I shall therefore henceforth stick strictly with the program. Please turn to Rule Three."

I was dead now. The boredom was paralyzing. Literally incapacitating. The judge fluttered in and out of my view as I battled gravity for control of my own eyelids. I was losing badly—as the fresh pool of drool on Rule 3.3(a)(2) demonstrated. I had three choices: I could leave immediately and lose the credit, in which case I would have to kill *another* half-day at this later in the year; I could begin sawing at my wrists with my car keys in a vain attempt to end it all; or I could begin thinking about sex.

Believe it or not, most of the time my fantasizing starts with my wife. This had been particularly true since our post-childbearing sexual rebirth a few years ago. But, for me, a good fantasy must have an element of possibility to it, and my advances were still being so resolutely rebuffed by Kelly that I had stopped advancing. I couldn't work up a good fantasy about my wife because I couldn't see it happening. That's what started me thinking about the present Stewey had given to me.

Inside a birthday card that had been backdated nearly three months, Stewey had enclosed a business card and a gift certificate. The gift certificate was from a place called The Healing Touch, and it said that the bearer was entitled to "3 half-hour relaxation therapy sessions with the therapist of your choice." The heavy business card was embossed with the name AMANDA DERBY, PH.D., who held herself out to be the proprietor of that business. Both items had been pushed to the back of the top drawer of my desk, where I had been unsuccessfully trying to forget about them.

"Trust me," Stewey had said again when he handed me the envelope. During the intervening week I had resolved that this was not in my best interests.

"Can you name any time when my trusting you has worked to my advantage?"

"I told you to marry Kelly."

"No. I told you she'd said *yes*, and after you picked your chin up off your home fries, you told me to hurry up and book the band."

"Same difference."

"Look, I'm doing better now, anyway."

"Kelly gave in?"

"No."

"Then how could you possibly be doing better?"

"I don't know. I think it was the *Shan Gri La*."

"A temporary, post-traumatic reaction. Not to mention, she got you off. I give you another week, tops."

"Thanks for the vote of confidence."

"I'm just being realistic. Male hormones are resilient little soldiers. Duty will call."

I knew he was right. But memories of his high school *Hustler* collection, with its faceless, close-range anatomical studies, colored my judgment of his judgment.

"I assume you've been to this place?"

"Some would say I *frequent* it."

"And Donna's never caught you?"

"Donna gave me one of these for *my* birthday this year."

Admittedly, this information threw me momentarily. What I considered to have been the absolute purity of my love for Stewey's wife in a previous life, and my subsequent adjustment to her falling for Stewey, never accounted for the possibility that she was attracted in some way to his basic baseness.

"Look, I appreciate your concern." I pushed the gift certificate across the table to him. "But I know your taste in adult entertainment, and I'd like to avoid feeling like I need to be scrubbed down with steel wool."

"Hey, can't a guy's tastes change?"

"A hypothetical guy's, or yours?"

"Whatever you think of me—and you're wrong, by the way—I know what *you* like, and that's all that matters."

He had a point. Worse yet, he knew that I knew it.

He pushed the card back my way. "You can thank me later."

Stewey had gleefully refused me any specifics, and so my fantasy had nothing to go on, really, as Judge Fagenbaum proceeded to reinvent boredom as we know it. But by the time he was winding down (after squeezing in a quickie about a "gentleman by the name of Arnold Palmer") and the newspapers in the back of the room were being refolded, my imagination had succeeded in installing Dr. Amanda Derby as the sovereign of a sort of adults-only *Brigadoon*.

And in the ultimate hormonally induced male rationalization, I concluded that today might be the one day in the next hundred years that her mythical city of pleasure and plenty would appear, so I'd better get back to the office quickly and make myself an appointment.

When I got there, Hank was gathering her things to head out for lunch. I could smell her before I was all the way through the door, and she was in a hurry: two sure signs that she had a lunch date. She was wearing a simple gray silk blouse, pleated pants that hid the thickness of her legs, and pumps that pushed her height to nearly five feet. Her short hair, which she had begun to color since going gray at the temples, was combed to the side like a young boy's. She was pursing her lips in such a way that I knew she had just reapplied her makeup—nothing more than a touch of lipstick that matched her own natural lip color. The perfume, the scent of which I recognized, was her one feminine weakness.

In the nearly twenty years I had known her, Hank had only had one relationship of any consequence: an eighteen-month, long-distance love affair in the mid-nineties with a player on the women's pro golf tour. I had introduced the two of them after Fox Run had hosted a minor pro-am event, and I suffered from not-insignificant pangs of guilt when it ended badly for Hank. Since then, her love life had been, as far as I could tell, nonexistent. She lived alone in a large but sparsely furnished apartment near the university, one of the few sections of this ultraconservative city that could be said to be tolerant of "alternative" lifestyles. Hank's lifestyle—which, when she wasn't with me, consisted primarily of walking her two dogs and painting countless watercolors that she refused to show anyone—was hardly alternative. And though she seemed to have a date for lunch every couple of weeks, nothing ever appeared to come of them. She handed me a stack of pink message slips, always the penance for a morning out of the office.

"Are any of these important?" I asked.

"To me?" This meant "no" in the language we had gradually invented between us. Virtually constant sarcasm had become our way of battling relational claustrophobia. We spent more time alone together than most retired couples, who, if you'll notice, often communicate as if each can't wait for the other to die.

"Who's the lucky lady?" I asked, sniffing the air. "I hope she likes Brut." This meant "You smell nice. I hope this one works out."

"None of your business. And you're smelling the stuff you gave me for Christmas last year in lieu of a bonus, you cheap bastard." Read: "Thanks." You get the idea. The following exchange took place without either of us ever looking at the other—I flipped through the stack of messages, and she was slowly closing the door behind herself to let me know that her time, and therefore mine, was limited.

"Listen," I said. "I may have to go out again for an hour or so this afternoon."

"I'll try to carry on. Have you billed enough yet this month to cover my salary?"

"Including benefits?"

"There are benefits?"

"Some."

"Like you leaving again this afternoon."

"Like me not making short jokes when you wear pumps."

"Bye."

"Bye."

The door finally closed on Hank, and I finished going through the messages on my way back to my desk. She was right. There was nothing that couldn't wait.

As had become my habit, the first thing I did was check my online stock portfolio. In the few short months since the consummation of my "deal" with Kelly, and my corresponding rededication to work and financial planning, I had progressed from a level of relative disinterest in the financial markets to a virtual fanatic. I was no "day trader" as that term has come to be understood, but I watched my stocks as if I were. I charted and recharted my picks on different timelines with different moving averages, monitored daily volume for momentum, read every minor news item that might have the slightest bearing on any of them and kept an almost constant peripheral watch on the real-time ticker of my own holdings that scrolled across the bottom of my screen. George Snyder, the U.S. equities analyst on my father's staff whom I was utilizing to narrow my field of choices, kept reminding me that I was "in this for the long haul" and that constant monitoring would only affect my sleep patterns. But I was hooked.

"I can see how my father became addicted to this," I had told George during one of our almost daily telephone conversations (which were, he would be quick to point out, always initiated by me).

"Your father's not addicted to the markets, Michael; he's a *student* of the markets. There's a big difference."

"You're belittling me again, George. You know I could get you fired."

"No you couldn't." George was in his late twenties, looked about sixteen and had balls Wile E. Coyote might have difficulty rolling off a cliff.

After tossing aside the messages Hank had handed me, I fell into my chair and jiggled my computer mouse, clearing the Pebble Beach screen saver and revealing both the market's overall status and my personal stock ticker. At first, I thought there must be a mistake. I watched the ticker through one more time. Nope. There it was again. Jesus. Bio-Life Solutions (BLSN on the NASDAQ) was a stock that George had encouraged me to buy at 10½. And again at 7. And again at 4. He was so convinced of the strength of the company's fundamentals and drug pipeline that I had gradually acquired ten thousand shares at an average buy price of about six dollars—more than twenty percent of my entire portfolio. It had ended the trading day yesterday at 3½. Their products, which focused on women's health and fertility issues, weren't the problem, George assured me; it was the fact that their U.S. marketing partner was doing a terrible job of promoting them. Once they succeeded in severing that relationship and finding a more suitable partner, prof-its would follow. Right now, impossibly, it was showing on my ticker at a current price of 9. Volume was running ten times its daily aver-age. If what I was seeing was accurate, I suddenly had an unrealized profit of $30,000.

I picked up my phone and hit the speed dial to George.

"I'm surprised it took you this long to call," he said.

"I was at a seminar all morning. You could have called *me*."

"Yeah, right."

"What's going on?"

"I have an idea but I don't know for sure yet. The company has scheduled an investors' conference call for eight o'clock tomorrow morning. Like I've said, I think Bio-Life is worth something north of twenty dollars, but that's long term. Institutional buyers didn't just wake up this morning and decide I'm right. Some positive leak is driving this thing."

"What's your best guess?"

"I don't want to take any chances on passing anything along to you that turns out to be inside information, even if it's just a guess now. I'll tell you when I know what I *can* tell you, tomorrow after the conference call. For now, just enjoy the ride."

"Should I sell?"

"You didn't buy in ignorance; don't sell in ignorance."

"You know I'm old enough to be your father in parts of West Vir-ginia."

"Do you want respect or advice, Dad?"

"I'll call you tomorrow."

"My insignificant, workaday life wouldn't be complete without—"

I hung up on George and raised my fists skyward. I had just made in one morning as much money as I made in three or four average months at the office. Well, not "made," exactly. It had just kind of appeared on my computer screen. But what a *rush*. And what a difference from the way I had been making money for the past twenty years, billing my life in six-minute increments and then listening to ungrateful clients telling me, "It couldn't have taken you *that* long."

Flushed with adrenaline, I opened my top middle drawer and fished toward the back for the envelope holding Stewey's gift. I found it, and Dr. Amanda Derby's card fell out. I was again struck by its "officialness," so much so that I picked up my phone and dialed the number as easily as I might have returned one of the calls now stacked on my desk. The voice that answered could have been the seasoned receptionist in the office of one of my big-firm colleagues.

"Good afternoon, The Healing Touch. May I help you?"

The legitimacy of both the business card and this greeting almost made me careless.

"Yes, my name is . . ."

Alarm bells sounded as I pictured the troll-like keeper of the *Shan Gri La* standing guard in the reception area.

I started again. "A friend of mine gave me a gift certificate, and I was just calling to see . . ."

"Could you please read me the number in the bottom left-hand corner of your gift certificate, sir?"

Sure enough. There was a number.

"Oh-one-seven-one-seven."

"One moment, please." I could hear her tapping a keyboard.

"Yes, Mr. Benedict. I see that you have three free sessions courtesy of Mr. Trammell. Would you like to schedule one of those now?"

Again, powers of description fail me. Of course, I wanted to kill Stewey. No. I take that back. I wanted to storm the nearest Wendy's like the Bastille, Stewey's head on a pike, French fries spewing like entrails from his mouth, nose and ears.

"Mr. Benedict?"

What good would hanging up now do? I breathed deeply and tried to speak without vengeance in my voice.

"How is it that you know my name?"

"We require all purchasers of gift certificates to provide the name of the beneficiary for tracking purposes."

"I see."

"It's for the protection of the therapists. I'm sure you understand."

No. I didn't. "Certainly."

"I should point out that because you are coming in on the recommendation of an existing client, in this case Mr. Trammell, there are certain procedures and information that will not be required of you."

"Like what?"

"Well, Dr. Derby can explain all of that to you when you come in for your first session."

"I'll be seeing Dr. Derby herself?"

"Yes, everyone is required to meet with Dr. Derby one half-hour before the appointed time of the first session, and at least once every two months after that."

"I see. To what purpose?"

"Again, I'll leave that to Dr. Derby. Has Mr. Trammell not given you any information regarding our services and procedures?"

"No. Mr. Trammell has not."

I was almost certain that I heard her suppress a laugh, then cover the receiver to say something to someone else in the room.

"That's all right. As I said, you will be briefed by Dr. Derby. Would you like to schedule an appointment?"

Whatever damage could be done, I thought in a moment of unparalleled naïveté, had already been done.

"Yeah," I said, feeling almost beaten.

"Fine. Now, when would you like to come in?"

Whatever appetite had driven me to pull out Stewey's card and pick up the phone had almost entirely dissipated. But, again, it seemed that I was no more able to resist my curiosity—which had been piqued considerably by this odd conversation—than my desire.

"Would one-thirty be too soon? I mean, I could see Dr. Derby at one-thirty, and then have a session scheduled for two o'clock."

"I'm afraid that won't be possible."

"Well, when is Dr. Derby's first available appointment?"

More keyboard tapping.

"She could see you at three-thirty P.M. next Thursday, June the sixteenth. Are you available?"

Pique, pique, pique.

"Yes. As a matter of fact, I am."

8

Carpe *fuckin'* diem.

—Sal

The thirteenth tee sits level with the Clubhouse, the equivalent of two full stories above the twelfth green and high enough to overlook all of Fox Run. For most of the summer the view from here is of the light green of the golf course cutting paths, some straight, some angled, through the deep green of what from above looks like dense forest. But now, at the height of a western Pennsylvania autumn, the only visible green is created by the bent and Poa annua grasses planted by the hired hands of F. Porter Beason more than eighty years ago. Everything else, in this late-afternoon light, is Technicolor, surreal in its vibrance. I have brought a camera to this spot almost every fall of my life, a new one every few years, with more and more buttons to push and knobs to adjust, and then, gradually, fewer and fewer. But every advance in photography has failed to capture, even once, what I have seen a hundred times. It is to this frustration that I have attempted to redirect my suddenly fragile psyche as Sal, still breathing hard from his climb up the railroad-tie stairs, repeats the question that I have apparently failed to answer.

"You okay?" he pants.

"I'm fine," I say, though we both know that I am not.

Sal's eyes narrow and his thick white hairline drops toward his eyebrows.

"You're all of a sudden lookin' like one of my asshole son-in-laws on his weddin' day. Like you don't belong in the clothes you're in." He looks at me hard. Then his brow unfurrows as my condition dawns on him. "Jesus Christ. You looked at the goddam scoreboard, didn't you?"

"No!" I lie. "Sal, I swear to God, it's like it was looking at *me*."

He shakes his head. "You'll never learn. None of you."

"What's that supposed to mean?"

"All you folks who grew up here. You get to thinking this is important."

"Come on, Sal. You owe just as much to this game as I do, maybe more."

"Oh, I didn't say the game wasn't important. The *game's* important. It's *your* game that ain't." Sal smiles to let me know he doesn't mean this quite the way it came out. "I mean, ain't it supposed to be *fun* to go low? Why is it all of you stop havin' fun just when you're playin' your best?"

"I don't know. Doesn't uncharted territory make everyone nervous? I'm five *under*, for chrissake."

"Uncharted territory?" Sal blows a quick burst of air through his heavy lips. "That's just what I'm talkin' about, Mr. B. You ain't exactly discoverin' the New World here. This territory is well charted. Just not by you."

Sal pulls my three-wood but he can tell I'm not ready to hit, so he takes the damp cloth he keeps slung over his shoulder and begins to work at the face with it, removing imaginary dirt.

"I'm not sure I like you lumping me in with everyone else who grew up here, Sal. You've known me almost my whole life. I don't really belong here."

Sal looks up from his work and laughs. "You know how many of the folks I carry for feel like that? At least half. Almost *all* the nice ones. It's like they feel guilty for bein' a member of this beautiful place. I'll never understand it. Of *course* you belong here. Wish *I* did."

I consider interrupting the uncomfortable silence that follows to tell Sal that he *does* belong. Or that it's *like* he does. But I'm not quite naïve enough to say it, and he's much too smart to believe it. The knowledge that overwhelms me, though, and that I do almost share with him, is that he, like my father, is a man whom I would emulate if I could. Instead, I fumble in my pocket for a tee and reach for the three-wood he is already holding out to me like an offering.

The thirteenth is where many potentially great rounds at Fox Run go to die. Part of the reason is the thirteenth itself—a long, 440-yard dogleg-right, with white out-of-bounds stakes bordering the triangular tree line that both marks the border of the Beason family property and forms the crook of the dogleg. The hillside at the base of the Beason property slopes left, away from the dogleg, creating a difficult reverse-banked curve. Because of that slope, the hole was originally designed as a straightaway par-four. But F. Porter Beason liked the look of the hillside property and the view it would give him of his new kingdom, and so he drew a large, triangular lot for himself into the plans. The hole was then redesigned to circumvent his majesty's domicile, and we have all been trying, mostly unsuccessfully, to find the best way over, around or through the multigabled lives of the family Beason ever since. When I was younger I would take a driver over the trees lining the Beason property and (when I didn't hit it out of bounds onto their patio) cut fifty yards off this hole. But the trees have grown taller and I have grown smarter (at least out here) so that my play is now a high, soft three-wood well left of the corner, then a long-iron shot in from there. The thirteenth is the beginning of Fox Run's answer to Augusta's "Amen Corner," and, truthfully, there are more than a few prayers proffered here, including the one Sal must sense that I am offering up now.

"Keep trustin' it," he says.

But I am willing the ball left even before drawing the club back. I know I should stop—wait until I can find in my memory a perfect shot from an earlier day, one that my mind can play without thought and my body execute without effort. But I have crossed that narrow yet crucial divide between trust and imitation, now trying to make happen what I need to *let* happen. And I make it happen, all right: a dead pull left of the fairway, left of the dense tree line, almost to the doorstep of the dark, low storm shelter that serves this corner of the golf course.

"We're in play," Sal says, without looking at me. "Let's go play for five and maybe make four." He is already striding down off the tee, hoping, I think, that I will follow him and move on. But I am standing, staring after the shot, still in shock at the suddenness of the change in my mental state.

"Come on," Sal chides, circling his arm forward but not turning to look at me. "Forget it. Did you think you was never gonna hit another bad one?"

I follow but hang back, trying desperately to refocus, to reestablish the calm that produced the magic of the last eleven holes. But tranquillity cannot be willed, no matter what the Eastern religions declare, and my mind, fixated on one poorly executed shot, is a jumble of the impossible mechanics of the golf swing and the futility of trying to execute them in perfect succession, in perfect rhythm, with perfect tempo. What has happened over the past months to my instinct to forget—the quality my father saw in me that very first summer evening? And what is the infinitesimal difference between our two genetic codes that allows my father to forget, even as the British pound, or the Thai baht, or pork bellies are tanking against his billion-dollar long position, while his son can't survive the good fortune of a game being perfectly played? I don't catch Sal until he has almost reached my ball. He leans the bag against the outside wall of the storm shelter, quickly checks the lie and my options, then looks up at me. When he sees my face, his own becomes stern.

"Quit whining," he says.

"I didn't say a *word*."

"Like you said, I've known you since you was twelve. You're whining. We're not in bad shape here. We got an alley back to the fairway. We can even advance it a little. You play it right, you'll have one-thirty in; easy bogey, maybe par."

He's right. Even the lie's not bad. Instead of the heavy rough, my ball has come to rest on the hardpan pathway created by decades of footsteps, including my own, entering and exiting the storm shelter. I can feel my mind begin to relax. I have stepped into this shelter many times during midround cloudbursts, sometimes pleading for a slice of blue sky, sometimes glad for the interruption. Once, the lightning strikes came so fast and close that my father and I took off our metal spikes and stood hunched on the center square of wooden benches. I took my first tentative sips of beer in this shelter with Stewey Trammell. We had stolen it from an ice-filled cooler behind the pool bar during a party and had run, laughing as if already drunk, the six hundred yards or so down the Clubhouse hill, up over the thirteenth tee and down again to this spot. When we opened the jostled cans, they shot foam that struck the underside of the roof and left a stain that I can still make out. The Fox Run High School grounds are just across the fourteenth fairway and through the woods from here, and I once smoked pot in this shelter with a dangerous girl from my A.P. English class who, at the time, had befriended me mostly to anger her married boyfriend. And I once made love here with Agnes Humpstone on a thick, summer night, the rain clattering on the roof, the light from the Beason family compound knifing sharp through the side slats, before being arched and softened over Agnes's broad, rising shoulders.

"You still in there?" Sal wants to know.

"Yeah, I'm here." My hands and pulse have both steadied, at least for now.

"I like four or less offa that lie, Mr. B. You get it clean and it might squirt up on you a little and catch one of those low branches."

"Give me the four, then."

"Okay. You can even hood this closed a little, I think."

"Yup."

The chute through the trees isn't particularly narrow, but I've got close to fifty yards sideways just to get back to the fairway, so the shot has got to hold its line. The swing will be short and compact, the clubface square to the line and closed, sending the ball on a low trajectory up the gentle slope, through the trees and into the fairway. I can see the shot before I hit it, which seems a minor miracle in itself, considering my mental state a few moments ago, and I can feel that I have pinched the ball perfectly off the hardpan. It never wavers from its line through the trees, and even Sal has said, "Nice play, Mr. B.," before it rises just enough to catch the last low-lying branch between me and the fairway and ricochets down and left.

"Goddammit, that was *perfect*!"

"Yep. Too perfect," Sal says. "That's what I was afraid of offa that lie. Come on. Let's go check the damage."

And there is more than a little of it. Although the ball is sitting no more than ten yards off the fairway, my only chance at getting to the green is with a hook recovery shot around the heavy base of an old oak that blocks my view of the green. The ball is sitting down in the rough, which will make it even harder to turn over. Add to that the fact that I'll need to aim the ball at the out-of-bounds stakes along the right side of the fairway and trust that it will turn left in time, trust that I'm not sure I've got right now, and you've got a shot I don't feel capable of playing.

"Shit, Sal. Maybe I should just punch out."

"You do that and you'll still have one-thirty in. We'll be lookin' at double-bogey six, five if we're lucky. Safe was the smart play on that last one, but not here. Come on. Hook this son of a bitch up by the green. I seen you hit this shot a dozen times from near this same spot."

"Never with this kind of number on the line."

"Well it ain't gonna *be* on the line much longer if you don't pick your fuckin' chin up off the turf and start playin' again."

He was suddenly hot and I knew enough to shut up.

"Were you listenin' to me on the tee or not? You say you're not like everyone else here, then you start mewin' like a pussy soon as you get in a little trouble. You ever notice how few of the really great players—now I'm not talkin' about those country-club boys who're always in the money but never win a goddam thing—how few of the great ones *ever* had what you have? Shit. Arnie's dad mowed the fuckin' fairways at Latrobe; Trevino was a little spic caddy hustlin' every white guy in the place; Tiger played most of his early rounds by sneakin' on the Navy course with his dad after hours. You remember when he stiffed it from one sixty-five in the pitch dark on the eighteenth at Firestone? Everyone was so fuckin' amazed. But he'd hit that shot a *thousand* times before. He played in the dark every goddam *day*. These people grabbed it and *choked* it when they got the chance. *Carpe* fuckin' *diem*. That's what I always say. Sometimes I think the problem with you folks is that every day of your lives is so goddam beautiful, you don't know which one to grab ahold of." He pulls a club without any prompting from me. "Now, hood this little seven-iron, and hook the shit out of it."

So I do. Only in overprotecting against the out-of-bounds, I hook it too much, and it turns hard with the slope of the fairway, skips through the green-side collar and into the left bunker. Still, Sal was right to make me try it. I'll have an easier time getting up and down from there than I would have from 130 yards. He says nothing. He takes the seven-iron, hands me my sand wedge, then starts off toward the green. Sal is playing father again, and I feel sufficiently chastised that I don't dare lag behind. But despite the inarguable truth of what he's said, it's not the whole truth. At least not for me. There are other issues, though I don't expect that Sal can draw them out here when I can't name them myself.

But his tirade has succeeded, at least for the moment, in getting me refocused. I hit a good bunker shot to about five feet, then make the putt for bogey. Now, Sal's got his voice back.

"All right. We're still four under. Long as you're already lookin' at the scoreboard, I might as well say it. We're four under."

"So, great and wise Yoda"—I toss the ball to him to pocket; I want a new one for fourteen—"you got the answer for me?"

"To what?"

"How do I know which one of these beautiful days to seize?"

"You seize 'em all, Mr. B. You goddam seize them all."

The house where my wife and daughters are living without me is an imposing, square, brick structure, and the five wide steps that lead up to the porch make the house look as if it sits unnaturally high above the tree-lined sidewalk. In daylight, the old, irregular windows are the color of deep ocean water, revealing only what happens to pass close to the surface, and even then the images are vague and twice reflected, superimposed on themselves. But at night, those same windows are like a bank of television sets, all lit from behind. That is when I pace the sidewalk out front, trying to appear as a passerby might, but looking, I'm afraid, more like a shooting-gallery duck waiting to be picked off.

It's the first week of September, still early in my exile—before Kelly will start bringing the girls to me once in a while, before I will start picking them up at school two days a week just to steal a few minutes with them—so these nights are all I have. Every sixteen minutes, almost to the second, a cop car passes. Our little town has at least one cop for every crime committed in the past five years, which, when budget time comes around, borough officials point to as evidence that the force is just the right size. They have already gotten used to my appearances here and don't even slow down, sometimes even flicking their headlights in greeting.

Tonight is garbage night. In my absence, it's Megan's job to pull the cans to the curb, and her grudging, slump-shouldered weekly appearance on the porch is, to me, nothing short of fresh water to a man lost at sea. She'll talk to me for a few minutes, not long enough to raise suspicion, tell me what her sister is doing, how her mother is feeling. But tonight there is someone with her in the den. They both have books open. Megan is slouched on the loveseat next to the computer, jean-clad legs splayed impossibly. Her friend is sideways in my reading chair, facing away from me, leaning against one chair-arm, both legs over the other. The size of the sneakers should tell me what I don't want to know, but the truth doesn't register until they appear on the porch together. I duck behind the brick stairs, and if Megan has remembered that she is to be looking for me, there is nothing in her voice that gives it away.

"The garbage is around the side," she says.

"God, your mom looks in on us like every five minutes."

"I know. Sorry."

They come down the steps together and turn away from where I crouch, toward the opposite side of the house.

"I mean, what does she think we're going to do in there?"

"You're lucky she let you come over at all. And if I don't get a good grade on this quiz . . ."

"Okay. Chill."

Megan has started ninth grade at the high school just this past week, and she has apparently made a new friend.

"Here, get the heavy one."

They each drag one can to the sidewalk, then it must be the boy who goes back for the third, because Megan's voice is coming from the sidewalk:

"Want to come do this for me every week?"

"Sure. What'll you give me?"

"Oh, yeah. You wish."

"Come here."

"We have to go in."

"Just for a second."

"*No.*"

"Come on. Just a kiss."

"What else did you think?"

"Nothing."

"Better not."

"Come on."

I'm sure that she'll say no again; that I'll have to leap out from where I am hiding to save her. But the next thing I hear is quick, quiet footsteps heading back between our house and the neighbor's. And the next is a long silence that brings a throbbing heat to my face. And the next is my daughter laughing in a way I have never heard before. They are back around the corner and up the stairs before I can even think to make sure I am still hidden, but I have nothing to fear, because the world is invisible to them.

Once they are inside, their tableau re-establishes itself in the den just as if they have never left the room. Megan flips a page, then he does. She doesn't even appear to be looking at him. Kelly rises from the couch in the living room, disappears, then reappears in the hall to peer around the corner of the den. She says something to Megan, who looks up, bored, nods, then back to her book. From the chair, the boy's hand waves at Kelly, who crosses back through the hall, back into the living room, where she lifts Hannah from the couch and starts up the stairs. I am sure the doctor has warned her about this, but Kelly has never been able to resist a chance to wrap her arms around our children.

I cross the street so that I can see over the porch roof into the second-floor windows. When Kelly sets her down, only Hannah's head is visible, and I pace and watch them move between the bedroom and bathroom, the nightly ritual, then disappear together into Hannah's bed for a story. This is Hannah's favorite part of the day, a part she usually spends with me, and she would stretch it to an hour if she could. But Kelly is more firm than I, less susceptible to Hannah's pleas, and it seems as if it's one story, or one chapter, and done tonight, the bedside light left on for Hannah to read more on her own. Then Kelly pulls the shade, and it's over for me as well.

I look back at the den frame, and the picture hasn't changed. To the right, through the leaded glass of the front door, Kelly appears at the foot of the stairs, then stops in to say something to the boy, who sits up and begins to gather his belongings. It is only the movement in that picture that causes me to look up and see the shade rise again in Hannah's room.

She is so close to the window that all I can see is her silhouette. At first, her hands are cupped around her eyes, blocking out the light from her room so that she might see out, and it is only then that I realize that Hannah knows I am here. Then, everything else remaining still, she moves one hand and spreads all five fingers and presses them to the glass in a silent, motionless wave. A police car rounds the corner and flicks its lights at me. I raise a hand in greeting.

9

George sighed. "You give me a good whore house every time," he said. "A guy can go in an' get drunk and get ever'thing outa his system all at once, an' no messes. And he knows how much it's gonna set him back."

—John Steinbeck, *Of Mice and Men*

The week between my call to the offices of Dr. Amanda Derby and the designated date of my "session" was one of the most incongruous of my life. On the one hand, I was guilt-ridden, feeling almost as if I had an appointment to be unfaithful to my wife. (All right, ladies. I can hear you: *There's no "almost" about it*. But, like it or not, to most men there are as many shades of infidelity as there are shades of gray. And when you utter thoughtless platitudes like, *If you're* thinking *about it, you might as well be* doing *it*, we're wondering when we'd have time for anything else.) I don't think I ever had any intention of having sex with another woman. But having been given no worthwhile information by either Stewey or Dr. Derby's receptionist, I didn't know what to expect upon my arrival, and I wasn't sure I trusted myself to make a rational decision if the choices were not presented to me until I was already in a precarious position. The fact that I had escaped Mika and the *Shan Gri La* with minimal damage was not heartening to me in the least. My visit there had grown out of one of those thousands of everyday moments when we men think about sex, starting with our immod-

est musings on the prowess of the morning news anchor and culmi-
nating with our nightly plans, mostly unexecuted, of proposing to
our partners (who are largely oblivious to the massive buildup) that
we have a go at three or four of the warped scenarios we've con-
trived throughout the day. And if I concentrated hard enough on
the rationalization, it could feel like a victory that only one of the
millions of such moments that I had experienced over seventeen
years of marriage had resulted in something I wouldn't tell Kelly
about. This felt different. This was planned. The fact that Stewey
had done much of the planning only made it worse. I was living an
entire week with the knowledge that a woman other than my
ornery, pregnant wife was going to, at the very least, put her hands
on me. The odd result was that I don't think I have ever lived
through a week in which fewer sexual thoughts flourished. I de-
bated daily about canceling; but, again, it was my curiosity that was
spurring me on to complete something that my libido had started,
the flaccid state of affairs that currently reigned notwithstanding.

On the other hand, there was a different kind of energy, almost
sexual itself, that was being generated by the run-up of Bio-Life.
The conference call that occurred the morning after my call to
George had revealed that one of the company's lesser products (a
contraceptive cream sold primarily in Europe) had been, along with
the products of several other companies, part of a massive government study on AIDS prevention. The products each contained a
small amount of a common spermicide, nonoxynol-9, that had
been shown to be effective in hindering the spread of the HIV
virus, but that had also proved toxic in the required dosages. The
products were being tested on an ultra-high-risk class, African prostitutes, in a double-blind placebo study that had been going on for
nearly eight years.

George was already talking over my head. "What the hell is a
double-blind placebo study?"

"It means that nobody, not even the government, knows who
got the real stuff and who got cold cream."

"They can *do* that?"

"Never in the U.S., not with a deadly virus. But HIV is spreading like the common cold in Africa, and most of these women are going to die anyway. The governments down there are desperate, and ours is finally realizing that we could be next."

"So is Bio-Life the winner of this dirty little contest?"

"No one is saying. But they announced today that the portion of the study involving their nonoxynol-9 product will be the first one un-blinded, sometime in early August."

"So this run-up is just a result of people knowing they're going to know the answer, one way or another, in August? That doesn't make sense."

"There's one more thing. Although no one knows which group got the placebo, the government announced today that preliminary indications are that there appears to be a 'statistically significant' difference between the two groups. The assumption that investors are making, obviously, is that it's the lovelies using our stuff that are benefiting, and not the ones slathering themselves with Oil of Olay. That's what we'll find out in August."

"Jesus. Did you know about this when you told me to buy?"

"Yes and no. Everyone's known that the study was going on, but no one knew if or when it would ever end, or whether anything positive would come of it. My analysis of this company for you was based solely on their existing and pending marketable products. If this hits, it's pure gravy."

"This is unbelievable!"

"Maybe."

That morning, an hour after the conclusion of the conference call and ten minutes after I had hung up the phone with George, Bio-Life opened at 12, three points higher than its previous day's close. By lunchtime, it was at 17 and had traded more than ten million shares. It touched 20 briefly, just before the close, and settled at 19½. Hank looked in at a little after four.

"If you're going to stare at that thing again all day Monday, can I just stay home?"

"My dear, if this thing keeps going, I may be able to do away with you altogether."

"No, no." Hank wagged a stumpy finger at me. "After all these years, you are *not* depriving me of the pleasure of quitting."

"Don't you have some administrative duties you could be taking care of?"

"I ordered pens and legal pads from OfficeMax this morning. What kind of operation do you fantasize that we run here?"

"Then why do I pay you to do two jobs?"

"Because last time I went on vacation you ordered enough paper to send a photocopy of the tax code to every member of the Allegheny County Bar, and enough coffee to keep them all awake while they read it."

"We ran out. Whose fault was that?"

"You just couldn't find it."

"We ran *out!*"

"Have a nice weekend, pookems."

"You too, love."

When I got home, Kelly immediately knew something was up. Over the past several weeks, we had settled into the kind of brother-sister relationship that every husband dreads: It was understood that we were going to fight; it was understood that, regardless, we loved each other; and it was understood that we were not going to have sex.

"Look at *you*," she said when I came through the door and into the kitchen. "If I didn't know better I'd think Hank spent the afternoon under your desk."

"Fixing the rollers on my chair?"

"It could only be one of two things, and you're home too early to have played eighteen."

"Bio-Life closed at nineteen and a half."

"And that's good for us?"

"Very."

"How very?"

"Over a hundred thousand dollars."

Kelly is not easily surprised, but I saw her flinch.

"So sell."

My foray into the financial markets made Kelly nervous. Oh she of little faith.

"Not yet. There's an announcement coming in August that could send it through the roof."

"Could?"

"Should."

"That's not what you said."

"I'm saying it now."

"Because you meant to say it the *first* time, or because you don't want to fight?"

"Both."

"What is your father doing?"

"This is purely George's call, and what difference does that make anyway?"

"What difference does the opinion of one of the most successful money managers on the planet make in what I think about your decision not to sell." A statement.

"Look. My father has positions in every major stock, currency and commodities market in the world. I'm watching seven or eight stocks like a hawk. Don't you think I'm capable of that much?"

"What if you don't know what you're watching for?"

"That's why I have George."

"George is twelve."

"He's twenty-seven. And he was hired by the man that you think is God."

Without meaning to, I had changed the argument, but this was one she was always ready for too.

"No. I just think he's a smart, lovely man. You're the one who's convinced that he sits in judgment over you."

"Of course he does. How could he not?"

"Michael, has your father ever expressed disappointment in any life choice you've ever made?"

"The man barely speaks."

"I said, 'Has he ever *expressed*.' Not everyone places the same value on words that you do. I don't remember my father ever telling me he loved me, but I *knew* it. He's been dead most of my life and I *still* know it. Men of that generation just don't communicate that way. Your father's silence isn't *brooding*, Michael. It's concentration. It's contentment. You can see it on his face—or at least I can—he's working *all* the time. But he's doing what he loves, and he just wants you to do the same. *Whatever* that is. Why do you feel the need to use his success as an excuse to diminish yourself?"

"You don't understand. You didn't grow up with someone who's maybe the best in the world at something. There's a certain unavoidable pressure that—"

"Just *sell*, okay?" She hadn't lost the thread after all. "That's my vote. And sell your fucking golf clubs while you're at it. Go back to being a mildly unsatisfied attorney who can't wait to get home to his wife and kids at the end of the day. There's *honor* in that, Michael. Even if you can't see it."

I couldn't, of course. That was the whole point. And what was happening with Bio-Life was only serving to make me less visionary. By Monday it wasn't just the large, well-informed institutional investors who were taking positions in the stock. The talking heads on CNBC (who admitted that they'd never heard of Bio-Life before Friday afternoon) had gotten word of the conference call and were talking up the economic possibilities for the company, which, they admitted, were "almost unlimited." On Tuesday, *The Wall Street Journal* ran a front-page article on the government testing and restated the same preliminary findings that George had given to me on Friday.

George himself was quoted in the article as a representative from my father's fund, which had been "the largest single investor in the company since early last year." That exposure sent other "informed" individual investors like myself scrambling for their laptops, and the stock price accelerated straight up. By Thursday afternoon, as I was restlessly awaiting the time when I would depart for my appointment with Dr. Amanda Derby, the stock had hit 32, my gain had surpassed a quarter of a million dollars, and George was calling *me*.

"I'm selling half of the fund's position," he said.

"You're *what*? What the hell for? The announcement's not for almost two months."

"Look, we bought this thing thinking it might reach the mid-twenties in a few years. We're at thirty-two after a little more than *one*. Have you ever heard the saying 'Bulls make money; pigs get slaughtered'?"

"Only since I was six."

"Old lessons are often the best ones."

"But this thing could go higher, couldn't it? I mean, this might be my one chance at something really special."

"Oh, it could go a *lot* higher. If this stuff really does prevent the spread of HIV . . . ? That's why we're keeping half."

"So what's the risk?"

"Drug and tech stocks always seem to rise in advance of news, so that when the news actually comes, there's almost always an anticlimactic pull-back. I just thought you'd want to know what we were doing to protect ourselves."

"Thanks. I'll think about it, and then maybe we can talk some more."

"We always do."

"Go sell your stock, chicken."

In trying not to appear overanxious (to whom, I am not sure), I had been waiting until the last possible minute to leave for my appointment at The Healing Touch. After George's call, I was going to have to hurry to make it on time. But make it where? I suddenly realized that I didn't know where I was going. Stewey had told me that it was "in town," but I had never looked at the card for an address. I looked now. There was none. Only the telephone number. I dialed it quickly and recognized the voice on the other end as the receptionist I had spoken with the week before. I was again struck by her professional manner—just the right balance of efficiency and flirtation in her voice—and I momentarily fantasized about replacing Hank.

"Ah, Mr. Benedict! We've been wondering if you'd call."

"Yes. I have a three-thirty with Dr. Derby, and—"

"You need to know where to find us. Of course."

"Yes. I have Dr. Derby's card, but there's no—"

"That's right. We like to have all of our first-time clients call us from a public phone near our offices, just to make sure they're serious."

"Is this tape going to self-destruct in ten seconds?"

"Very good, Mr. Benedict! It just helps to maintain our privacy, which I'm sure you'll agree is to your benefit as well. We found that when we gave our address at the time the appointment was made, we got a lot of loiterers checking the place out in advance, and then many of them never showed. Dr. Derby didn't like the fact that so many non-clients knew where we were, so she went to this method. She figures if you've got the courage to call from across the street, you're on your way. Just don't forget a couple of quarters!"

"Check."

"Very good. If you'll just give this same number a call from the pay phone on the corner of Grant and Forbes, we'll talk you in from there."

"Roger, Moneypenny. Bond out."

"Moneypenny out!"

I grabbed my suit jacket off the hanger and headed for the door, hoping that Hank would see that I was in a hurry and not ask any questions. I really am delusional at times.

"Where are *you* going in such a rush?"

I opened the door to indicate that I would not be delayed. "Up to Grant Street," I said (which was true).

"You've got a hearing?"

"Yeah." (Which was not.)

"Why haven't I had any prep work?"

I was slowly closing the door on Hank's queries, as she had done to me on her way out to her lunch date the week before. "It'll probably be after five by the time I get back, so you can leave whenever you need to."

"That's all you had to say."

Five minutes later I was at the appointed corner dropping two quarters into a pay phone I'd never noticed before. For some reason, there was no feeling of being watched as there was the afternoon of my escape to (and from) the *Shan Gri La*. Stewey's refusal to tell me what to expect at The Healing Touch, the secrecy of the location, even the receptionist's oddly professional manner all combined to create a dreamlike state in which my actions were almost involuntary. When she answered after only one ring, I had to literally shake my head to refocus, like a cartoon character clearing cobwebs.

"I can see you, Mr. Benedict. You look very nice today. Did you dress just for us?"

"Yes. I mean, no. This is pretty much my uniform uniform. Where are you?"

"I'm looking out the window behind my desk. We're on the seventeenth floor of One Oxford Centre, just across the way. Do you know which one that is?"

One Oxford was the high-rent district. It housed one of the largest law firms in the city and at least another dozen small and medium-size firms.

"I've spent a lot of time in that building. I'm surprised I didn't at least recognize the name of your business."

"Well, our name doesn't appear on the directory downstairs. Just come on up to seventeen, turn right out of the elevators, then right again. Ring the buzzer by the door at the end of the hall."

I walked, still in somewhat of a daze, through the surface parking lot between Forbes and Fourth Avenues, then across Fourth and
through the revolving doors of One Oxford. I passed the escalators
leading down to the food court and up to the exclusive mezzanine
shops, and turned in to the first bank of elevators serving floors one
through twenty-three. There was an elevator waiting. I got in,
alone, and lit the 17 with the warmth of my index finger. The doors
closed. I felt my feet surge into my ankles, my stomach compress
into my diaphragm, and then my body was light and flying upward,
weightless during the instant that the elevator slowed, then settled.
The doors opened on an empty hallway that contained no signs of
business activity of any kind, and I half expected Stewey to jump
out of a darkened doorway and end the prank right here, but there
was no one. I followed directions: right, right again, and found myself looking down a long hallway. The lights were dim and the double doors at the end seemed small and far away, as if I might have to
drink a potion to enter. But when I reached them, they were large
and substantial, made of a heavy wood stained dark. There was
nothing to indicate who occupied the space behind them, though
there appeared to be a slight discoloration in the wood where a line
of letters might previously have provided a clue. The twin brass
knobs seemed to glow in the dusky light, and I almost expected
them to feel warm to the touch. But they were cool. And locked.
And when I reached to press the buzzer to the right of the door-
frame, I was momentarily shaken by the sight of a round, convex
intercom speaker. But it was the receptionist's soothing voice, and
not the rasp of the gnomelike madam of the *Shan Gri La*, that welcomed me before I even had the chance to announce my arrival.

"Come in, Mr. Benedict," she said. The door hummed, the lock
released and I was admitted to the offices of The Healing Touch.

I was expecting a burst of light when I entered, but instead was
welcomed into a room of soothing, muted warmth. The floor-to-
ceiling windows that stood behind the mahogany reception desk
had been covered with heavy tapestry drapes that hung from

antique-brass rods. The curtains had been pulled to within a foot of touching, and a modicum of sunlight diffused through the sheer behind. The rest of the light in the room emanated from ornate, shaded sconces set above leather couches to my left and right and from the green-hooded reading lamp on the reception desk. Wine-colored carpet covered the floor, and oak wainscoting rose to almost shoulder height on three walls. A tall, attractive woman dressed in a slate-gray business suit stood, smiled and extended her hand from behind the desk.

"Miss Moneypenny, I presume?"

"Welcome, Mr. Benedict. It's Leah, actually. Please make yourself comfortable. I've already notified Dr. Derby of your arrival." She motioned toward one of the couches, then sat down and picked up the phone. "Yes, Rebecca, could you please hold your session a moment until the waiting room clears? Thank you." And then to me: "It's not always possible, but we try to keep clients from crossing paths. It's more important to some than others. And you?"

I sat down and picked up a copy of *The Wall Street Journal* from the coffee table just to do something with my hands. "Me? Oh, I may just be here this once." Delusions were coming in bunches today, which was why I dismissed the sudden feeling not only that I would be here again and again, but that I had been here before.

"I understand, Mr. Benedict, but—"

"Yes, that would be preferable for me as well."

"Very good." Leah's phone fluttered softly and she picked it up. "Fine. I'll send him right back." She hung up and made a mark on a chart sitting in front of her. "Mr. Benedict, you can go on back now. Just proceed all the way to the end of this hallway." She motioned to her right. "Don't be concerned about all of the doors you pass. They're all empty offices. The treatment rooms are on the opposite side of the reception area."

"Thank you."

"I'll see you shortly."

I was glad for the warning from Leah because it was disconcerting walking past all of the closed doors in the narrow corridor. Again, I was struck by the sense that I had been here before and, despite the silence, I couldn't help but imagine that if I opened one of these doors, I might find Mika, in a dark room with cinder-block walls, grinding her elbow into the unsuspecting shoulder blade of a new customer. "You *rike?*" What was I doing here? What did I expect to find here that I hadn't found at the *Shan Gri La?* When had I become willing to risk so much to pay someone else to do something I had been successfully doing to myself for forty years? I heard her voice before I even realized I had knocked.

"Come in."

I had concocted many different versions of Dr. Amanda Derby over the past week, settling, absurdly, on an image of one of those doctors you see only on daytime soaps: hair pulled back in a severe bun, trendy but efficient glasses perched on a prominent nose, the white lab coat hugging tightly enough to hint at what would be revealed when the hair came down and the glasses came off. But I never expected the person before me now.

I would guess that she was my age, perhaps a few years older. Certainly she was not unattractive, but neither was there any pretense of glamour about her. Stray wisps of gray hair escaped from a simple brown ponytail, and she wore no makeup that I could detect. There was a natural ruddiness to her cheeks, as if she had pinched them before I entered, and the smile that she gave me as she extended her hand came not from her mouth but from her eyes. In contrast to Leah's professional appearance, she was dressed in jeans and a simple white blouse, reading glasses dangling from her neck. In short, Dr. Amanda Derby looked more like a seasoned attorney who had just stopped by the office on a Sunday morning to clean up some paperwork before the start of a new workweek than a woman who might be in the business of selling sexual gratification to the likes of me and Stewey Trammell.

"Please sit, Mr. Benedict." She nodded toward one of the two large armchairs in front of her desk. "I have been looking forward to meeting you. You come highly recommended by Mr. Trammell."

"Really?" I sat down on the front half of the chair, as if she were my junior high school principal. "As what?"

"Oh, as a friend, mostly, I suppose. And as 'a lover of beauty,' I think he said."

"Stewey said that?"

"A trifle sarcastically, perhaps, but words to that effect, yes." She opened a slim file that appeared to have a single piece of paper in it and slid her reading glasses onto her nose. I noticed that she wasn't wearing a wedding ring. "Because of Mr. Trammell's recommendation, we can skip over some of the usual formalities, but I'd still like to ask you a few questions and then make sure you know what we're all about here."

"That would be helpful. Mr. Trammell has taken great pleasure in telling me nothing."

She looked down at her file again. "He says you are going through a period of difficulty with your wife."

"I'd say it's more that she is going through a period of difficulty with me."

"You should know, Mr. Benedict, that I don't believe that a woman who is withholding sex is ever playing fair."

"In this case, you might be wrong."

"How so?"

"She's not really *withholding* it. I mean, that's how it started out, but now it's just sort of understood. And she had good reason."

"As I've said, I don't believe there is such a thing. But what started it, if you don't mind my asking?"

"Look, I don't really see why you need to know why I'm here. I don't know if *I* know."

"Mr. Benedict, we only have a short time together, and I need you to be willing to be open and honest with me."

"Again, I don't see why—"

"Because Mr. Trammell has paid my staff and me to perform a

service for you, and I can't properly perform that service without certain information. Furthermore"—she placed her elbows on her desk and leaned toward me, measuring her words—"I am extremely protective of my staff, and I can't do justice to that duty without preliminary and continual monitoring of our clients' progress. Treatment of the kind we offer can itself become a problem if we're not careful."

"I'm sorry. I'm not trying to be difficult. I guess I'm just having trouble equating my friend Stewey with what I know so far about your operation here, which, admittedly, isn't much."

"I'll tell you anything you want to know. But I get to ask the questions first."

"Fair enough."

Amanda Derby sat back and removed her reading glasses, letting them fall to her chest. "You were going to tell me about your wife."

"Kelly."

"Kelly."

"She's pregnant."

"Congratulations." She paused. "And how precisely does that impact on your presence here? Is your wife not interested in sex during pregnancy?"

"As a general rule, no. But this time there's more to it than that."

"Explain, please."

"Our youngest is eight."

"So this child wasn't planned?"

"That would be safe to say. I guess I was finally getting used to the idea that we were done. Kelly lost one five years ago. Late. We both had difficulty with that."

"Can I assume that you were less than enthusiastic at the news of this most recent pregnancy?"

"I practically told her that I didn't want the baby. I was getting used to us being adults again together. And for whatever reason I'm more frightened than Kelly is by the possibility of losing another one. I can't watch that happen again. So, there's that. And then there's the fact that I've stopped trying."

She didn't appear surprised by this. "Why?"

"I don't know. I spent most of my pre-sexual life as every beautiful woman's best friend, including Stewey's wife, I might add. It's funny. I tend to look on that period as if I experienced one sexual rejection after another, but I never even *tried*. This is that kind of rejection, with Kelly. I don't try because it's not going to happen. And I guess I thought I was done with that. I don't want sex out of pity. I'd rather *pay* for it than have that. I guess that's part of why I'm here. I want her to come back when she's ready."

Amanda Derby smiled for the first time since she'd greeted me. "What?"

"Nothing. I'm just looking at another note from my conversation with Mr. Trammell. It says, 'Michael is in touch with his feminine side and thinks that's a *good* thing.'"

"I could tell you a thing or two about him, you know."

She closed her file and sat forward. "No matter what Mr. Trammell has or hasn't told you, you must have some idea of the services we provide, but I do want to make one thing clear."

"Please. That would be a nice change of pace."

"You are *not* paying for sex. At least not to my way of thinking. And if you believe that you *are*, you may as well go elsewhere. We are providing *relief*—lovingly given, in a relaxed setting, where the rules are clear—so that you can go home and more objectively address the nonsexual aspects of your current difficulties. It is my experience that, for men, when sex is part of the problem, it is often *all* of the problem." She leaned forward again. "Let me be blunt. If you treat her with the utmost respect, your therapist will touch you in any way that you want to be touched. You can tell her, or you can let her follow her instincts, which, I can promise you, are good." My face was growing warm. I was no longer in the principal's office, but in the nurse's office being offered condoms. "No part of your body will penetrate any part of hers, or vice versa. Is that clear?"

"Yes, ma'am."

"Because men are more visually oriented than women, we find that it helps when our therapists perform their sessions nude, but that is *completely* up to her and may depend upon her level of comfort with you. Is that equally clear?"

"Equally."

"Whether or not you can touch her is, likewise, her choice."

"I wouldn't dream of presuming, I swear."

Her shoulders slackened. "I don't expect any problems, Mr. Benedict. It's just that, no matter how clearly I lay this out, we have some men who make certain, shall we say, assumptions—who think this little recitation is just for my own protection."

"Stewey?"

Dr. Derby looked surprised, then almost scolded: "A *perfect* gentleman. You know, Mr. Benedict, Mr. Trammell may not be as different from you as you think."

"All you need to know about Stewey is that he's got his wife buying him gift certificates to come here and get *relief*, as you so gently put it. My wife would have my balls in a nice rice pilaf if she knew about this."

"Mr. Benedict, you may not feel comfortable telling your wife about your visits here, but if you are going to feel guilty about them, they're not likely to do you much good."

"Do I really hear a woman telling a man not to feel guilty about a hand job from someone who is not his wife?"

"You need to stop thinking of it as a capital-H *Hand Job*. It's *just* a hand job, Mr. Benedict—something you've been doing to yourself for the same purpose since there was enough to grab hold of. I'm just providing you with a little company, a little inspiration, sort of like turning the faucet on when you need to urinate."

"Very romantic."

"That's my point. This isn't about romance. There's nothing here that threatens your feelings for your wife, or hers for you. In fact, if you let them, your visits here will let you focus more pointedly on those feelings as they exist *outside* of your sexual distance from each other."

"Did anyone ever tell you that you rationalize just like a man?"

She almost smirked. "All the time." She glanced at her watch, then at my file. "On Mr. Trammell's recommendation, you'll be seeing Samantha for your first session. He's chosen different therapists for your other two, but you can certainly stick with Sam if you like her. My office hours begin at noon, but the young ladies are not available until twelve-thirty. Most afternoons, there are four therapists here, then four others replace them for the evening hours, from five until ten." She picked up her phone. "If you're ready, I'll have Leah tell Samantha you're on your way."

She was on her feet, extending her hand before I could ask any of the myriad questions that were swirling almost visibly before me, before Rod Serling (certain to be concealed in one of the many darkened doorways of The Healing Touch) could even begin his narration. I left Amanda Derby's office and retraced my path down the narrow, deserted corridor to the reception area, where Leah, with a subtle nod, directed me across to an adjacent hallway. "The second door on your right, Mr. Benedict. Please remove your clothing and lie down."

The room was small and rectangular, large enough to accommodate a massage table and the path around its circumference, where two adults might have to touch in passing. Mirrors covered the two longer walls, and the only light came from candles standing in each of the four corners. There was a faint scent of vanilla that seemed to be coming from the candles, and another of mint that I couldn't trace. As I had been doing for most of the afternoon, I followed instructions. I removed all of my clothing. I lay down on my stomach. I hadn't noticed the music until now, something calming and indistinct that seemed to both blend with and consume other sounds. Was I hearing human voices on the other side of these walls? Or was it just the intended subtext of the music? From my position it seemed impossible that others could be close, the mirrors expanding to infinity the width of the room, the candles likewise multi-plied, though without a corresponding increase in light. I closed my eyes, instantly shrinking the room and dismissing whatever meta-phor that vision might otherwise have forced upon me. The thought that I couldn't escape, though, was that nearly forty years after Jenny Teagle and Addie Crupp, here I was, lying on a table, waiting to play doctor.

Can I make you believe this? Can I make you believe that there was, if not romance, then at least intimacy in what happened in that room? That I kept my eyes closed and never heard her enter? That she whispered my name and then hers, and that her fingers then grazed my skin as a blind woman's might, taking care not to manipulate or distort, but merely to remember? That she climbed up onto the table with me, and that her lips touched nearly every-where that her fingers did; and that where they couldn't, she cre-ated an illusion so compelling I was sure that she was making an exception for me. That when the scent of mint grew more domi-nant, the fingers that had barely disturbed a single cell on the sur-face of my skin closed around me, warm and slick, and that I pushed up into that warmth as if into her, while the rest of me fell away into anonymity and forgetfulness. That she collapsed into me and nestled her hair into the nape of my neck like an old lover, while my breathing regained its evenness. And that it was at once more than I ever could have expected, and not nearly enough.

10

Its inhabitants are, as the man once said, "whores, pimps, gamblers, and sons of bitches," by which he meant Everybody. Had the man looked through another peephole he might have said, "Saints and angels and martyrs and holy men," and he would have meant the same thing.

—John Steinbeck, *Cannery Row*

I view it as a part of my penance that I am writing this in a house in which I am surrounded by pictures of myself as a younger and better person. The folly that I didn't (or wouldn't) see at the time that these events were taking place is blinding here, among these old images, and if I had any guts, or weren't such a sap (it's hard to say which), I'd take them all down. Mostly, I think, I'm afraid of the debate with my mother that would surely arise, and the accompanying feeling, at age forty-five, of having no better argument at my disposal than: "But it's *my room*, Mom." So, there I am, hugging the Junior Club Championship trophy like a stuffed animal, my eyes squeezed shut with a perfect joy I can still remember but no longer feel. Or I am struggling to hold up a string of puny bluegills, the bottom half of my seemingly gigantic father in the background, holding two Zebco rods like little canes. And there is my white-tuxedoed arm draped around the bare shoulders of Donna O'Connor, who agreed to go to our junior prom with me the year before she discovered her round knight of the round table. Outside of this room, countless others line the upstairs hallway walls, interrupted only by entrances into rooms that hold more: a high school scholars' banquet; three graduation days; innumerable family vacations; at least a dozen of my father and me holding golf clubs—at The Homestead, the Greenbriar, Pinehurst and Pine Valley. My parents always told me that I could be anything I wanted to be. I was smart; I had family; my family had money. I had nothing but infinite possibilities and choices. And, somehow, I have chosen this.

I work here on the weekends and on Tuesdays and Thursdays. Hank now stays home on those two days (the culmination of a hard-fought negotiation in which she agreed to take two days off in return for me not reducing her salary), and I work until ten minutes before the end of Megan's last class at the high school. The first time she spotted me standing beside my car, behind the line of Blue Bird school buses, I could almost see her resisting the urge to run to me, conscious of the watchful eyes of her peers, who, truth be told, were concerned only with who might be watching *them*. Thereafter, she adopted a shuffling slump that she has perfected over the ensuing weeks, and which I have dubbed—to no visible effect— "Dead Teen Walking."

Today, I am a few minutes late, and I have to shout to keep her from getting on the bus. The expression on her face—as she shoulders her way out of a group of students who appear to range in age from ten to eighteen—tells me that announcing my presence with actual words is going too far, even for me. Why is it that we fathers not only tolerate but sometimes intentionally seek to elicit this precise reaction from our teenage daughters? Why is my response to her scowl to smile even more broadly and wave both arms over my head? For me, it is a fascination with the heretofore-unheard-of ability to utterly embarrass a woman without, for once, losing any real ground. She makes her eyes as narrow as she can without closing them, leans forward against the weight of her backpack and looks directly at me during the whole of the time that it takes for her to cover the fifty or so yards between us. In doing so, she looks frighteningly like her mother plowing her way through grocery bags on the kitchen floor.

"*Dad*. You don't have to *yell*," she says by way of greeting.

"But I did, pumpkin. You were about to get on the bus."

"Oh, *God*! Not *that*!" In Megan's mind, the birth of the art of sarcasm coincided precisely with her first menstrual cycle, and she has been working hard at perfecting it in the three years since.

"Come on. Hop in."

"I'll *get*. I won't *hop*."

"Suit yourself," I reply, forearms up, my hands hanging limp like little paws in front of my chest. "You don't know what you're missing."

"Dad. Don't you *dare*. I *swear*, I'll never ride home with you again."

I give one tentative little hop, knowing this one *could* lose me some ground, then walk the rest of the way around to my side and get in. She stands by the passenger's side door, watching for any further transgressions that might justify flight, then hoists her backpack off her shoulders and falls in next to me with the force of someone roughly five times her body weight. I have learned that this is mostly for show—to prove unequivocally to her friends that she is resisting to the last—and that she will be, if not exactly unrestrained, then at least receptive to exchanging a few pleasantries with her father once we are clear of the premises. It is always up to me to begin.

"How was your day of almost-higher education, pumpkin?"

"Fine."

"Any major discoveries or epiphanies to report?"

"Nope."

"Any broken hearts?"

"Some. Not mine today."

"Good."

I make a left turn out of the school driveway, rather than the right her bus would make. Kelly and I have an unspoken agreement regarding these pickups and deliveries: As long as I deposit our daughters at the corner within ten minutes of when the bus would do the same, she will pretend not to know the difference.

"What about urgent notes from friends in need?" I ask.

"Jason was unfaithful to Amy and she's a wreck."

"Unfaithful. You mean like—"

"Not *sex*, Dad. *God*, you're so paranoid."

"Sorry. I guess it's just hard for me to assume that no one's doing what I wasn't doing at your age. And for a long time thereafter, I might advise."

"No *Tales from the Crypt*, okay, Dad?"

"Check."

"Anyway, Amy's mom wouldn't let her go to the Homecoming after-parties with Jason, and he ended up hooking up with Muriel Squeams. *Major* scandal."

"Unfortunate name."

"*Major* slut."

"But no sex."

"*Dad.*"

"Sorry. How about you? The after-parties, I mean."

"Yeah. I went. Mom feels guilty, so she lets me do more stuff now."

"And?"

"It was fun, I guess. I only stayed until like twelve-thirty. I didn't have a date or anything."

"What about . . . what's his name again?"

"Matt? *So* yesterday, Dad. Try to keep up."

"Sorry." Though I was mostly sorry to have wasted generous portions of fatherly worry on the subject of Matt without ever having (officially) met him, my night hiding in the bushes notwithstanding.

"Anyway, Mom didn't want me riding home with this senior who was bringing Tina home, so she and Hannah came to get me."

"Hannah was up until twelve-thirty?"

"Yeah. She was in her pj's." I could hear the smile in Megan's voice. "She was psyched."

To me, it was a miracle that her adolescence had done nothing to quell Megan's reverence for Hannah. She had wanted a sister from the day she could make herself understood on the subject. And though she could not have comprehended fully, she seemed to grasp that we were having difficulty complying with her request, so that when Hannah finally did arrive, Megan treated her as much like a divine gift as we did. Our friends warned us that the novelty would wear off soon enough. But it didn't, and it hasn't.

We ride in silence for a while. It has been only two weeks since my round with Sal, and November has just begun, but it already looks and feels like winter coming on. In western Pennsylvania, fall is a one-month season lasting from late September to late October. Only the oaks are holding stubbornly to a few curled, brown leaves. Dark-gray branches reach toward us from either side from the light-gray sky, and the road seems to be pulling us into a black-and-white photograph that is Pittsburgh in November. When we crest the top of Delafield, pass the turnoff to my parents' house and head down the other side into our sidewalk community along the Allegheny River, Megan, uncharacteristically, breaks the silence.

"Mom says you talked."

I can tell that she is looking straight ahead through the windshield, making an effort at nonchalance, but expecting the opposite from me. I am not sure that I can comply without giving her the wrong impression.

"We did."

"At the Club. After you played one day."

"My home away from home, once removed."

"That's all she would tell me."

"I'm not sure there is more to tell yet."

"Yet?"

"I'm just like you, pumpkin. Or maybe I shouldn't presume that. Are you hoping? Because that's all I'm doing. Just hoping." We have almost finished the broad, back-door circle to our neighborhood, finally rejoining the route the bus completed just a few minutes ago. "What you said before? About getting to do stuff? You know your mom's got nothing to feel guilty about. You know that, right?"

Megan turns to look out her window. "You mean, do I know this is your fault? Yeah."

"Good. That's good."

"Just what's *good* about that, Daddy?" Now she turns fully to face me, but she can deliver only a glancing blow. My eyes are on the road. The bus stop is just ahead. "What's good about knowing who to blame when you don't know what *for?*"

"Sweetie, it wouldn't do anybody any good—"

"*Bullshit*, Daddy! Amy *hates* her dad. How am I supposed to know if I'm supposed to hate you?"

Our house is four doors down on the cross street but invisible from here. I make a show of concentrating while I pull close to the curb at the corner, trying to come up with an answer. That's what we're supposed to do, right?—give answers to all the hard questions, even if we don't really know? But what do you do with questions you don't want to help them find the answers to?

I shrug. "I don't know, sweetie."

"Whatever."

Megan pushes the door open, pulling one burden after her and leaving the other behind. She throws her backpack over just one shoulder and adopts a straight-legged limp to keep it steady. She has shared with me that she and her mother are in a standoff over last year's winter coat, which still fits but is no longer "cool." So, despite the cold, she is wearing the same hooded sweatshirt that she wore to my parents' house two weeks and thirty degrees ago, and her ponytail rests in the hood.

I put down the passenger-side window and call after her: "See you Thursday!" She turns up the walkway to our house, toward the front door that I can't see, and, just when I think that she won't, she looks toward me and raises a hand.

． ． ．

I am not such an anomaly standing on the walk in front of Woodland Elementary School. There is a fairly substantial cadre of parents, mostly of first graders and younger, who have not yet gotten used to the idea of their children jostling along at thirty-five miles an hour, three to a seat with no restraints. Most are mothers, but the "New Economy Fathers," working at home or in high-tech suburban offices in jeans and sneakers, are beginning to make their presence felt. Fortunately, I recognize none of them, other than from my twice-weekly sightings here. Most are much younger than I, waiting, I suspect (as Kelly did for Megan nine years ago) for their first school-age child to emerge from the bedlam. Younger siblings seldom enjoy such coddling, though the thought that takes hold before I can stop it is that, but for the inexplicable frailty of a fragile womb in a strong woman, I might be waiting for both Hannah and Jessica to come through those heavy doors. The beginnings of this vision have visited me before but, for some reason, today I don't resist it, and Jessica appears to me as clearly as if I had watched her grow into this person. I don't know where she got it but she has curly blond hair, and her eyes are brown and wide and curious, still like an infant's. She waits just inside the door of her kindergarten room as her classmates pass, looking for her sister. When she sees Hannah, she springs toward her and takes her hand, and they walk together to meet me, Jessica's short legs moving fast to keep up. The image is so powerful that I am surprised to see Hannah appear in the doorway alone.

Hannah is in third grade and has been riding the bus since her first day of kindergarten. And despite the unfortunate genesis of these pickups, Hannah's reaction to them—which is to bolt toward me and jump into my arms like a puppy—makes me feel a little bit like I am paying off an old debt to her.

"Daddy!" The weight of her own backpack never fails to surprise me.

"Hey, sweet pea." Her arms are wrapped around my neck, her legs around my trunk, so that I could let go without letting her fall. I pat her backpack all over, as if trying to guess its contents. "You trying to sneak one of your friends home in this thing again?"

"*No*, Daddy. It's *home*work!"

"Homework? You mean like coloring and stuff?" I have shifted her to my left hip now, and we are moving toward the car. Hannah is small for her age, especially considering her mother's height. Still, her legs dangle almost to my knees, and I carry her like this only because she still lets me.

"Hel-*lo*." She is knocking on my temple with her small, curled fist. She has begun to adapt her sister's sarcasm into her own harmless version. "Anybody home? Math? Reading? Science? Ever heard of them?"

"I think at your age all I had on me when I got home was the Spiderman comic rolled up in my pocket."

"This is the *Information* Age, Dad."

"That explains many of my difficulties."

"Miss Lang says we're way smarter than she was when she was eight. And she's a *teacher*."

"And she's just talking on the *average*. Just think how smart *you* must be compared to her when she was eight."

"Dad, I'm *not* the smartest one in my class."

"Impossible."

"Ian can multiply double digits in his head."

"A simple parlor trick. Does he write stories like yours?"

"No. I *am* the best story writer."

"My entire point in a nutshell. I'll take letters over numbers any day of the week. If I'm going to Vegas, maybe I take Rainman Ian. Anywhere else, I'm taking you."

My Camry is sandwiched between two luxury SUVs that look like they could have taken the beachhead at Normandy. Hannah likes to get in by herself, so I set her down behind the car, hoping she won't ding the Expedition on our right too hard.

"Hop in, sweet pea."

"Here, hold this," she says, stripping off her backpack and handing it to me. Unlike her sister, Hannah is still a willing participant in this old pantomime. Without prompting, she adopts the pose that almost got me disowned an hour ago, top teeth over bottom lip, and hops around to her door. She likes to be on the passenger's side so that we can see each other in the rearview mirror. The rear-door handle is at her chest level, and she curls both sets of fingers under it and does a full-body pull and lean to unlatch it, her two long pigtails the only parts of her staying perpendicular to the ground. There is no reason for me to leave my insurance information behind, because Hannah acts as her own doorstop, pinned between the upper half of her door and the lower half of the Expedition's. Carefully, she extricates herself by rolling clockwise, and then, still standing, pulls her door halfway closed by shuffling backward so that she'll be able to reach it from inside. Satisfied that she won't need me, I get in, buckle my seat belt, then make myself look busy while waiting for her to meticulously accomplish the same.

"Ready, sweet pea?" I ask the face in my mirror.

"Yup."

"Seat belt clicked?"

"Yup."

"Bum flat on the seat?"

"Yup."

"Helmet securely fastened?"

"*Dad!*"

"Elbow and shin pads in place?"

"Dad, come *on*! You don't want to get caught behind the stinky *buses*, do you?"

"Right. We'll dispense with all but the most important items. Socks turned inside out?"

"Dad! Hurry! I think the first one's starting to move!" This was our twice-weekly game of chicken with the evil yellow buses. We never lost, but you wouldn't know it by the pitch of Hannah's voice. "*Go*, Daddy!"

"Nonsense. Those old cargo vessels are no match for this nimble little number."

"*Go*, Daddy! *Go!* They're starting!" I pull out and accelerate, more with my voice than with my foot, and merge easily in front of the lead bus.

"See. No problem. Another victory for Japanese agility over American heft."

"Whew! That was a close one. Wasn't that a close one, Dad?"

"Maybe the closest yet. Which is to say we were only in a very *small* amount of danger, in case some other grown-up asks."

She looks up at me in the mirror. "You said not to tell her you pick me up."

"I said nothing about your mother. I'm just covering all of my bases in case you're ever questioned by the police, stuffy suits from the school, those types."

"*Dad.* Everyone at my school is a *lady*."

"All the more reason for caution. In fact, I'm thinking we should stop these races altogether."

"No! No! No!" she squeals, and the smile on her face is big enough to reveal a gap in her bottom row of teeth I hadn't noticed.

"Excuse me, young lady, but are you aware that there is a hole in your face?"

Hannah pushes her jaw forward to give herself a temporary underbite, then pulls her lower lip down for my viewing pleasure. "I jusht losht it lasht night," she says, still holding her lip.

"I'm afraid you're going to have to learn to be more responsible, young lady. If you can't keep track of your own teeth, what's next? Ears? I mean, you can *spare* teeth, but—"

"The Tooth Fairy left me two dollars, even though I know it's Mom."

"Two dollars! Is she *mad*? Mr. Greenspan keeps trying to warn us about inflation on the horizon, but no one chooses to listen. Just what might someone of your vintage and stature do with two entire dollars?"

"I'm saving up for Christmas. Mommy and me picked up her pearls from being rehung at the jewelry store, and she saw this bracelet she just *loved*. She even took it out and put it on. It was the sparkliest thing I ever saw. But she said it was way too much money, and she was just trying it on for fun, but I'm going to get it for her."

Admit it. There are times when we love our children more than others—times when something approaching rapture explodes within the chest cavity for no better reason than that they will never say certain words or do a certain thing in precisely *that* beautiful way again, and we feel utterly powerless and overwhelmed by the evanescence of those moments and our inability to hold on to them in any meaningful way. I have tried. Frustrated by the "milestone video" we took of Megan's early years—first smiles, first food, first steps—I was determined, with Hannah, to capture some of the daily, fleeting wonders that always made me draw, hold and expel a single long breath, as if not breathing caused time to stop. I set up a video camera on a tripod and moved it all over the house, filming hour upon unedited hour—of Hannah studying her hands as if trying to decipher code, of Kelly or myself feeding her at night in the rocker at the foot of our bed, of Megan holding Hannah in her small lap and reading her books from memory. *Now* I would remember. But remembering and reliving are two very different things, and the first time I watched an hour or so of my efforts, I was struck by the realization that, even a month later, I was not the person who appeared on the screen. There I was, holding her, rocking her, no doubt experiencing the moment I had intended to capture, but unable to pass it forward. That's why, after Hannah says this, I hold my breath until my vision of her in the rearview mirror begins to blur.

"What's the matter, Daddy?"

"Nothing, sweet pea."

"Will you give me a dollar for A's on my report card? Mom is. We get them next week."

"Sure."

"Are there any chores I can do at Nanna's house?"

"I'm sure Nanna could come up with some, and I'm sure she'd overpay you handsomely. And do you know what? Sometime before Christmas, I'll come get you a little early, and we'll go pick the bracelet up together, okay?"

I know that it's a mistake as soon as I've said it.

"But won't you be home by then, Daddy?"

"I sure hope so, sweetie. I don't know. I'm definitely working on that."

"Mommy misses you."

I hope that she can't see my eyes grow wide. "How do you know that, sweet pea?"

"I was crying a little bit at story time last night. Mommy doesn't do the voices right. I said I missed you, and she said we all do."

"Mm."

"That means she misses you, right?"

"Maybe."

"So I said, then why doesn't he come home, and she said I'd understand when I got older."

"There's no right or wrong, you know, sweet pea, on the voices. She just does them differently."

"How much older will I have to be, Daddy?"

"That's hard to say."

"Will you be home by then?"

I can't look at her, nor can I speak, and, by not repeating her question, she shows a level of understanding of which she is probably unaware. We are quiet for the last minute or two of the ride, and when I steal a look in the mirror, Hannah is looking absently out her window, the end of one pigtail stuck in the corner of her mouth. The elementary school is closer to our house than the high school, and this trip with Hannah, no matter how circuitous my route, is always much too short. But I don't want Kelly to worry, so I pull close to the curb where I dropped Megan just an hour ago and get out, pulling Hannah's backpack behind me. By the time I reach the sidewalk, she has already pushed her door open with a sneakered foot and stepped out. She reaches her arms up to me, and suddenly I *am* reliving a moment, or maybe thousands of them since the day she took her first steps, when she reached up for me in just this way. All children do it. It's the way they remind you, over and over again, *Don't forget I'm yours. Pick me up, hold me and, even when I'm old enough that I won't let you anymore, don't let go.*

11

People by and large become what they think about themselves.

—Dr. Bob Rotella with Bob Cullen,
Golf Is Not a Game of Perfect

For all avid golfers, there are holes on their home courses that qualify as nemeses. For me, there are two such holes on Fox Run, and one of them is the fourteenth. I used to warn guests about this hole—the left tree line set so close to the edge of the rough that its upper branches encroach onto the fairway, the white out-of-bounds stakes that parallel the base of the tree line on the right, and the tee set slightly cockeyed to aim players out of bounds. I used to, that is, until I realized that I was only placing in their minds obstacles that I had magnified for myself over thirty-five years of play. That's the way it is with nemesis holes. Most often they are not the most difficult, but are instead holes on which poorly played shots over a period of years gradually gather to form a mental barrier against success. Thus, I found that when I said nothing my guests seldom had much trouble with this hole. But when I pointed out to them what *I* saw, they would instinctively tighten, try to guide the ball into the now-constricted fairway and, invariably, hit one of their poorest shots of the day. Worse yet, I had given them a head start on acquiring demons it had taken me years to assemble, and when they returned to Fox Run, it was always with memories of the "diabolical fourteenth."

There are no guests today, unless you count my demons. I am coming off the bogey at thirteen, but it was a *good* bogey, considering I had struck forestry with my first two shots and found a bunker with my third. I should be approaching the tee with, if not renewed confidence, then at least a sense of satisfaction for having kept the round alive with some good, hard work. But even on the best of days I don't approach the fourteenth with any sense but foreboding. Right now, the voice that has been speaking to me since my walk up the railroad-tie steps to the thirteenth tee is still whispering scoring scenarios, and it has been joined by another, more dangerous voice that is reminding me that the last good full swing I made was on the twelfth tee, seemingly hours ago.

"I'm thinking about two-iron, Sal."

"What for?"

"You know my history here. I just want to keep it in play and get to fifteen."

"I got no problem with that. Just stay aggressive with it. You try and guide the deuce, and it ain't goin' any straighter than driver."

He's right, of course, but I know that any wood is going to feel like a billy club in my hands right now. I'll aim two-iron at the left edge of the fairway, away from the out-of-bounds. If I feel good over the ball, I may even decide to cut it back a little toward the center.

But I don't feel good. In fact, I feel as if I am in the midst of a nightmarish version of a lesson with our club pro. He has adjusted my shoulders just so, my hips just so, my knee flex just so, until I am a tableau of the perfect, learned stance, with no idea whatsoever of how to draw the club back. Is it possible to have lockjaw below the neck?

"Mr. B.?"

"I'm all right." I step back and try again. No difference. There'll be no trying to cut it now. Just keep it in bounds. Aim it further left. Stay aggressive.

The instant the ball comes off the club, it's already spinning left. A pull hook. When it enters the trees, it is a sinking line drive.

Although the trunks of the trees are maddeningly close together, my ball manages to avoid the first few and goes in deep.

Once you get started, it's amazing how easy it is to hit one bad shot after another.

After that first meeting with Dr. Amanda Derby, and then my "session" with Samantha, I was overcome by the sensation that something immutable had been recast. Two weeks before, while on my way to the *Shan Gri La*, I had sensed that all eyes were on me. But now, as I walked back down Forbes Avenue, thinking about how I might answer the question "How was your day, dear," I became the suspicious observer of everyone I passed. How many of these people, looking straight ahead and outwardly intent on the business of their day, were, in fact, walking simply to air out their skin or their clothes or their regret? Suddenly, everyone looked guilty to me, or at least no less guilty than anyone else. And despite the convenient justifications I had been given by Dr. Amanda Derby and her admonishments that guilt would only impede my "progress," I felt that I had become part of a community of deceivers. And this knowledge, rather than making me less likely to betray again, only made me feel that I had plenty of company; that what I had been before—an imperfect but mostly unsullied husband and father—was an aberration to which I was unlikely to return.

I used my three "free" sessions from Stewey in less than two weeks and was required to see Amanda Derby again before setting up my own account. This time, she allowed *me* to ask some of the questions, making it clear that she was doing so not to encourage any type of intimacy between us, but because the information might aid in my own "recovery."

Dr. Amanda Derby's story and the genesis of The Healing Touch was much like any good male rationalization: Each step proceeded reasonably from the one prior, and it was only when you reached the end of the chain and looked back that it seemed impossible to have gotten here from there. She became a board-certified psychoanalyst in 1986, joined a small practice and found that she was pretty adept at helping women identify and address their issues, but had minimal success with men. She even went so far as to ask her partners to stop referring male patients to her. There was one man in particular who made her want to quit her practice. She treated him for months, listening to him go on and on about how his wife refused every sexual advance he made. His wife ridiculed him, slept with him only to assert power or when she wanted something. He was a sweet, weak man, and he paid Amanda Derby thousands of dollars to listen to him, but nothing she was telling him was doing him any good. So one day . . .

"And I *still* don't know why, I reached over and touched his cheek, and then all of a sudden his face changed, and I'd never seen a look of such pure gratitude in my life. Then he closed his eyes and leaned back and I kept touching him, until finally . . . well . . . I finished him off. Right there in the office."

"That was the natural next step?"

"It seemed that way at the time. I was just following my instincts. And he was, maybe not cured, but *better*. Not right that instant, of course. But when he came back the next week—after we got over the initial awkwardness—he said that the attention I had paid to him, and just the physical release itself, had given him a feeling of confidence that enabled him to become more assertive at home. I knew I had made a mistake, but my job was to help people. And this was *helping* him. So we kept doing it—always at the beginning of the session or he couldn't concentrate—and it *kept* helping . . ."

So she tried it, selectively, with some of her other male patients, setting strict ground rules in advance, and it seemed to help almost *all* of them. Obsessives, aggressives and submissives all became less so; workaholics gained perspective. And not one of them tried to push the relationship further. This was a release with no strings, no guilt. This was their *doctor*.

Of course, it was also illegal, and after almost a year without in-cident, one of her patients suggested to his wife that if she were as understanding as his analyst in sexual matters, their life together would be much more fulfilling. She was brought before the disciplin-ary board and told that she could allow her license to lapse and leave the profession quietly, or have it formally taken from her. She chose the former.

"As you might expect, I had patients contacting me constantly about unofficial sessions. To support myself, I started seeing some of them in my home. When I hired a couple of young college students to help me out, word spread. I hired a few more, got out of the 'la-bor intensive' part of the job, and eventually had enough of a busi-ness to move down here, where most of my clients are located. I'm not allowed to call them patients anymore. Why are you looking at me like that?"

"You still think of them—us, I guess—as *patients?*"

"I do."

"End of rationalization."

"I suppose you could look at it that way."

"But they're not seeing *you*. They're seeing some young nymph. No offense."

"My patients *do* see me. Every two months, at a minimum. And they pay the same two hundred and fifty dollars for that half-hour that they pay for the half—"

"They pay *what?*"

"Your friend gave you a very generous birthday present, Mr. Benedict. It's part of the way we keep this from becoming a place where men go in search of *nymphs*, as you call them. Any man just looking for sex can get much more for his money elsewhere. And I'm frankly surprised that you would speak in such terms about my young ladies after having had the pleasure of their company."

Thus chastised, I took my leave of Dr. Amanda Derby and began my tenure as an official "patient" of The Healing Touch.

It was frightening how natural the transition proved to be, how easily the rationalizations came to justify the actions of a man I wouldn't previously have recognized. Even now, starting the sentences that need to be written here with "I" is discomfiting, and I find myself tempted by the detached objectivity of the third person. It would be almost effortless to say that "he," Michael Benedict, didn't care whether or not the drug that The Healing Touch was offering was a cure; that he only knew he was addicted. That despite his frugal nature, his visits actually accelerated once he began paying for them himself—twice, sometimes three times, a week. That when Bio-Life hit 40, he celebrated by selling a mere 250 of his 10,000 shares for $10,000 and set that money aside as a present to himself, in recognition of his brilliant investment savvy, as a "slush fund" to do with as he pleased. That he requested a different therapist every time until he had seen them all, then started at the top of the list again, then chose Samantha. That, until her, he was a victim of the strip-club "New Girl Syndrome" all over again except, instead of a few singles stuffed into a garter, this was $250 a pop. That no less an authority than Stewey Trammell, the man he viewed as having guided him down this path, warned him that he was headed for trouble. *What about all that guilt?* you might properly ask. *Isn't this all somehow inconsistent with the shame that he professed on the street that first day?* And I, the dispassionate but omniscient third-person narrator, would anticipate your confusion and remind you that guilt and addiction have coexisted nicely for the length of human history; that it is the very nature of addiction that guilt can only effect remission, not cure. I would tell you that in those early weeks his remorse persisted, ironically, for precisely as long as the sexual relief itself. He was trapped in his own moral and sexual conundrum: As long as the relief lasted, he felt guilty about the physical act that had brought it on; once his desire returned, shame was replaced by the convenient rationalization that he was the victim of his wife's decision to withhold that which he now sought elsewhere. A man in such a state (I could say, in a nice turn of phrase) prefers to attribute blame to causes of the exogenous variety.

But catharsis and confession are ineffective in the third person, and it is time to admit that there was another rationalization I was working on at the time—one that I believed lent something approaching archetypal legitimacy to my behavior. And that was my growing belief that I was doing nothing more than every fellow hunter/gatherer would do, given the knowledge of its availability, the promise of secrecy and the means to afford it. Dr. Amanda Derby and The Healing Touch helped me to establish the quasi-validity of this pretense by stripping away societal mores in the name of "medicine," re-elevating instinct over guilt in an atmosphere not of clandestine squalor, but of gentility. It was easy for a man to come away from an experience like the one I had with Mika at the *Shan Gri La* claiming repentance. In truth, it wasn't guilt that prevented a return visit; it was disappointment. I convinced myself that it was this kind of anticlimax (if you'll excuse the pun) that kept most men from continuing along the path of their fantasies, a path down which I was now hurtling like some non-penetrating Caligula devotee. The stories are so familiar as to have become Hollywood stock: a much-anticipated night out with the boys provides, at best, a tease, at worst, a parade of overweight strippers and watered-down light beer; escort services advertising "sophisticated companions for the discriminating executive" send, instead, desperate single mothers with smoky voices and sagging breasts; and affairs begun with nothing but hormonal zest elevated by the absence of commitment ruin marriages or become ruined marriages of their own. There was no such unavoidable letdown associated with a visit to The Healing Touch.

At least, not at first.

"We're in the pinball machine, Mr. B., but we got another bogey or two to give if we need to. We'll just take the cleanest way out, even if it's backward."

Despite his earlier claim that he never thinks about my next shot until he is five paces from it, Sal is telling me this a hundred yards short of the trees. His intuition exceeds his considerable knowledge of the game, and he knows that the demons are present. Not only that, he knows which ones they are. He wouldn't be talking otherwise. He senses that the little scoreboard gremlins are being devoured by the more dangerous ogre of self-doubt, and he knows that silence only invites it closer.

"It went in clean, so maybe we'll take that same path right back out. We'll have two hundred in, maybe two-ten. Making bogey here won't be any tougher than it was on thirteen. A little longer third shot, but if we miss the green, it ain't gonna be any harder to get it up and down. You with me?"

"Yup."

Though I am not. Sal is quiet for a moment, but he doesn't let it last.

"I'm surprised how much light we got left. When the shop told me two-thirty, I thought the sun would be setting behind seventeen by the time we got there, but we're in good shape. It don't take as long when you're makin' birdies, I guess."

"I guess."

"Look. See here? We got an alley right back this way." Sal has walked beyond where my ball is sitting, and he is making a cutting motion with his right arm to show me the path. "We're close enough to the fairway you don't got to worry so much about the low branches. Just the line this time. Here, just punch this through." He hands me a six-iron and I take it without a word. This isn't like the first hole, when I decided that I didn't care. The problem now is that I care too much. The extraordinary stretch from holes two through twelve took me to a place I'd never been before. Because of the way I had always approached the game, my good rounds felt like hard work. They were satisfying but not exhilarating. This one had been so *easy*, and I want that feeling back. But I am, quite literally, lost in the trees.

Sal moves aside, and I stand in his footprints, looking back along the line he has cut. It's an easy shot, and there are no real choices to be made.

"Just right back through the gap, Mr. B., and then we're safe."

"Gap-down" was the term George used to describe the impossibility of what I was seeing on my computer screen.

"The market is pretty good at anticipating things like earnings news and the progress of new product development. But when something unexpected like this happens, bids dry up and sellers become desperate. Instead of following a chartable price line, the line breaks and is re-established down at the price at which a willing buyer, if any, will buy. That's what you're seeing."

"So this isn't a mistake."

"Afraid not."

"Jesus Christ."

When I had left the office the night before, Bio-Life had stood at an all-time high of 50½ in anticipation of the imminent unblinding of the placebo study. My investment was worth more than half a million dollars. The stock had been heavily traded over the past week, indicating, according to George, that it was moving into weaker hands. Institutional investors were taking their gains and getting out, while less sophisticated traders (he didn't say "like you," but the inference was clear) were looking for a further jump on the news.

When I turned my computer on at ten o'clock the next morning, I was puzzled to find that Bio-Life hadn't traded a single share. Even more strangely, the "Ask" price was still close to 50, but the "Bid" was just 9. Then I saw the news item:

August 12, 2005 (*Fremont, CA*) Bio-Life Solutions, a pharmaceutical company specializing in women's health products and based in Fremont, California, announced today that clinical trials of its Prevo-Gel product being conducted in several African countries are being halted effective immediately. Prevo-Gel is an approved nonoxynol-9 contraceptive being tested on African prostitutes as a method of preventing the spread of the HIV virus. Initial indications several weeks ago from the double-blind placebo study demonstrated a statistically significant difference in the frequency of HIV occurrence between the two test groups, but the un-blinding of those results late yesterday unexpectedly revealed that it was the placebo group that had faired better. The company immediately issued a statement defending the safety of its product and stating its belief that, despite clear instructions to the contrary, certain subjects of the study had been over-applying the product, resulting in potentially toxic levels of nonoxynol-9 not associated with normal use. The company reiterated its belief that Prevo-Gel should continue to be considered as a viable HIV inhibitor in future studies, but that it was joining with African authorities to call a temporary halt to the current study "for the safety of the subjects involved."

Had he not been on my speed dial, I'm not sure I would have been capable of dialing George's number. During the time that I waited for him to answer, the first shares of the day of Bio-Life traded—at 9½. By the time George had calmly finished his definition of *gap-down*, it had dropped to 6, my average purchase price.

"Jesus Christ!"

"You said that already. Take it easy."

"Take it *easy*? You don't understand. This is my kids' *college* money."

"And you haven't *lost* any of it yet. Yes, you missed a chance to make a quick buck by hanging on too long . . ."

"I sold a little bit at forty."

"Great move."

"No. *Not* a great move, George. I've already spent the money."

"Michael, that's one of the things you *do* with extra money."

"College money, George! I know you just *graduated*, but some of us need to be thinking about the *future*."

"Stop being so hard on yourself. Did you buy something nice for your wife?"

"Not exactly."

"Either way, you're right back where you started."

"But you said the company was worth twenty-plus *without* this!"

"Why are you shouting at me?"

"Because *you* got me into this!"

"And *you* didn't get out when I told you to. Look, no one could have anticipated this—though '*control group*' does seem a bit of an oxymoron when applied to hookers. Some of them were apparently smearing themselves with this stuff twenty times a day. At least *someone's* business is booming."

"Not funny."

"Try to remember that this is still the same company you started buying in March. Buyers will be scared to death of it for a while because they'll feel they've been misled. But in a couple of years—"

"Years!"

"—when revenues for their existing products start to ramp up, this spike on the chart will just be an interesting footnote."

Interesting footnote: On November 1, 2005, its offshore production facility in the Yucatán Peninsula having been, respectively, flooded then flattened by hurricane Wilma, Bio-Life Solutions filed for Chapter 11 bankruptcy and de-listed its stock.

Sal's earlier estimate proves accurate: After my punch out of the trees, I've got almost 210 yards to the green for my third shot. A light breeze has come up, meaning that two-iron is the right club, but I know it won't feel right in my hands after the tee shot I just hit with it. Sal must be thinking the same thing but, knowing the frailty of my confidence, he'd never voice such a choice in the negative.

"I think hard-three gets you there easy," is all he says.

The last three-iron I hit was the perfect tee shot on number five, and it is that shot I am replaying, again and again, as I stand behind the ball to get my line, take my stance and eye my target. But on the fifth tee there are no white stakes to worry about. I catch the ones here at fourteen in my peripheral vision, and they suddenly become an unwanted part of the shot I am picturing. Then they grow to the height of the trees they parallel. Then they acquire the properties of high-powered magnets that can suck in a urethane-covered sphere with the force of gravity. I step away.

"Don't even *think* about aiming this left," Sal says. "This game ain't as hard as you're makin' it right now."

"I'm having visualization issues."

Sal is working the zipper of one of the pockets on my bag. "Mind if I hit one while you work them out?"

"Sorry?"

"There's nobody behind us, and I've always wanted to see if it felt any different to hit a ball out here on a day other'n Monday."

I step back. "Fire away."

Sal drops a ball on the fairway. I am disconcerted not so much by the fact that Sal is breaking sacred protocol (which he is) as by my own inability to read his motives.

"I'm going to need a little more club than you." He pulls my three-wood, sets the bag down and takes a few practice swings. "You got a little extra head-weight on this thing?"

"A little."

"Thought so." His thick, gnarled hands grip the club like a base-ball bat. His swing is compact and mechanically solid. When he ad-dresses the ball, he takes one quick look at the target, then starts his backswing the instant he looks down. The club never gets more than about halfway back, and his lower body, which has logged countless encumbered miles around this golf course, no longer has the flexibility to rotate. But he generates surprising clubhead speed with his thick wrists and forearms, and the ball shoots forward as if off the end of a whip. It stays on a low line, boring through the new wind without an inkling of a waver right or left. When it lands ten yards short of the green, it takes an unlucky bounce left and rolls into the green-side bunker. I reach into my pocket and toss another ball at his feet.

"Don't mind if I do," he says. Again, he takes one quick look at the flag, coils halfway up and releases. The flight path is identical, but the wind has fallen away and the first swing must have loosened the joints in his shoulders and hands, because this second shot lands well beyond the first and holds its line on the ground, rolling up the apron to the center of the green.

"Nice shot. What's your point?"

"No point."

"You take lessons as a kid?"

"Yup. Hundreds. Still do."

"From who?"

"Every good player here. You as much as anyone." Sal pulls the bag upright and thrusts my three-wood down inside as if staking a claim.

"Ah. The point," I venture.

"Look, Mr. B. I've carried for my share of pros, and most of 'em don't swing it any better'n you do. A lot of 'em would look downright herky-jerky next to you on the driving range. I mean, you swing it so pretty sometimes it hurts."

"A well-rehearsed illusion, my friend."

"Bullshit. Your swing has looked mostly the same since you was twelve years old. You could play just about any given day the way you played today if you could adjust the bolts on your head once in a while."

"Thanks."

"I mean it. You ever see a shrink?"

Someone comes to mind, but I don't think she qualifies.

"Not for my golf game."

"Ever try talkin' to your wife?"

"As you know, not currently an option."

"Your mother?"

I can't help but laugh. "Sal, what my mother knows about golf is roughly equivalent to what you know about psychoanalysis."

"But she knows *you*." Sal squints at me with what he apparently thinks is great meaning.

"And this revelation entitles you to look at me as if you just discovered a baldness cure?"

He smiles and rubs his woolly white head. "Bad example, Mr. B."

"Mind if I hit, Doc?"

"Be my guest."

I must admit that watching Sal hit two straight ropes with such perfect simplicity seems to have helped diminish thoughts of the impossible complexity of my own swing, and the fact that I have just watched them both rise on an unerring line to the flag gives me a more immediate picture on which to concentrate.

"Nothin' but center of the green from this far," Sal reminds me.

"Got it."

The swing starts out better. But as the club reaches its apex, the winds kicks up again, and the ball, although solidly struck, begins fading slightly right as it rises. The wind only gives traction to the spin and takes it farther right, toward the upper limbs of the locust trees that line that side. If it catches the wrong side of a branch it will fall out of bounds.

"Shit."

"Spit it out!" Sal yells. "Spit it out!" And, as if in response, the ball glances off the lower half of a dead, leafless limb and falls straight down, just short of the right green-side bunker.

"You know what I always say, Mr. B. You gotta talk to 'er."

"I like to talk," Samantha said, somewhat hesitantly, in response to my question. It was a question I hadn't asked in a long time, and one wouldn't think that a woman in Samantha's line of part-time

work would be easily flustered. But this was a place of almost limit-
less contradictions, and I had learned during an earlier visit that
the lithe beauty standing over me—whose hands had stopped at my
question, her spiraling chestnut hair partially hiding from my reflected view the tattoo of a blue lightning bolt that appeared over
her left shoulder and ended at her left nipple—blushed easily and
taught preschool in the mornings before arriving at The Healing
Touch. (When I had expressed my surprise, she assured me that little boys that age didn't see any difference between her and their
mothers. I assured her otherwise.)

"Talk?" I said and reached down and back from my prone position to find a smooth calf.

Samantha smiled at the mirror. "You're already embarrassing
me, Michael. Don't make me be more specific. That feels nice."

"Good. What if I want you to be more specific? Isn't the customer always right?"

"In your case, yes."

"Well?"

Samantha was the "therapist" I had seen on my first day, and the
only one of the six who worked afternoons at The Healing Touch
I'd seen more than twice. She was older than the others (which still
placed her only in her late twenties) and there was a shared inten-
sity to our sessions together (real or imagined on my part) that was
both indelible in its own right, and came closest to replacing what
was missing for me at home.

It is hard to characterize the letdown that accompanied my second sessions with the others, but there was a bizarre familiarity to it
as well. Certainly the women were, without exception, stunning to
look at, and there was always that juvenile excitement that accompanied my first session with each. But what is it about me that invites confidences? Is there something about the ordinariness of my
face that tells otherwise guarded, beautiful women that they have
nothing to fear from me? That they can stand naked before me, both
literally and figuratively, without apprehension? I began hearing

about unfaithful ex-husbands, abusive boyfriends, professors at local universities who traded grades for a little "extra credit," even grumblings about Dr. Amanda Derby herself. Have you ever been sexually gratified by someone who is simultaneously describing to you her difficulties with a lover or, worse yet, her boss? It began to make me feel (if this is even possible in the context of a hand job) patronized. In a way, it was just another form of having Donna O'Connor change her T-shirt in front of me. And it stopped being enough. Amanda Derby was wrong. Kelly's imposed abstinence hadn't left me craving relief, but *connection*. I doubted that the doctor would approve, but I had chosen Samantha as someone who might be willing to nourish that appetite.

"Well?" I said again, in response to what appeared to be her embarrassed silence.

"Well, what?" She smiled like she knew.

"What would you think about trading places?"

"You mean, like in *The Prince and the Pauper*?"

"No. I mean like you lie down here." I sat up and slid off the table.

"So far, I like it." She lay face down and blew out a long sigh, relaxing into the white sheet that covered the firm, padded surface of the table.

"Now you talk." I moved her hair away from her neck, pressed and circled my thumbs there, then down over her shoulders.

"God, that's nice. Would you be offended if I slept instead?"

"Did you bring your nap rug today, Miss Samantha?"

"Careful."

"Sorry. But stop trying to change the subject." I lightened my touch and brushed down her back, around her hips and down both legs, feeling her skin rise to meet my fingertips. I took her right foot in my hands and pushed both thumbs into the arch, up over the ball to her toes, one at a time. Then the other foot, then up to her calves. "You tell me what you like . . ."

"You mean more than this?"

"What you want me to do, maybe what we'd do together if we weren't here, or if I were someone else." My hands moved up over her thighs.

"Mm. You wouldn't have to be someone else," she said.

"No?"

"Uh-uh."

Then she started to talk. I did everything she asked, never straying from the rules of the house. I kissed the back of her neck and down her spine, my hands moving down the sides of her small breasts, over her ribs and past her narrow waist to her hips. She parted her legs, and I blew lightly between them, my fingers tracing back and forth along the moonlike lines at the top of her thighs. She turned over, and I kissed up over her belly, between her breasts to her throat, which she stretched long for me and turned from side to side. And then, without being asked, I moved my lips to where the lightning bolt came over her shoulder and grazed them along its jagged line to its barbed tip, and she arched into me, pushing her breast hard into my mouth, and I took one of her hands and moved it down over her stomach and between her legs, and my hand over hers felt her fingers push inside. And then she began telling me, her breath coming fast and her hand moving under mine, what we would do, together, if we could, if we weren't here, if I were her lover and not a married man who suddenly had to pretend that this was his wife, and if thinking that and feeling the body beneath me begin to shudder didn't make me want to weep with both penitence and gratitude, and if the sound of her didn't fly out of the room and out of the building and up the Allegheny River to Fox Run and back through twenty-five years to the night that Dee Dee Svenson rose beneath me like this; and if the breast at my lips and the belly under my arm didn't swell and her sound become Kelly pushing a lifeless little girl feet first into the world as if it were arriving and leaving all at once; and if this woman who was, after all, not my wife, and whose name I probably didn't know, didn't pull me to her, still breathing fast, and kiss me on the forehead like the child that I was.

. . .

I touch my ungloved palm to my forehead, and it is damp despite the cool October air. I am bleeding strokes like a hemophiliac with an open wound, and Sal, the equivalent of an E.R.-attending on the golf course, has been unable to stem the flow. For my fourth shot here at fourteen, I am left with a delicate twenty-yard flop shot over the right-hand bunker to a pin cut close to the right fringe. My chances of getting up and down from here are, at best, one in ten, especially since I can't seem to steady my hands. A swing like this can be performed with mechanical perfection, but if the hands aren't soft and confident, disaster awaits. Get too tight and mechanical, and you are likely to drive the blade of the club into the belly of the ball, sending it screaming across the green. Overcompensate for your nerves by exaggerating relaxation into "floppiness," and you might take a pelt of turf right out from under the ball and leave it within a yard or two of your feet.

Are you thinking what I'm suddenly thinking?

So what? Right?

How is it that hobbies for some become obsessions for others— obsessions that take on a beauty so compelling that everything might be sacrificed in their pursuit? I remember watching a documentary with Kelly that chronicled a group of amateur climbers who got caught in a treacherous storm as they attempted to scale the peak of Mount Everest. They refused to turn back. They had trained, they had sacrificed, they had spent money they didn't have for this one opportunity, and Kelly and I looked at each other in disbelief as the film cut to the pregnant wife of one of the climbers, patched through to her husband via short-wave radio and telephone, as she said good-bye to him and listened to his last breaths. I remember thinking: "What an *idiot*." And yet, am I so different? This round, I realize in a moment that combines equal parts self-pity and self-recognition, is my Everest, and I am running out of air. I should be radioing base camp for help, but instead I am dying here, as elsewhere, by my own hand. And for what? I have no real chance of making it as a professional player. Never did. Take me away from the comfort and familiarity of Fox Run and I don't have a prayer. Kelly knew it the day we made our deal. Sal knows it too, knows that a pretty swing is different from a reliable one. For the briefest of instants, I see myself from a thousand feet up, as if standing in an architect's model of Fox Run, an aimless rodent in a green-carpeted maze, and I can see the way out. The problem is, there's nothing waiting for me there.

Ironically, it is this very attitude of resignation that stills my hands and allows me to execute the flop shot, if not with focus, then with enough detachment to loft the ball over the bunker to the center of the green, twenty feet left of the hole. Sal, who has remained silent during this sudden shift in my demeanor, extends his hand to accept my wedge.

"Nice shot," he says, as if unsure.

"Thanks." I say this without looking at him. My mood is shifting yet again. Something resembling anger is beginning to replace my detachment. Strangely, anger—at least self-directed anger—is an emotion I have rarely felt since leaving my home. There has been guilt, regret, more than my share of self-pity as the victim of the imperfections that I have come to view as grafted to my chromosomes. But I am still standing outside of myself, close now, no longer looking from above, and what I see makes me want to do violence to the person I have become not by fate but by choice. Sal is wiping the grass off the blade of the club but staring at me, trying to pull my eyes to his.

"Are you back, or are you gone?" he says.

"What do you mean?" I am looking at my hands.

"You know what I mean. You took a nice easy swipe at that ball, but I'm not sure why. You're packin' it in, aren't you?"

"What difference does it make, Sal? Really."

I want to breathe those words back in before Sal can hear them. It may not seem like much, but I have demeaned the game that is his life's work. My own self-anger, thus detonated at the feet of an innocent target, dissipates as swiftly as it had gathered. And after what fills Sal's eyes passes just as quickly, he gathers my anger up for himself.

"You're right," he says. "A minute ago, you woulda been wrong, but now you're right. I get paid the same fifty either way. This don't mean shit to me." He shoulders the bag and turns toward the green.

"Sal, I'm sorry."

He stops and turns.

"Do you have any idea how many poor bastards would give anything to be where you are right now? Even if you two-putt here, all you gotta do is par in to do something the rest of us—your father included—would die for."

"But what are we *doing* out here, Sal, you and me? Can you tell me that?"

"We *were* playin' one beautiful round of golf." He points a short, callused finger at me. "I got news for you, Mr. B. Everything's meaningless. Or nothin' is. It's up to you." He shrugs, hands me my putter, then walks to the left side of the green and takes my driver out before laying the bag down. By doing so, he is telling me that he will send me off the other side of the green to make the long walk to the fifteenth tee alone. He will save himself that walk by taking the shortcut through the trees, directly to the spot along the fifteenth fairway where my drive is likely to come to rest. This practice is customary when players have each other for company. It is equally customary for a single player and his caddy to walk to the fifteenth together. I feel admonished, and diminished, by the gesture.

Sal holds my driver in one hand and pulls the flag with the other. He points out the line, silently, then steps away. I am distracted by his inattention, even more by my part in it, and I make a hesitant stroke that comes up three feet short.

"Inside left," Sal says quietly, as if to himself. I know it is the correct read—that, firmly struck up this gentle grade, the ball will fall only slightly to my right. And yet, drawing the putter back the mere three or four inches that I will need and returning it back to this same spot feels as if it requires surgical meticulousness, and the ball veers weakly away before reaching the front of the hole. I tap in quickly with the back of my putter blade for a triple-bogey seven. I am now just one under par.

"Too bad," Sal says, replacing the flag.

"Yup."

"I'm gonna go on ahead, if you don't mind."

"No problem."

"I'd like to use your phone to make another call on the way, if that's all right."

"Sure. I'd still like to finish, though. I mean, if you're calling to give her an estimated time."

"Oh yeah, 'course. I didn't think—"

"Are we okay, Sal? You and me?"

"Fine, Mr. B. We're fine."

I knew that I had been here before, and not just to see Dr. Amanda Derby or Samantha or the others, but before that. And now, at noon on a sweltering Tuesday in mid-August, with the lights turned up and the suite empty, I remembered. These offices had once been occupied by a small firm of plaintiffs' attorneys, Zubrow & Klutch, that had been invisible in the Pittsburgh legal landscape until its senior partner became one of the first lawyers in the country to file massive numbers of personal-injury lawsuits against all of the major asbestos companies in the United States. When some of those early cases survived summary judgment motions by the fifty or sixty joint defendants (including one represented by the law firm where Kelly and I met), huge block settlements began to be crafted, and for the next ten or fifteen years, the partners in that firm, who had been practitioners of mediocre talent and repute, made millions of dollars. When the last of the asbestos companies filed bankruptcy in the early nineties, leaving hundreds of thousands of asbestos-disease sufferers to fight over a few pennies on the dollar, the partners of Zubrow & Klutch retired to Florida, invisible once again.

Dr. Amanda Derby herself buzzed me in. She had let it be known through Leah that there were issues to be discussed regarding my treatment, and had specifically asked that I be her first appointment of the day for my "checkup." In the harsh overhead light, the carpet appeared worn and the color uneven. The heavy drapes behind Leah's desk were frayed and faded, and the desk itself was badly chipped at the corners and appeared to be made of a wood laminate covered by a mahogany veneer. Even the oak wainscoting was mottled and in need of a fresh coat of finish.

"Sorry about the atmosphere, Mr. Benedict. The cleaning people just left and Leah's not here to reset the mood yet. We show our age in this light, don't we?"

"You took over Z&K's lease?"

"I was wondering if you knew them. We bought their furniture too, for next to nothing. They seemed in a hurry." Amanda Derby came out from behind Leah's desk. She wore light khakis and a peach-colored scoop-necked T-shirt that revealed the beginnings of summer freckles, and her hair, again pulled back in a simple ponytail, had begun to lighten.

"I think they were just in a hurry to stop working," I said. She offered her hand, and I shook it. "Like me. Only I don't get to."

"I heard that they were quite successful at one time."

"They were lucky."

"I don't believe in luck, Mr. Benedict, good or bad. Fate, yes, but not luck."

Amanda Derby opened her office door and held it for me to pass. "Please excuse the mess," she said. "I'm just arriving myself."

The "mess" consisted of three or four files on her desk and a few Post-it notes on one arm of her chair. Otherwise, the room was in perfect order. She sat down, moved the yellow notes from her chair to her computer screen and pulled one of the files to her. "Please, sit," she said. She took her reading glasses from her top middle drawer, hung them around her neck, then slid them on. She opened the file that was on her lap, then tipped herself back from the molded edge of her desk with a sandaled foot. "I see that you have been here quite a lot."

"You say that as if you don't want my business."

Dr. Derby looked at me over her glasses. "For reasons to which you can now attest, Mr. Benedict, I don't have much difficulty cultivating repeat clients. My problems are with those who become, shall we say, overly attached to treatment."

My face grew warm at the implication, and I tried to defend myself by alluding to her own first-day advice.

"You're not saying that I should feel *guilty* about that, are you?"

Not even a smile.

"No. But one of the reasons I require our clients to see me periodically is so that I can head off issues like this. I have found that overuse of our services is often accompanied by a growing lack of discretion, which isn't good for you *or* me."

"I understand. But I really don't think that's going to be a problem anymore."

"No? The week before last, you were here three times."

"I've had something of a reverse liquidity event since then."

"Excuse me?"

"The week before last I still thought I was rich."

"I'm sorry to hear that you are having financial difficulties, Mr. Benedict, but I don't think that limiting the frequency of your visits just because you can't afford them anymore directly addresses the issue."

"Which is?"

Dr. Derby let her glasses drop to her chest. "You've been seeing a lot of Samantha."

Over the past few weeks I had seen Samantha (and only Samantha) six or seven times for extended, hour-long sessions that had become, at least for me, increasingly intimate. I might even have called what we did together "making love" if defining that term didn't also require me to define the term "fidelity."

"She's a lovely young lady," I said.

"Yes, she is. But your treatment, Mr. Benedict, is not meant to be a form of recreation, or, even less, a direct replacement for what is missing at home." I stared at her but could think of nothing to say. I felt as if she had just sprouted a claw and ripped the voice box from my throat. "I believe that you are a good man, Mr. Benedict—a little lost at the moment, but a good man, nonetheless. Unfortunately, I think that your time here might be exacerbating your problems. This is the wrong kind of medicine for you. You are, in essence, taking cough syrup for the alcohol."

It is far down on the list of priorities, I am sure, but with the mapping of the human genome now complete, some obscure researcher (probably a man as wretched and befuddled as I) will someday think to locate that one step among the millions on the spiraling helix of his DNA that makes him such a lummox and his spouse a veritable soothsayer. For if you are a man in search of the truth, you will find it surrounded, like the tough outer skin of an unfertilized egg, by a nearly impenetrable circle of women, attached and hinged at the shoulders, and facing inward. And you, one flaccid, ineffectual sperm among millions, will peck and poke hopelessly at the flexible but inaccessible circle, perhaps even managing a onetime herculean push that stretches and thins the membrane enough for you to gain a fleeting impression of what its constituents see every day. But the circled clique will bounce back and fling you out and beyond recovery so quickly and with such force as to render you utterly unsure of what you have glimpsed, leaving you to scrabble back for another vain attempt.

When I answered Amanda Derby, it was as if exhausted by the lifelong accumulation of such attempts, and I knew at once that this would be the last time I would see her.

"Do you have any children?" I asked. Her face softened at my question.

"No, Mr. Benedict. I don't."

"Have you ever been married?"

"When I was of *marrying age*, I was handling the genitalia of at least five men a day. I wasn't sending signals, and nobody was asking."

"So you were having bouts of conscience while telling them that they should not?"

"*I* wasn't doing it for therapeutic purposes."

"Maybe you were."

She smiled, but slowly, as someone seldom surprised by the truth. "Maybe."

"Let me tell you something. Even if you're lucky—which, by any measure, I am—when you walk out of that church or synagogue or courthouse office with a new ring on your finger, a piece of you disappears. I'm not just talking about men, either. I think Kelly would tell you the same thing. And then it happens again when each child is born, but you don't really notice it, you don't really miss anything, because these beings you're tending are so much more perfect and worthwhile than what you've lost. But then they stop growing *because* of you and start growing in *spite* of you, or because of the world, or whatever, and you find that you've got time on your hands to start looking aimlessly around the house for those pieces you've misplaced. Only you haven't misplaced them; they're just *gone*. And for no good reason, other than that now you've got the time, you start to miss them. Or worse yet, you start to think about replacing them with something else that you know is going to feel like an artificial limb, but you do it anyhow."

"Which is your artificial limb, Mr. Benedict?"

"Take your pick." I shrugged. "Right now, I'm the frigging Six Million Dollar Man."

Amanda Derby made a note in my file. "I'm limiting you to two visits a month."

"I was thinking maybe I should quit it altogether. Recovering alcoholics can't be weekend drinkers, can they?"

"Better yet."

"Would you mind thanking Samantha for me?"

"Not at all."

"I'm going to miss her. That seems impossible, doesn't it?"

"That's part of your problem, Mr. Benedict. I think you miss everybody. Let me check the reception area for you." Amanda Derby picked up her phone, punched a button and waited. She put the receiver back down and looked at her watch. "Leah must be running late. Let me walk you out."

"Don't bother. I can find my way."

She rose from behind her desk. "Here, take this," she said, handing me my file. "We don't keep these any longer than necessary. There are no copies."

I opened the file and fingered the three white, lined sheets of paper that detailed my exemplary attendance over the past three months. Each appointment appeared in thin blue ink in what must have been Leah's looping hand. In the spaces between, and in the margins, cryptic notes had been scratched with a heavy black felt-tip. Most were not immediately legible, but at the top of the last page, in large block letters that were underlined, Dr. Amanda Derby had written: WATCH.

I closed the file and held it out to her. "I'm not sure I even want to leave here with this. Can I trust you to dispose of it for me?"

"Certainly."

"I have a few clients who could learn something about record-keeping—or *not* keeping—from you."

"You're going to be fine, Mr. Benedict."

"Ah, yes. 'Fine.' A word meaning both 'exquisite' and 'okay.' You said you believe in fate. Which are you predicting for me?"

"Take care, Mr. Benedict," she said, extending her hand. I noticed for the first time that it looked older than her face, and when I took it, I don't know why, I turned it over and kissed the weathered, tanned back of it, my lips parting over her middle two knuckles. Immediately, I knew that it had been an impertinent gesture, but that uncertainty only made me pause and hold it there longer. When I finally straightened and turned to let myself out, I tried not to look at her. But as I pulled the door closed behind me, I could see that she was looking down at her hand, cradling it in the other, as if I had broken it.

The hallway was still bathed in white fluorescent light of the type that reveals every body flaw in a department store changing room. Like a child, I stretched both arms out like wings and pulled my fingers along the smudged walls, momentarily losing touch and balance at each doorway. The reception area was still bright and empty. There was no sign of Leah, though as I crossed the worn carpet to the doors, I heard a sound like someone fishing through her purse outside.

When I had left my office, just before noon, Hank had looked to be readying herself for a lunch date. And now, as I began to open one of the large double doors to leave The Healing Touch for the last time, her fragrance seemed to thrust its way through the widening fissure even before I saw her. And because the sight of her—her back to the door, waiting, the side of her face becoming visible at the sound of the turning latch—made me catch and hold my breath, her perfume swirling in my head like an imprisoned reefer hit, I had to grip the doorjamb to keep from falling into her.

My first instinct, as with any animal that has been futilely on the run, was to believe that I had been caught, trapped. Until I realized, with the deliberate slowness of her thick scent falling from my nostrils, that we both were. I had known Hank for as long as I had known my wife, and yet the word "vulnerable" had never once come to mind when looking at her face until now. It was as if she was pleading with me not to judge her at the very instant that she might most easily have determined to judge me. And then it was gone so quickly I couldn't be sure that I had ever seen it.

"I suppose that you have more explaining to do than I," was what she said.

"No question," I admitted. "Maybe later. Would it help to know that I don't think I'll be coming back here anymore?"

"Yes. Would it hurt to know that I will?"

"No."

"Good. Because I've got nothing to be ashamed of. Unlike some. I'm a single woman. I get lonely."

"Of course."

There was a long pause. I was still inside, holding the door open. Hank looked down, then over my shoulder into the reception area.

"There's no one here yet," I said. "Except Amanda. Dr. Derby."

"Yes. At twelve-thirty, I often have to wait."

"I could let you in."

"No. That's all right. Leah will be along shortly."

More silence. Why I felt the need to make further conversation, I don't know, but I was frozen. Although I was inside and she was out, it was as if she were a sentry charged with the security of the entire world beyond this threshold.

"So," I said. "Who are you here to . . . ?" Hank's chin jerked upward. "Never mind. I don't want to know."

"No."

"So, then. Will I see you back at the office?"

"Of course."

"Yes. Of course."

I stepped out and let the heavy door close behind me. With Hank standing there, immovable, the sound didn't bring the finality I was hoping for. Instead, it sounded like the beginning of me stepping back out into the world over which she was standing guard. And as if sensing this—as if this recognition on my part were some kind of password—Hank stepped aside.

"You smell nice," I said as I passed. "Really."

"Thank you."

I didn't look back, but I knew that she was watching me, and it made the wide floor feel like a balance beam beneath my feet. When I made the turn into the elevator bank, I caught a glimpse of her, arms folded, small and expectant in front of the broad entry, like a child who has been banished to the hall by a teacher, and I realized that, except when she was with me, she spent most of her life alone like this, waiting for someone to let her in.

An elevator came. I got in and dropped into the marbled and chromed lunchtime bustle of street-level and made for the revolving doors. Below me, in the lower-level food court, I could see table after table of heads sitting atop dark-suited, crouched shoulders. The down escalator was dense with more dark suits, but because of the early hour the up escalator was nearly empty. It was only this sparseness that allowed Leah and Samantha, white paper bags in hand and late for work, to stride up and past the few others, as if the stairs moved faster for them. At my current pace, I would meet them at the top of the escalator. I had never seen anyone from The Healing Touch outside its offices before, and I didn't know how to react. Not two minutes ago, I had thought that I had left them behind, but here they were, bearing down (or, in this case, up) on me like a couple of elegant, instantaneously resurrected demons. Leah, as usual, was dressed in conservative gray. But Samantha looked like a colorized rose in a black-and-white movie: red dress, red lipstick, auburn hair trailing like flames. She was beautiful in the mirrored candlelight of The Healing Touch; but here, surrounded by ordinariness, the sight of her was staggering, and I stopped just to look. What was the protocol? Should I say hello? But they passed close enough for me to discern Samantha's scent, and both offered nothing more than a glance toward me: two models of discretion. Samantha, perhaps, registered momentary recognition, if not warmth, but her eyes caught me then let me go so quickly that anyone watching would have been sure that she had no idea who I was.

12

Confession is good for the soul only in the sense that a tweed coat is good for dandruff—it is a palliative rather than a remedy.

—Peter De Vries

In 1996, on the occasion of the seventy-fifth anniversary of the establishment of the Fox Run Golf and Hunt Club, F. Porter Beason III commissioned and oversaw the dedication of a stone marker and plaque at the fifteenth tee bearing the name of his grandfather beneath the inscription THE LAST BREATHER (which referred, presumably, to the gentle fifteenth itself and not the elder, deceased Beason). During an early-morning ceremony, a single bagpiper led F. III and a slow, shuffling cadre of Fox Run elder statesmen (replacement joints outnumbering original teeth) across the five hundred yards from the eighteenth green to the fifteenth tee. It was a solemn and somber procession, until several of its constituents lost momentum somewhere along the moderate slope of the fifteenth fairway, and one of the assistant pros was dispatched to procure a small squadron of electric carts to complete the journey. Once everyone was settled and attentive, F. III unveiled the marker and explained that his grandfather had always loved stepping onto this tee. From here he could see, on the hillside beyond, the two things of which he was most proud: the Clubhouse and his home.

Whether he would still be so proud of the latter, knowing that it was now inhabited by F. III, early-retired from his burdensome duties as manager of the family foundation, was irrelevant: He had chosen the perfect moniker for this simple downhill par-four that gives the illusion of leading you home, but is, in fact, a brief respite after the perils of thirteen and fourteen, and before the grinding length of the three finishing holes. Even today, knowing that I need to make at least one more birdie, and knowing that this hole presents my most likely opportunity, there is a profound sense of relief as I round the corner behind the tee, alone. Perhaps the source of my relief is the same as it was for F. Porter Beason: the generous fairway leading down the slope, then back up to the elevated green and the Clubhouse beyond. Perhaps mine results from the figure of Sal emerging from the pines halfway down the fairway, my cell phone still to his ear, raising his free hand to signal not only his readiness, but his forgiveness. Or, perhaps, my relief is nothing more than resignation—to the likelihood that whatever magic had been touching me has moved on.

Whatever its genesis, my newfound comfort is just that: comfort. It isn't focus; it isn't confidence, exactly. It is, instead, that rare confluence of indifference and ardor that all of us who love this game feel on any stolen fall afternoon that is quickly turning to evening. It is not a feeling that affects, or is affected by, performance, so Sal would not disapprove. He would argue that I am disguising surrender as contentment. But sometimes surrender is a necessary first step.

Back at the office, I left a scribbled Post-it note on the arm of Hank's chair: *Gone home*—and I went, not knowing why until the moment I got there. Seeing Hank at The Healing Touch, then seeing Leah and Samantha out in the "real world" rising toward her, was like witnessing my two lives hurtling inexorably and inevitably toward each other. They weren't, of course. Hank would never reveal anything, if not because she cared for me, then because she required my discretion as well. I had no reason to doubt that Amanda

Derby would destroy my file. And to Samantha, I now understood, I was a paying client and nothing more. But somehow these practical assurances had nothing to do with the atmosphere of inevitability, the sense of unqualified necessity that followed me back out onto the street, that clung to me like the staggering August heat as I climbed into my car, and that circulated cool through the air-conditioning vents, warm through my lungs, again and again, until I pulled up in front of our house to find Kelly sweeping the porch steps, and finally recognized its source:

I was going to tell her.

I was already speaking when I was only halfway to where Kelly was standing, before she had even cleared the quizzical look from her face that resulted, at first, not from what I was saying, but from the mere fact of my being there, at two o'clock in the afternoon of a workday. It was as if what had been following me, clinging to me, circulating through me just kept right on moving, as if the words rushing from me were its next, natural, predetermined incarnation. I told her everything, sweat cascading down my forehead and up through the tight weave of my white shirt, without thinking, without stopping, without even discerning the effect of my revelation on her—selfish, even in this moment of contrition. It is only now that I can see her lean heavily on the handle of the broom as the meaning of my words begin to take hold, see her let go, let it drop, and press firmly with the fingers of both hands on the top of the growing belly that holds the new life whose frailty frightens me more than any consequence of my confession, see her sit hard on the cement steps, one hand moving to her face, the other up to me, held out like a crossing guard's, protecting innocence, telling me to stop. I remember now that I touched her bare shoulder, that moisture instantaneously rose between us like a fluid partition, even before she could recoil from me as if bitten. Then, with the posture that only a woman carrying a child can adopt, the bearing that recognizes the relative insignificance of everything outside the border of her own womb, she stood, went inside, closed the door behind her, then emerged, not five minutes later, with a duffel bag packed neatly, I assumed, with everything I might need for the next few days. She walked past me with it to my car, opened the passenger's side door, placed it carefully on the seat, closed the door, then strode past me again, up the stairs and back into the house. When the door closed, it was with the thud of finality that had been missing outside the door of The Healing Touch. Hannah appeared briefly at the living room window wearing a bright-orange bathing suit with a huge yellow sunflower sewn to the chest, the upper petals of which tickled her chin. Before she could answer my hesitant wave, two gentle hands slipped under her arms and pulled her away.

I didn't know what to do next. Whatever confessional forces had driven me here, their power had been exhausted in the brief moments it had taken me to act as the enabler of the collision I had foreseen, to deliver the facts of Mika and Amanda Derby and Samantha into my marriage like ravenous cells, without considering the effect of their introduction any more than I had considered my response to the fact of Kelly's pregnancy four months earlier. I was again, in essence, looking to her for answers, asking the same question: "What are we going to do about it?" Now that she had told me, I was left, finally, to ask myself the same question. And as if to prove that the "sensibility" quadrant of my brain had been entirely eradicated, I drove to Stewey's.

Stewey and Donna lived in the oldest section of the borough of Fox Run, less than a mile from the neighborhood in which we had grown up together. Stewey's house resembled Stewey: big, irregular and in need of maintenance. It had lodged no fewer than four owners in the twenty years before Donna and Stewey moved in, and each had annexed an addition, so that the house, like Stewey, had been steadily but unevenly tacking girth on all expandable regions. Stewey had bought the house talking of five children, but their family had never grown beyond the one daughter they had at the time, Shelley, who had just finished her freshman year at Lehigh. As a result, three of the five distinct wings of the house were shut off and dark, and even the exterior of those sections appeared forgotten, as if the neglect were seeping through the clapboards from the inside. That I expected to find him at home at that hour was further evidence of my impaired mental state. But as I drove into the semicircular gravel driveway, pulled the overnight bag from the seat next to me and got out to approach the front door, I believed that I was Felix Unger to Stewey's Oscar Madison and that he would be there to greet me and to usher me into this new, diminished period of my life with a huge, welcoming paw and a corned-beef sandwich.

Of course, it was Donna who answered the door.

People who meet Donna Trammell now find her unremarkable. She has become, in Kelly's words, "comfortably frumpy." But every time I see her she is, at first, still Donna O'Connor, seventeen, wearing nothing but cut-offs and a powder-blue lace bra, holding up the two indistinguishable T-shirts from which I am to choose. Which is to say that I am always momentarily speechless. The circumstances of my visit on that day, and the fact that I was expecting to see Stewey, baseball cap on backward, wiping a fried-sandwich-greasy hand on his gray sweatshirt before welcoming me in, did nothing to improve my communication skills.

"Michael?"

I looked at Donna, then at my duffel bag. I had received it as a tournament favor from the last Fox Run Men's Invitational, and my name was stitched on the zippered top. I noticed a slight imperfection in the stitching of the B in BENEDICT. There was a single line of red thread mixed with the gold. I was still looking at it when she spoke again.

"Michael, are you okay? What's in the bag?"

"I'm not sure," I said, realizing for the first time that I wasn't. I could have been carrying plastic explosives triggered to the zipper for all I knew. "Kelly packed it for me."

"Are you going somewhere? Look at me, Michael. You're scaring me."

So I looked. She wasn't wearing a baseball cap, but she did have on a sweatshirt that had to have been Stewey's. Her hair was cropped short now, not in a purposeful, stylish way, but in the kind of cut that women refer to as "easy." The sleeves of her sweatshirt were rolled and bunched behind her wrists, and the waistband fell almost to the cuffs of her bermuda shorts. Her legs were thick and tanned all the way to her white ankle socks and sneakers. I realized that I was looking down again and forced my eyes up to meet hers. When I did, it was as if a high-speed glass elevator had just rocketed me up ninety floors, and I felt unsteady at the new height. A bead of sweat stung my right eye.

"Sorry," I said, winking like a mental patient. "I was looking for Stewey. Of course, he's not here. Is he?"

"No. He's at the office. Why would you—?"

"I think I've been kicked out."

"Of your *house?*"

"Yeah. I'm pretty sure." I looked at my duffel bag again. "Yeah."

"Jesus. Come in out of that heat. You look like you're about to melt."

Donna pulled the door wide open, then took my free arm to lead me in. The effect was one of stepping from a sauna into a walk-in refrigerator. In an instant, the wetness that was coating my face and torso evaporated, and every pore clamped shut.

"Thanks."

"Sorry about the air," she said, crossing her arms over her chest. "Stewey needs to be kept refrigerated during the summer months."

I felt myself beginning to recover. "No. It feels good."

"I used to turn it down whenever he left the house, but then I had a nonstop string of colds every summer. I've found it's easier just to add clothing. Here, let me take that." Donna reached for the leather handle of my bag and set it just inside the entrance to the den, where I knew there was a pullout couch.

"Are you sure this is okay?" I said.

"Mostly." She motioned for me to follow her to the kitchen.

"Though I suppose it should depend on what happened. Are you going to tell me?"

"If you don't mind, I'd rather wait and tell Stewey, swear him to secrecy, then have *him* tell you."

"Suit yourself. You know you're always welcome here, Michael."

"You don't have to commit yourself yet. Kelly won't exactly see it as a badge of your friendship that you are harboring a fugitive."

"*You* were my friend first. Remember?" Her smile was, even still, compassionate and not the least suggestive.

"That I do."

She opened a cabinet and took down a heavy mug. "Coffee?"

"No thanks."

The Trammell kitchen could have been photographed (at any time of the day or night, I suspected) for a designer magazine. Cherry cabinets, rich hardwood floors and muted accents of mustard and goldenrod were warmed by dimmed, recessed lighting. The countertops, including the center island around which Donna and I sat on stout, backless stools, were ceramic Mexican tile, some with hand-painted fruit or flowers interspersed randomly. Copper-bottomed pots hung according to size above the island and next to various tongs, pincers, forks and spatulas. The only nod to Stewey was the stainless-steel commercial refrigerator that was big enough to accommodate a hanging steer.

Donna sipped her coffee, holding the mug in both hands, and looked up. "So," she said.

"So," I said.

In the ensuing silence, Stewey's refrigerator hummed behind me like an idling freighter.

"So, what do two old friends who haven't really talked in a while talk about while trying not to talk about something else?"

"I don't know."

Donna squinted at me. "Are you sure you're okay? I mean, physically."

"Sure. Fine."

"Because you look a little peaked."

"It was just the heat, I think."

"Can I get you something cold?"

"Don't bother," I said, immediately wishing I had answered otherwise, if only to give one of us something to do. We passed another few moments in silence.

"How about kids?" she said. "We could talk about kids."

"Okay. Kids."

"How are your girls?"

"Great. Yours?"

"Great." Donna nodded. "Yeah, she's great."

"That's great." I nodded with her. We were two heads plugged into the same iPod. "She's home? Shelley?"

"No. I mean, yeah. She's home, but not right now. Actually, she's with her father today. She's been going in with him once a week. Sort of an informal internship. He'll be home early today. With her. In fact, when I saw you at the door, I thought maybe the two of you had talked."

"No. That's nice. That's nice for them."

"Yes, it is." Lines appeared at the corners of her round eyes, then vanished again as she brought the cup to her mouth, sipped, then set it back on the island, still encircling it with her hands. "What about Megan? Is she ready for the big move up to the high school?"

"She is. I'm not."

"No? It's not such a bad place. We did all right."

"I suppose. I'm just not prepared for her to be in a place where boys think about girls the way I thought about . . . girls."

"She'll be fine."

"I guess."

"And little Hannah?"

My body had adjusted to the temperature, and the initial alertness the cold had brought had begun to fade. I crossed my arms and trapped my fingers under my armpits, as much for support as for warmth. "Maybe I will take a cup of coffee," I said. "Just to hold."

"I'm sorry. I'll turn it down."

"No, really. I don't want you to do anything on my account."

"Are you all right?"

"Perfect."

"You're perspiring again. Maybe you should see a doctor."

The dizziness came on in a surging rush, and I had to grip the countertop to keep from tumbling off my stool.

"I think maybe I just need to lie down," I said. "Could I possibly lie down?"

"Of course. Come on—I'll get you a blanket." Donna put an arm under mine and led me back to the den. She sat me in a green leather chair, and I closed my eyes and listened to her toss the pillows from the couch, then pull out its creaking skeleton. I must have dozed, and she must have left the room to get bedding, because when I opened my eyes, a thick white eyelet comforter stretched out and away from her hands and seemed to pause, suspended, over clean white sheets. Then she was helping me out of my suit jacket, tugging at my tie and loosening the button at the collar of my shirt. I was still shivering as she helped me under the covers. Then I felt her lips touch my temple, dry and motherly.

At first, I dreamt the disjointed, semiconscious dreams of the fevered, unable to force my eyes open to see the voices I was hearing. Hank was handing me a file, telling me that a client was waiting in the conference room to speak to me. Then the voice was Amanda Derby's and the file was mine, and I could feel her tapping it as I held it, pointing to something important I was to read but my eyes still refused to open. And then it was Kelly over my shoulder, and there was a stack of Hannah's artwork in my lap. "Look, Michael! Look!" they were all saying. I could feel my forehead arching up, trying futilely to pull me into consciousness. "I just need to lie down," I told them. "Just for a minute." And when I did, when they finally let me, I fell into a bottomless sleep and found myself standing in a silent snow, holding Hannah's hand. We were on the bank of a frozen pond, where I had taken her to ice-skate many times, and she was pulling me down the small slope to test the surface. "Come on, Daddy! Let's go!" she squealed. "Easy, sweet pea. Take it slow." I knew that the ice was solid, but we tested it together so that she would always remember, always be safe. The snow stopped. She crept out a few paces in her boots, while I sat and opened the shoulder bag I had brought. I took out her white figure skates, then my black hockey skates and set them beside me. "Look at me, Dad!" She had gotten down on all fours. "I'm a polar bear!" She was no more than ten feet from me, but she seemed to be getting smaller. With each shuffle of her hands and knees, she receded farther into her white snowsuit, until she crawled out of it, a naked infant. I stood to call to her, and the sun suddenly blazed behind me like a torch. I was instantly hot and wet inside my heavy coat, and the milky-white ice of the pond cleared in a growing semicircle that started at my feet and swept out beyond Hannah and across its surface like the leading edge of an explosion. The ice groaned and cracked under my feet as I ran toward her. She kept crawling, growing smaller still, then fell to her side, squalling, plump and slick as a newborn, and when she rolled to her back, her face wasn't Hannah's but Jessica's. The weight of my steps as I neared her broke the ice beneath both of us, and I saw her slip silently under at my feet before following her in. The shock of the water drove the breath from my chest but I stayed under, sinking, flailing my arms and legs in all directions, until I felt a soft thud against my heel. I reached down, found a limb with one hand, then her torso with both and pushed her over my head. I kicked upward in terror, no longer able to control the instinct to breathe, and, as my lungs filled with water, I thrust her up through the skin of the surface.

Stewey sat wedged in the green leather chair, reading the sports section under an antique-brass lamp. His huge, slippered feet, which rested on a green leather ottoman, were crossed almost daintily at the ankles. I sat up and pulled the comforter around me.

"Jesus Christ, it's freezing in here."

"Oh, good. It's alive." Stewey folded the newspaper and regarded me with mock suspicion. "So, what am I supposed to think when I come home early to find you rumpled and sleeping after an afternoon visit with my wife?"

"What time is it?"

Stewey consulted his watch. "A little after nine."

"At night!"

"Or so these darkening windows would indicate, yes."

"Why didn't somebody wake me?"

"Somebody tried. You were uncooperative." Stewey tossed the newspaper to the floor. Despite his attempt to make the gesture appear cavalier, a mere conversation starter, his round, expressive face betrayed concern. "Donna filled me in on what happened. So, what happened?"

"I told her."

Stewey looked puzzled. "She said you didn't."

"Not Donna. Kelly."

"Why would you have to tell Kelly?"

"I don't know. I just couldn't keep it from her anymore."

"She didn't *know* why she kicked you out?"

"Of *course* she knew. After I told her."

"Are you still asleep? Told her *what*?"

"Everything."

Stewey opened his mouth as if to continue this disconnected exchange, and then the connection struck him. "You *told* her?"

"That's what I've been telling you."

"Everything?"

"Yeah, everything."

"Are you insane?"

"Not anymore, I don't think."

"You *told* her?" He was still incredulous. "That might be the stupidest thing you've ever done."

"How can you say that? Donna knows *you* go. She buys you *gift* certificates, for chrissake."

It is difficult to describe the change in Stewey's demeanor here, but it was profound. I thought I saw guilt, then shame, then I was sure it was self-pity. He looked, to me, like a basset hound facing a raised, rolled newspaper.

"She *sends* me," he said. "There's a difference."

I didn't get it.

"I don't get it," I said.

"You never did."

Stewey freed himself from between the arms of his chair, stood and crossed the room to close the French doors that separated the den from the foyer. Then he pulled the ottoman to the foot of my temporary bunk and sat down heavily. He seemed to gather himself before speaking. He looked at the floor, then fixed me with a gaze a doctor might use to tell you you've got six months to live. In thirty-five years, I had never seen this look on Stewey's face, and the effect was almost comical.

"Donna doesn't like sex," is what he said.

Now I knew he was kidding. "So who'd like sex with you?"

"With anybody." His face hadn't changed. "I mean, I was her first, so there's only *been* me, but it's not *me*, if that makes any sense."

"You're *serious*?"

"Dead."

It would not be an overstatement to say that this revelation rewrote, instantaneously, numerous heretofore-fragile moments from my youth.

"Since when?"

"Looking back? Probably since forever. We never did much when we were dating. But what did I have to compare it to? I still felt like the neighborhood fat kid, and the fact that she even agreed to be *seen* with me seemed like some kind of miracle. She wanted to wait until we got married? Well, that meant we were *getting* married, and I wanted that more than anything in the world. Then when we *did* get married, neither of us had any experience, so I figured I was just doing something wrong. She wanted a baby right away, and everyone says sex is no good when you're trying to get pregnant, so that didn't seem so unusual. Then when Shelley was little there was no *time*, and every couple we knew was having the same problems. But then I got the new job, and we moved in here, and everything was going to be different. Only it wasn't."

I worked hard at processing this new information, at recasting every assumption I had ever made about Stewey and Donna and the two of them together. Stewey caught me.

"Why are you looking at me like that?" he said. "It's not as if she's got cancer."

"I don't know. It's just that I always thought—until I met Kelly—I always *envied* you."

Stewey stiffened. "Look at yourself now, buddy. You *still* should."

"I didn't mean . . ."

He rose. Even as my best friend, standing over me he was imposing.

"There isn't *one* other thing I would change about her, okay? How many guys do you think have a list that short? And how many wives would willingly send their husbands to be touched by someone else to help save a marriage? Huh? The only son of a bitch luckier than me is you, and you're blowing it."

"You're right. I'm sorry."

"I mean, where does someone in your current condition get off pitying *me*?"

"Come on, Stewey; you know that's not the way I meant it."

He sat down. "Yeah, I know. Shit." He put his huge, round head in his huge, round hands, a softened Charles Atlas holding up his own world. "We tried everything, but no one wants to just help you move *forward*, you know? They all think you've got to go back and find the goddam *source* of the problem before you can address it. And I didn't want her to go through that. Not for anything. I mean, just in case there *was* a source other than going to Catholic mass every Sunday. How many people do we know in therapy who are really happier now that they know exactly *why* they're so fucking miserable?"

"But how did you end up with Amanda Derby? Can I assume she's not on your HMO's list of approved specialists?"

"We got to the point where we just decided to live with it. Or *I* did. I'm not sure Donna ever quite knew what all the fuss was about. The last doctor we saw used to work with Amanda Derby when she was in private practice, and he recommended her as— I think this is what he said—'a treater of symptoms, not problems,' and he made us agree we wouldn't reveal the source of the referral. I wasn't too sure about the idea, but we went to see her together, and Donna loved her." He shook his head. "Can you believe that?"

"How long have you been seeing her?"

"Almost three years."

"Jesus."

"Donna and I get to concentrate on what we're really *good* at together. Don't get me wrong. It's not like we never . . . It just became so discouraging, you know?—trying to be together like that—with her expecting nothing from me in return and me feeling like she deserves so much." Stewey looked away from me, toward the beveled doors. "Anyway."

"Anyway."

"So," he said after a moment, "what are you going to do?"

"I don't know."

"What did Kelly say?"

"Nothing."

"Nothing at all?"

"Nope."

"Shit."

"Yeah. Somehow I don't envision Kelly and Amanda Derby hitting it off right now. Though, come to think of it, they both kicked me out today. Suppose that should tell me something?"

Stewey appeared not to have heard me, or at least he didn't answer right away. His eyes were surveying the walls of his den, which, I noticed now, served as a shrine to his high school and college football careers. I followed his gaze, which seemed to have fixed on one of the largest framed photographs in the room. It was of Stewey, helmetless but in pads and covered with mud and grass stains, beaming as he held aloft his current wife and then-unblemished captain of the cheerleading squad across his thigh-size forearms, like a single, weightless piece of cordwood.

"You know, Mikey," he said, finally, "when I sent you there, I never thought anything like this would happen."

"Stewey, don't be ridiculous. I'm an adult, most of the time. There's no need for you to apologize."

"Let me finish. I don't know Kelly, you know, like *that*, other than stuff you've told me. And maybe I figured you embellished a little. Maybe, in a way, I was hoping I had company."

"You do have company. Only, unfortunately for you, it's for the foreseeable future."

"I'm serious."

"So am I."

"You can stay as long as you need to. You know that."

"Thanks." I pulled the comforter tightly around me. "Aren't your guest rooms properly zoned so that your patrons don't have to share the same habitat with Frosty the CFO?"

"I'll talk to maintenance. You need anything else?"

"No, I'm fine."

"The phone's on the table behind you. The TV remote's there too."

"What more could a man want?"

"We'll be in the living room if you feel like talking."

"Thanks. I think I'll just stick to my quarters tonight."

Stewey used the foot of the bed to push himself up off the ottoman. "Night, Mikey."

"Night."

"Everything's going to be all right, you know. I mean, it's you and *Kelly*."

"Yeah."

Stewey left the room and closed the doors gently behind him without looking at me through the glass. I sat back against the shell of the couch. I never traveled on business anymore, and I realized that I hadn't been away from home overnight without Kelly since Hannah was born. She would be asleep by now, having been given some temporary excuse as to why Daddy wasn't home for stories tonight. Kelly, under normal circumstances, would be reading her own book in the living room. Megan would be on the phone, toggling between call-waiting beeps like a baseball GM negotiating a three-team, six-player deal. I was sure that Kelly wouldn't answer the phone if she heard it ring, but Megan had never engaged in a telephone conversation too important to ignore a chance at another. I could get in through her. Without giving myself time to think about what I might say, I reached behind me, picked up the phone and dialed.

"Hello?" Bingo. Megan.

"Hi, pumpkin."

"Daddy? Where *are* you?"

"I'm at the Trammells'."

"What happened? I went into the kitchen while Mom was making dinner, and she was crying, but she wouldn't tell me anything. What's going on?"

"Can I talk to her?"

"I don't think so."

"Could you just tell her I'm on the phone?"

"Dad, she told me if you beeped through to just hang up. I'm not even supposed to be *talking* to you. What are you two fighting about? Can I help?"

"What's she doing right now?"

"She's reading her book."

"She is? Really?"

"Dad, what *happened?*"

"Just tell her I called, will you? Let her know where I am and that I need to talk to her, okay?"

"I'll tell her but she doesn't want to talk to you."

"And could you kiss Hannah for me?"

"She's *asleep*, Dad."

"I know. She'll go right back. Just sneak in and kiss her and tell her it's from Daddy, okay?"

"I guess."

"Promise me, Megan."

"*Okay*, I promise."

"Good. Thanks. I love you, pumpkin."

"Love you too, Dad."

"Did you go swimming today?"

"Dad, Amy's on the other line."

"Sorry. Tell your mother, okay?"

"I *said* I would, Dad."

"Right. Bye then."

"Bye, Daddy."

I set the phone on my lap and stared at it. For what must have been fifteen minutes, I looked at nothing but the phone, in something of a trance, willing it to ring. When it did, my entire body jolted and I nearly fell out of bed. A moment later, Stewey was peering at me through one of the panes of the door, his forehead and chin distorted by the beveled border, pointing at the phone in his hand. I picked up.

"Hi."

"Don't say *anything*. It's my turn this time."

"Okay."

"*Nothing!*" She paused to make sure that I understood and would comply, then she began. "First, I want to make it clear that I *knew* something was going on. I know you, Michael. Don't *ever* think you can hide anything from me. You wear guilt like an overstarched shirt. My mistake was thinking that one of your stock picks had gone bad and that you were afraid to tell me what had happened to the kids' college fund." (I felt myself slipping on another stiff shirt, but I remained silent, as instructed.) "Second, I want you to remember that I am saying, on this *very first* day, that I recognize that I am not entirely blameless in this situation, but that nothing, *nothing*, short of pulling out my pinking shears and going Lorena Bobbitt on you, could ever demonstrate the anger and humiliation and *betrayal* that I feel at your choice of how to deal with our problem. Remember all of those times I tried to talk you out of your paternal inferiority complex? Well, *forget* them. Third—is this third or fourth? *Don't* answer!—I am five months pregnant, and I will *not* subject this baby to the stress of trying to work through this right now, or even the stress of my having to *look* at you every day and think of where you've been and the *filth* that has touched your body. I need to not see or speak to you for a long time, no matter how hard that is on the children. We will leave the house by noon tomorrow, and the back door will be open. Get what you need and be out by three. On the issue of whether or not this is permanent, I'm not deciding that yet, because if I did, the answer would be *yes*, and carrying a baby that's going to grow up in a house without a father is another stress I'd just as soon avoid right now." She paused. "Oh, and don't *ever* put Megan between us again like you did tonight."

That was it. She hung up. I put the phone down and stared at it some more. A moment later, Stewey appeared at the door again and questioned me through the glass: thumbs up, then thumbs down. When I made no motion in reply, he went away. Fifteen hours later, I gathered two suitcases, two hanging suit bags and seven banker's boxes full of belongings from my grown-up home and transported them to my childhood home. Seven hours after that, I was sitting at the dinner table with my mother, my father having abruptly excused himself to read *The Wall Street Journal* in the den, telling her a censored, skeletal version of my misdeeds, both to be sure that she didn't blame Kelly and because she had never once in my lifetime failed to figure out exactly what I had done wrong anyway. A week later, I started calling every evening, when I knew Megan would be on the phone, to talk to both girls before bed. In September, shortly after school started, I began my twice-weekly pick-ups at Fox Run High and Woodland Elementary, cut back to three days a week at the office and began jotting down notes, then sentences, then whole paragraphs in an effort to make some sense out of what had occurred. Throughout, I continued to play and to practice almost daily, more to consume time (which there seemed to be far too much of) than in pursuit of my original ambition, until the day in late October when an old man in red suspenders helped me to glimpse perfection, only to have me begin to look away.

As I get ready to hit my tee shot at the fifteenth, Sal still has my cell phone to his ear. I can see that he is hanging back along the tree line so that the caddy-master can't see him from his perch outside the Clubhouse. Although the rules tend to relax at this time of year, it is technically improper (but for Kelly's pregnancy) for me to have my phone on the golf course. If this were the high season, and *Sal* caught using it, something akin to a stoning would likely follow.

My newfound comfort allows me to take a free and easy swing. But, as I said, comfort and focus are two very different states of mind, and the resulting shot is one that Stewey (even Stewey as he has been reconstituted for me) would have lovingly and accurately labeled a "condom shot": It didn't feel too good, but it's safe. The ball comes off the bottom half of the club and takes a low but straight line down the hill. The slope makes up for the mis-hit, and it ends up in perfect position. Frankly, I find that I couldn't care less. Sal heads for the fairway and tucks my phone into his pocket.

When I reach him, I notice that he doesn't have a club pulled yet, nor is his hand resting on the one he's about to recommend. He has had plenty of time to step off the distance, to account for the downhill lie and the back-tier pin position. There is nothing unusual about the shot that might require discussion, yet he seems distracted.

"You've got about one-twenty to the middle, Mr. B., one-thirty back to the top shelf."

"Downhill lie—sounds like a perfect hard wedge."

"Yeah, maybe."

"Maybe?"

"I don't know. Wedge might spin off that top shelf all the way back to the front."

"Short is always better than over the back when the pin is there, Sal. You taught me that when I was fourteen. I'll take the wedge."

"Yeah, but we need birdie here, Mr. B." Sal is looking everywhere but at me. "I'm just sayin' you might at least take a minute and think about the nine."

I am looking hard at him, trying to pull his eyes to me, but I can't.

"Everything okay at home, Sal?"

"Home? Oh, yeah. Fine."

"Sal?"

"Yeah?"

"The wedge?"

"One minute." He sets the bag down. "Let me get you a distance from that sprinkler head. I marched it in from the one-fifty, but I never trust those damn things."

"Sal, it's not that big a deal anymore." But he's already on the move. He's not in any hurry either. Once he reaches the sprinkler head, he turns and makes a show of taking slow, perfect, one-yard steps. When his right foot finally lands heavily opposite my ball, he nods as if justified.

"Yup. Damned one-fifties. It's one-seventeen to the middle, one-twenty-seven back shelf."

"Okay, so you've proved that it's a *more* perfect wedge. Thanks."

He looks like he's about to say something else, but I pull the club myself and step back to take my line.

"Hold on," he says. "Let me see that clubhead."

"What?"

"Hand me the club a minute."

"Sal, what *is* your problem?"

"Nothin'. I just thought I saw some turf in the grooves. You want me to give it a quick wipe?"

"You're the one worried about me spinning it too much. Now you want to clean out the grooves?"

"I'm just askin', do you want me to give it a wipe?"

"No, Sal, I don't. Now could you please step back so I can—" My cell phone flutters and Sal goes for it like Doc Holliday going for his pistol.

"I think it's for you," he says.

"Of *course* it's for me. Who is it?"

Sal looks at the green Day-Glo display. "Looks like your mother."

"Christ. Let her go into voice mail."

"She's just gonna call back." He could have been saying this because he knows my mother, but I get the feeling that he just plain *knows*. I take the phone and Sal turns and begins marching off the yardage yet again, this time to a more distant sprinkler head. Reluctantly, I put the phone to my ear.

"Yeah, Ma."

"Your father watches porno."

"*Excuse* me?"

"I said, your father watches porno."

"Yeah? Well, your mother wears army boots."

"I'm serious."

"You're looney."

"Go ahead. Deny it if you want. You're good at denial."

"Ma, why in God's name are you telling me this?"

"Because it's true. And because Sal told me to."

"*Sal* knows Dad watches porno?" From twenty yards down the fairway, Sal looks up involuntarily. If he didn't, he knows now.

"No, silly." Great. "I was just telling him about how hard you are on yourself—and rightfully so most of the time, I might add—but that you never give your father credit for being human. You come by it honestly, you know, all this obsession with sex, sex, sex. Your father used to try to get me to watch it with him, when we first got the VCR. He'd try to get romantic with me, but I always started to giggle."

I am beginning to feel ill.

"Ma, I really don't need to hear this."

"When I'm not around, I'm sure he's enjoying it by *himself,* if you know what I mean."

"Ma."

"I don't know what you men find sexy about those movies. They're ridiculous. They're about three steps below the Three Stooges as far as I'm concerned."

"We like *them* too, Ma."

"True enough. Let me get your father. He has something to say to you."

"Jesus, Ma! I can't talk to him *now.*"

"He and Marge Two are relaxing in the den. He's got no idea what I just told you, so don't ask him about it."

"I'll try to keep myself from discussing the Pamela and Tommy Lee video with my seventy-year-old father."

"Who?"

"No one, Ma."

"Michael, your father is one of the only true live-and-let-livers in the universe. All you have to do to please him is not to lose those girls of yours. And I'm speaking specifically now of the ones living in your *house,* not the ones—"

"Ma, I *get* it. There's no call for sarcasm."

"Let me get him." I instinctively pull the phone away from my ear. My mother, ever conscious of saving time, even in milliseconds, neither moves the receiver nor covers the mouthpiece when summoning someone to the phone. *"Mike!"* Still down the fairway, Sal looks up again. "Here he is, dear. Good luck with your game. I hope you win."

"Ma, I'm not . . ." but she's already gone, of course.

"Michael?"

"Hey, Dad."

For just a few seconds, he says nothing. I can hear my mother whispering in the background. "Your mother wants me to tell you that I love you."

"Is that why you're telling me?"

"Yes."

"Otherwise you wouldn't."

"Wouldn't love you or wouldn't tell you?"

"Is there a difference?"

"Jesus, you can be stubborn."

"Sorry. Thanks, Dad. Really."

"I hear you've got a good round going."

"I *did*. I've got a little work to do to get it back."

"I'd kill to be able to hit the ball like you do."

"That's what Sal said."

"Sal's a smart guy."

"I'll tell him you said so."

"Make sure you bring the card home."

"Sorry?"

"The card. Make sure you bring it home. Marge Two and I want to hear about every shot, don't we, girl?"

"She made it into the kitchen?" Marge Two is about the same age the original Marge was on our wedding day and somehow walks without bending a single joint.

"She goes where I go."

"Okay, Dad. I'll see you soon."

My father hangs up and I listen to the dial tone for a moment. When Sal sees me drop the phone to my side, he stops pretending to be busy and walks back toward me. He puts out his hand for the phone, and I put it in my own pocket.

"I think I'll hang on to this from here in, if you don't mind."

"Everything okay at home?" he says, somehow fixing a look of concern on his face.

"Very funny." Now he is smiling. "Don't say *anything*."

"That's the best she could come up with?"

"It's my *Dad*, and I said not to say *anything*."

"It's *everybody's* dad."

"He said he thinks you're a smart guy."

"The feeling's mutual." Sal looks down at the ball between us. "You gonna hit or what?"

"You should have this thing measured to the inch by now, Doc. What's your diagnosis?"

"Hit the wedge. You never want to be over this green."

"Thanks."

Muscle memory is a funny thing. Even more imperfect and unpredictable than visual, auditory or sensual recollection, muscle memory, when allowed to take over, enables athletes to do what is impossible for others, over and over again, without conscious thought: a gymnast hurtles through the air in a blurring series of twists and rolls, then lands like a driven stake; a third baseman dives to snare a line drive too quick for the television cameras to pick up, then wheels to throw from his knees, without so much as a look, to double the runner off first; a basketball player, two defenders and eight limbs hemming him into the baseline corner, takes one step back and lets fly a blind jumper that spins up, over and down, as if sucked through an invisible arc of tubing that spits it through the net. But add fear, and the same gymnast might balk before takeoff; insert a single failure in a crucial situation, and the same third baseman may be unable to execute even the most leisurely throw to first without bouncing it in the dirt or making it a third-row souvenir; put the game on the line, and the same basketball player, his defenders now relegated to their assigned spots along the key, may be unable to hit the front rim with a simple free throw. What sets an elite athlete apart is not so much the ability to perform *without* conscious thought, but in spite of it.

But just as a momentary loss of focus or hint of self-doubt can bring instant amnesia to muscle memory, sometimes a simple adjustment or even a single perfectly executed shot can resynchronize everything. For that reason, it is difficult for me to control the surge of adrenaline that accompanies the wedge shot I hit in to the fifteenth green. As soon as it comes off the club, I know I'm locked in again. There is almost no sound, other than the gentle *puffff* of the blade taking a shallow pelt of firm, autumn turf that flips high and chases the line of flight before landing ten yards down the fairway. The ball starts on a low, boring trajectory off the downhill lie, then rises, spinning, and lands on the top shelf, five feet from the back flagstick, before taking one quick hop forward and a jolt backward that brings it rolling back down the hill, fifteen feet below the hole.

"That's it," Sal says, watching it, as much to himself as to me. "That's the swing."

When we get to the green, I see the line before Sal points it out. It's as if the hole is the center of gravity itself, as if all I have to do is start the ball in motion and it will be pulled up the hill and into the cup. But my pounding pulse transfers too much speed, and it catches the left side, spins around the back edge and comes back at me a foot or two. I tap in for par.

"I thought you had that one, Mr. B.," Sal says.

"Don't worry, Sal. I got it all right."

I don't know what brought it back. I refuse to believe, perhaps stubbornly, that it had much to do with the content of my mother's call. Rather, I prefer to credit the mere fact of Sal's call to *her*, this woman who, just maybe, he once loved a little bit. If my round meant that much to him, what excuse did *I* have? Whatever the reason, I know one thing: Now that the feeling is back, I don't want to lose it. This is the present tense in which I want to live. But I know that I will need Sal's help to stay here.

13

It's enough to be on your way.
It's enough just to cover ground.

—James Taylor

Sal still looks unsure, but I can tell that he's wavering. The sixteenth tee is no farther from the caddy-master's lookout than the fifteenth green, but the sight line is obscured by two low maples, each still holding fast to a spherical cluster of deep oranges and yellows side-lit by a mellowing sun. Sal has walked to the middle of the tee, and he is moving his head up, down, right and left, without rotating it, like someone looking successively through each false pane of an invisible, mullioned window.

"Relax, Sal. He can't see you here. Besides, what's he going to say when he finds out I *asked* you to?"

"I just feel funny, that's all. It ain't my place."

"Number one: bullshit; number two: I'm *making* it your place. Come on. It'll help me keep my mind off the scoreboard." His face registers the logic of this last argument. "You can even set the stakes."

That does it.

"Anything?" he asks.

"Name it."

Sal still has all of his teeth, and his grin shows me nearly every one. "Loser on each hole humps the bag on the next."

"Done. What about ties?"

"Whoever's carryin' it keeps carryin' it."

"So you get this first one?"

"I ain't won nothin' yet, have I?"

Sometimes, the trick to eliminating unwanted thoughts is to replace them with others. Golf has none of the qualities present in so many other games that rely on natural ability to react, instantaneously, to another player or moving object. There is no other sport in which there is almost nothing *but* time for conscious thought. That's why, even for professionals, protecting a huge lead can be harder than coming from behind. Greg Norman's admirable reaction to his collapse at the '96 Masters was to admit that he just didn't have the game that day, but I never thought that explained it. He was six shots ahead going into Sunday. It should have been easy. But he had no opponent on which to focus, nothing to keep him in the present tense, until it was too late. By the time Nick Faldo caught him, the pressure brought on by the proximity of what had been unthinkable at the start of the day was too great. And it was the specter of the unthinkable, and *not* his next shot, that anyone who follows golf could see being played out behind the dazed, coral-reef blue of his eyes even before it happened. Scaled down to fit my own world, that is what started to happen to me on the thirteenth tee, and that is why Sal's hands are now curled around the grips of my two longest irons, swinging them together, first slowly then faster, loosening the muscles in his wrists, shoulders and torso.

"I'll even give you the honor, old man," I say. "Fire away."

"I don't need no gifts from you, other'n the strokes I'm entitled to. I'll take the honors on seventeen, after I hand you the bag."

"Fair enough. What do you think your handicap would be?"

"I'm up to a twelve now."

"Established? Really?"

"I got software."

I should have known.

"Okay, so you get a shot on me here and another on eighteen. Let's go."

"Let's go yourself. Hit it."

The sixteenth is a 430-yard par-four that plays even longer because of its steady uphill grade. Realistically, the birdie I need is unlikely to come here, but my only thought is of this tee shot. The driver again feels like a balanced, natural extension of my own arms, and the sensation at impact is not of hitting the ball, but of slinging it with elongated limbs. It rockets out along the precise flight path I have already seen in my mind and bounds nearly to the 150-yard stakes, 280 yards away.

"That's it, huh, Sal? That's the one we've been looking for."

"Sorry. Didn't see it."

"What do you mean, you didn't see it?"

"You're spottin' for yourself off the tee now. If I watch you hit it, I'll swing too hard. It takes me three to get there anyway."

Sal puts the two irons back in the bag and takes a few tees and an old ball from the zippered pocket.

"Take a new ball, Sal." I hand him the driver.

"Nope. I'm gonna beat you with your own clubs and a dirty ball. Now, clear the tee."

The swing he puts on it is an exact replica of the two he made from the fourteenth fairway, and the ball takes off on a low straight line that carries it 220 yards down the center. He is picking the tee out of the ground before the ball lands. He slides the driver into the bag and feigns difficulty lifting it onto his shoulder. "Man, it's gonna be nice not luggin' this load down the last two."

"Pretty big talk for a man sixty yards back."

"Layin' zero."

"You're gonna need that stroke."

"You begrudgin' me?"

"Never."

"Come on, then."

Sal leads us down the blacktopped cart path and over the narrow stone bridge that crosses Fox Run Creek just in front of the ladies' tee. His gait is, as always, uneven, but his pace has quickened. By the time he reaches his ball, I am ten paces behind and thankful that his adrenaline rush has helped me to steady my own. He doesn't look at a sprinkler head for distance, nor does he appear to take into account any of the prevailing conditions. He sets the bag on its stand, pulls the three-wood and launches another perfect line drive that rolls to within ten yards of the green.

"Nice shot," I say, having just caught up.

"All I can do from here."

My tee shot is more than sixty yards beyond Sal's, just 148 yards from the front-left pin, but this is no place to go for the flag. The left-hand bunker is deep and, once out of it, the green runs downhill to the hole. I'd much rather miss right and have a long uphill putt. Then again, the seventeenth is a long par-three. I make birdie there maybe once a year. If I don't go for it here, I'll be left gunning for birdie on the long, par-five eighteenth.

"What do you think, Sal? Should I fire one at the flag here?"

"You don't get it, do you?"

"What do you mean?"

"You want to play a match, we're playin' a match. Askin' your opponent for advice in match play is automatic loss of hole, so we'll just say I didn't hear you."

"You know you get mean under pressure?"

"No pressure on *me*."

I compromise by choosing an aggressive line, then hitting a high, fading eight-iron that lands softly on the front part of the green, maybe eighteen feet right of the hole. It's a perfect spot from which to putt. I look over for Sal's reaction, but he is already halfway to his next shot. When he sets the bag down, pulls out the sand wedge and addresses the ball, I assume he's just checking his lie before deciding what to do. There are at least three ways he could play this delicate little shot. But before I can stop walking— and so comply with one of the cardinal rules of golf etiquette that some Fox Run members believe must have been chiseled into the reverse sides of the tablets Moses lugged down off the mountain—he hits a beautiful little bump-and-run that hops once on the hillside, starts rolling on a line just left of the flag, then takes the slope and dies two feet short of the hole, dead on line. I'll give him that putt for a four (a three with his stroke) and now I'll have to make mine just to tie.

"Sorry, Sal. I didn't know you were ready to hit."

"Didn't bother me."

"Obviously. Nice shot."

"Most days, I'm teein' off with about two hours of daylight left. And most of the places I play you don't get lies good enough to flop it. So I bump everything when I'm in close. And I do it quick."

Up on the green, I tell Sal to pick his ball up. Then he pulls the flag for me and I still half expect him to point out the line. He doesn't, of course, and I don't need him to. I stroke the ball perfectly and start walking after it, ready to pick it out of the bottom of the cup. But the greens have started to dampen in the early-evening air, and my ball and I both reach the hole and stop short at the same instant. I almost trip over my own feet trying not to step on it.

"Shame," Sal says. I tap in for par and look up in time to see him give my head covers a little pat before walking past the bag toward the next tee.

When I sling on the double straps, the bag feels heavy but good, pulling my shoulders back and stretching my chest out in an almost military posture. "I don't know why you're complaining," I say to Sal when I catch up. "If you'd use both straps, you'd have an easier time of it."

"From the guy who just carried it ninety feet."

"I'm just saying."

"I hate them things. I like the clubs where I can see 'em, not trailin' behind me like a papoose."

"Suit yourself."

"No, suit *yourself*. I'm done for the day."

"That so?"

"Yup."

"I assume you need everything here?" I say, referring to the length of the hole.

"Yeah. Give me the driver, caddy."

The seventeenth runs downhill, so it doesn't play all of its 230 yards, but the deep trench in the center of this double-green makes it difficult to roll it on the back half, where the pin is today. I figure Sal will have a tough time reaching it from the back tees. He gives it a good run, though, hitting yet another low liner that runs down through the dip and back up the other side. But just at the top of the far crest it loses momentum and falls back.

"Man, you're boring," I say. "Do you ever hit it crooked?"

"I'd trade you for your extra sixty yards any day."

"I might have to think about that."

"Don't."

"What's your best round ever here?"

"Sixty-eight. From the whites."

"You're kidding. When?"

"August fifteenth, nineteen-sixty. Back when I *had* that extra sixty yards."

"Did you ever do it anywhere else? Break seventy, I mean?"

"Nope. I know you folks like to think you got the toughest course around, but it's easier to go low putting on these greens than on some of the dog tracks I played, especially back then." He sees that my hands are grasping the heads of two different clubs. "You gonna hit or what?"

"I'm thinking."

"Stop it," he says, already *knowing* what I'm thinking and unable, for the moment, to control his natural impulse to help me. I am always faced with the same dilemma here. Two-iron is barely enough club to reach the green, three-wood is too much and I carry nothing in-between. But club choice isn't Sal's primary concern, nor is it mine. I have said that the fourteenth is one of my nemesis holes, and Sal knows that it is impossible for me to step onto this tee without acknowledging the seventeenth as the other. Again, difficulty plays almost no factor. It's a long par-three, but the green is enormous, as wide as any fairway on the golf course. And yet, while I can rope this same two-iron down the center of any one of those fairways, I seldom find the green with it here, and then the hole *does* become difficult. The huge twin bunkers that drop off both sides of the green are each nearly eight feet deep, and you can seldom see more than the top half of the flag when you're down inside one of them. Unlike fourteen, it's not often that I blow up with a big number here. Instead, this hole has chipped away at me over the years, sapping my confidence with one bogey after another in crucial situations, until I have almost come to expect that result. Both seventies I shot earlier this spring carry a four on the scorecard at seventeen. What I fight here is not so much fear as resignation.

I decide on the two-iron, and the shot comes off crisp and low, heading for the front right corner of the green. It even hits there and I am sure that I will be putting, but it takes an impossible kick to the right, bounces once more, then disappears over the edge and down into the trap.

"Jesus, Sal. They're going to erect a monument to me in that bunker when I die."

"That ain't the worst of it."

"No? Then what is?"

"Carryin' this bag all the way up eighteen." He grabs the putter and heads off ahead of me.

"Smart guy," I call after him, knowing that he is. He's trying to goad me into staying sharp while keeping his own game face on, and it works. Aware of the fact that I won't get a good look at the flag from my position in the bunker, I start picturing the shot as soon as I reach the fairway. There are no thoughts of the mechanics of how to execute a high, soft bunker shot, but over and over I can see it arching up and out, landing just beyond the fringe of the green with no spin at all, releasing toward the hole and turning left as it slows. I don't try to manipulate or refine the image; I just let it play. Sal is hitting his putt now, and I vaguely register the result before shuffling side-footed down the steep face of the bunker and jumping in from the overhanging lip. The green is above my head now, and if I were relying on what I could see, I would have to take another run up the hill for a look. But the shot has already been imprinted. I dig my feet into the sand, noting both texture and firmness and overlaying those qualities on the image I am seeing. Then, before I have even thought to begin the motion, the heavy-bottomed lob wedge is taking a steep plane up and away from my body and descending, from its own weight, straight down to strike with a gentle *pupp* that lifts both sand and ball up, over and out, mimicking what I have already seen. Before I can even shake free of my self-induced trance to scale the hill, Sal is yelling in spite of himself. "Go in, you son of a bitch! Go in!" Now I take the slope in two jumping strides, stumbling and going down hard on the second, my arms stretched forward and clutching at the green-level turf like a man whose extension ladder has just fallen away and left him hanging over the cornice of a flat-topped roof. But I can see it: see it take the subtle break to the left five feet from the hole; see it decelerate as if hesitating to dare what it is about to do; see it seem to gather itself and surge around the final hooked corner of the break before jolting to a stop, briefly wedged between the flagstick and the inner razored edge of packed earth, and falling out of sight.

Something resembling a Pawnee war cry issues from Sal. "Hooohooooooo!" Then he does a light-footed rain dance that incorporates snatching his own ball from the green and mine from the hole. "You gotta talk to 'er, Mikey! Don't I always say that? You son of a bitch!"

"A little help?" I am still flung over the starboard side of the S.S. *Over-Privileged*.

"Every great round's got a shot like that! Out of nowhere! I been waitin'! I admit I was beginnin' to think maybe—"

"A hand, Sal?"

"Oh, sorry. Sure." He provides some ballast while I regain my footing. Once I am standing next to him, he reaches up and tousles my hair, as if I am ten years old and six feet tall. "You son of a bitch!" Then he jogs, somewhat asymmetrically, to the spot where I have left the bag standing and throws it lightly over one shoulder. "Don't you wish your father was here?"

Epiphany is antithetical to the slow-footed workings of the average male sensitivity. Incapable of experiencing such moments of clarity in real time, we are left, most often, to recognize them in memory.

Kelly had just dropped the girls off at my parents' house for one of their increasingly frequent visits to me. She had nodded a small, unreadable greeting and started to turn, Hannah wrapping her arms around me in the doorway, Megan brushing past on her way to the TV. Something about the way Kelly held my eyes, maybe for the first time in months, before turning to go, emboldened me. Everything I thought to say sounded awkward inside my own head, and I had been instructed to stop saying I was "sorry," so I settled instead on the one thing that was the most awkward, but also the most true.

"I love you," I said to the side of her face. She turned back to me and raised an eyebrow, her unreadable look now readable as a kind of resigned impatience. Hannah, her head still buried in my midsection, looked up and smiled.

"I love you too, Daddy," she said.

"Go watch TV with your sister for a minute, sweet pea."

"Okay."

Kelly crossed her arms, resting them on her belly. "Was that supposed to make one of us feel better?"

"I don't know. It seemed like the least wrong thing to say. How do you feel?"

"Huge."

"But okay?"

"Yeah. This has been a good pregnancy. All things considered."

"Why am I still so scared? About that, I mean."

"I don't know."

"Why aren't you?"

"I don't know that either. I just know it's going to be okay this time."

We stood in silence for a moment, but she didn't move to leave. Again, nothing seemed like the right thing to say, including what I chose.

"Can you still remember why you married me?" I asked.

"Jesus. You've never been one for small talk, have you?"

"I figure I may not have long."

She was quiet, even shook her head once, slowly, and I thought she was going to leave. When she spoke, the gentleness in her voice surprised me.

"Look, Michael, it took me a long time to figure this out, and even longer to become resigned to it, but men and women just love differently. I know you love me, and I know there's more to it than what I'm about to say, but I also know that at the very core of that love, from the beginning, was the simple fact that I was a pretty girl who liked having sex with you. The fact that I turned out to be a good choice was, for you anyway, mostly luck. And that's okay. Or at least it *was* okay, when I was sure I was the *only* pretty girl having sex with you."

Chastised, I didn't insist, except to keep looking at her.

"I know," she said. "I haven't answered your question." She paused, and I sensed that she was considering not so much the answer itself, but whether it was worth wasting on me. She shrugged. "I fell in love with you mostly because I knew you'd be a good father. And I kept loving you mostly because it turned out I was right."

"Not very sexy."

"That's where you are *so* very wrong."

And then she did turn and leave.

. . .

There is a feeling of power and of calm standing on the tee of the par-five eighteenth knowing I can play it any way I want. All I need is a par, and I can make five here in my sleep. Fox Run Creek crosses at the base of the final climb to the green, 550 yards away, then turns toward us and runs the length of the right side of the hole before passing the tee, ducking under Fox Run Road and resuming its purposeful trek to feed the lake in front of the third green, where Kelly once made her extended series of determined deposits. The fairway is broad and inviting though, with plenty of room to avoid the creek. To be safe, I could even hit three-wood, and Sal looks down at my hand as it rests on the head cover.

"You ever hit three-wood here?" he asks.

"Not really."

"You know what I always say."

"What's that?"

"Hit the fuckin' driver."

So I do, and it sails high and lazy in the thickening air. Sal, who I don't think has ever hit one high and lazy in his life, hits a video facsimile of every shot I have seen him hit today. It bounds along the left side on a line with mine but fifty yards short. There is no more competitive chatter from Sal. It seems that for him the match ended when my ball fell into the hole on the seventeenth green, and that he is playing now simply because he can. He lays up well short of where the creek crosses the fairway with his second shot, and after my second clears the water with thirty yards to spare, he lands his third just short of the green and rolls it up and on. He hands me the sand wedge I will need for my last full swing of the day.

Our pace slows to a savoring stroll, and I pull a windshirt from my bag against the chill. Someone, perhaps waiting for a dinner partner to arrive, is watching our approach from the ornate wrought-iron railing of the Clubhouse terrace, but other than this disinterested observer, we are the lone outdoor inhabitants of this wide expanse of acreage. Even the caddy-master appears to have been sent home early, a sure sign that the season is almost over. Sal will have to wait until tomorrow to be paid.

As we approach and then cross the creek, our soft-bottomed shoes impress silent, wet prints on the paved bridge deck. The sun has not yet set but has fallen behind the surrounding hills, and the light has entered that phase when it seems to come up through the ground and luminesce from anything holding to it. We come off the bridge together, and the figure on the terrace leaves the guard rail and begins to descend the same path Sal followed to meet me three hours ago. It is Kelly, of course. Though the fact that you have guessed this, and the fact that she may be here more for Sal than for me, doesn't make her appearance, leaning back into the slope for balance, any less astounding to me. I look at Sal and he sees the question. "At the turn," he says. "When you were on fire. To tell the truth, it didn't sound like she was comin'." When I still fail to articulate a sensible comment, Sal says, "You can take it out of my tip, the call."

"Yeah, sure," I reply, but over my shoulder because I am moving more quickly now. By the time I reach my ball, Kelly is crossing the practice green and I raise the head of the club in a hesitant greeting. She keeps walking. I take a hurried stance and look up once at the white flag that seems to glow, diffused and pulsing in the diminishing light. I swing and cut the damp turf and the ball spreads and smolders too as it rises, like fireworks going up. *Guess what color it's going to be, sweet pea—hurry up—Daddy guesses red.* But I look down and away before it explodes, before it descends, and there is my wife, standing above me behind the green, her arms crossed over her belly not in resistance but in a posture of waiting, of possibility, and suddenly the present tense, at least this present tense, is emptied of all meaning.

· · ·

There is an antique glider-rocker in the corner of our bedroom that my mother gave us the day Megan was born. During the first month of her life, Megan slept in a white lace-trimmed bassinet at the foot of our bed and, every two or three hours, in response to her gentle, newborn cries, Kelly would lift her from there and nurse her in the rocker. We joined with other first-time parents in lamenting the loss of sleep, the loss of freedom. But there was a rhythm to those early nights, a sense of purpose in our wakefulness that brought a perfect peace that nothing since has ever duplicated for me. I would rise with Kelly every time, almost stubbornly, determined that this new being would see that her cries brought my face as well. And then I would follow them to the chair and cup Megan's tiny head as she latched on to Kelly's swollen breast. Kelly would wince and blow air in short bursts to combat the strength of those first, desperate pulls. Then her whole body would yield and soften, and the rocking would begin. My utility, such that it was, having ended, I would kiss Megan's temple, and perhaps the tiny hand that always rested on Kelly's breast, and climb back into bed to fall asleep to the muffled *click-click, click-click* of the rocker.

The rocker was never moved to the nursery that would later become Megan's bedroom, nor was it moved to Hannah's room six years later. We never even talked about it. It had been waiting for us in that corner the day we brought Megan home from the hospital, and that is where it has stayed for fourteen years. Thousands of stories have been read in that chair, hundreds of bad dreams and skinned knees and hurt feelings rocked easily into memory by something so simple as the pendular motion of human touch. When do we outgrow that kind of healing? Perhaps we know, instinctively, when it will no longer have any effect. Maybe it only works on mistakes and injuries of innocence.

Six months after we had buried Jessica, I was awakened in the middle of a muggy August night by the sound of that rocker and the muffled cries that interrupted its rhythm. We had been doing well, or so we were told. Recently, we had even been asked to speak to a few groups of couples whose losses were more immediate than our own. One of those talks had just taken place the previous evening, and many had approached us afterward to say that we had helped. I watched Kelly smile at each of them, clasping their hands, but she had been quiet on the way home.

"What is it, hon?" I whispered, sitting up in bed. She didn't answer, nor did she stop rocking. I got out of bed and went to sit on the floor at her feet. We had passed many nights like this, early on. Lately, like I said, we had been doing better.

I knew not to look at her, not to push. Kelly cannot be coaxed into catharsis. I wrapped my fingers around one of her calves, the muscle like a tennis ball, and began gently kneading it. Then I waited. Gradually, I could hear her gain control of her breathing.

Finally, she asked softly, "Did you hear what that last woman said?" She was still rocking.

"No. I'm not sure."

"She said we had helped her to place her tragedy in *perspective*. She said she was starting to see how insignificant it really was." Kelly started to cry softly again.

"Mm. I remember."

"I never want to help anybody see that."

"I don't think that's what she meant, hon." I could hear the air handler click on below us, outside, and its hum was followed by a silent, almost instantaneous cooling in the room. "I don't think she knew how to say what she meant."

"Maybe."

Kelly stopped rocking. I can't explain why, but I sensed that there was something else. Twins often have a kind of telepathic empathy for each other that science has tried to explain through genetics. But I don't think that twins have anything on the long-married, and I tend to believe that their empathy is borne purely out of proximity. Spend enough time huddled close to another human being, and some of the electrical impulses that carry your thoughts and horrors and urges across one synapse after another are bound to begin hurdling that short, receptive gap. Gradually, the journey becomes familiar, natural, and intuition becomes merely an extension of self-awareness.

I stood, and Kelly let me pull her up. I sat in her place, and then she made herself small in my lap. Her cheek was wet against my bare chest. We started to rock.

"I wouldn't take her," she said. Her body went slack when she said this, and she began to cry with a sound that manifested a pain I could never imagine or name.

"Hey, shh. Who, sweetie? Who wouldn't you take?"

"Jessica. They tried to hand her to me, but I wouldn't take her. I was too afraid. She was so tiny. Then they took her away. I never held my baby. Michael, I never rocked our baby."

"Shh, honey. Yes you did."

"No. They tried to give her to me."

"Yes you did, honey. Every night. Right here." I was holding her head as tightly against me as I dared, as if I might absorb her grief. "Right here. Reading to Hannah. Remember? You rocked her to sleep every night of her life."

You can choose whether or not to believe this next part, but when I came up over the rise I wouldn't even have noticed my ball sitting within ten feet of the flag if it hadn't been directly in my path to Kelly. I bent and swiped it up as I passed. Then, not knowing how to begin talking to this person whose love I wanted fiercely to deserve, I placed it in the palm of the hand she had turned over between us. She looked at it, rolling it from the base of her palm out to her fingertips and back again, as if examining it for flaws.

"What was that putt for?" she asked finally, sparing me from having to begin what we would say.

"Birdie. And sixty-eight."

"No way you three-putt from there."

"Never can tell."

"You had nothing to lose."

"No?"

She closed her hand around the ball and tucked it in the pocket of the corduroy jumper that fell heavily from her shoulders, then seemed to reach out to me from her midsection, weightless.

"Where are the girls?"

"Home."

"Our home?"

"I'm not sure yet."

"That sounded different from no."

"Maybe."

Sal was on the green behind me now, but I felt him keeping his distance.

"Who's with them?"

"Just Megan. She said you once promised her that when she started high school she could look after Hannah on her own."

"I did."

"She's also begun to fancy herself precocious."

"Isn't she?"

"God, I hope not. This family needs a blissful underachiever in the worst way."

"I could be that again. I think I want to be that again."

"It isn't time for promises yet, Michael."

"No."

In the long silence, the outside lights of the Beason compound came on and turned the dew all around us to cut glass. Sal approached quietly, slid the bag from his shoulder and set it down next to me.

"I putted out for five and the win," he almost whispered. "It's all yours." He patted the head covers. "Night, Mr. B. Night, Mrs. B."

"Good night, Sal," we said together, then watched as he crossed the practice green and turned, unburdened, up the hill.

Epilogue

I ronically, Kelly has always favored writers who cast their protag-
onists as far out as they dare before reeling them back in, tri-
umphant and redeemed. But there is very little redemption in real
life, mostly just second chances, and I got one of those. Only time
will show whether true redemption will follow. On December 18,
2005, the four-month anniversary of my exile and eight weeks after
Sal took the healing process into his own callused hands, I was invited to move back into our home. A few days later, Melinda Claire
Benedict came head-first into the world, peered up at her father and
voiced several months' worth of pent-up disapproval. Those protes-
tations would continue, almost unceasingly, for sixteen weeks.
Strangely, Hannah was often the only one who could quiet her. She
slid eagerly from the role of the doted-upon to that of caregiver,
and we moved the rocking chair closer to the foot of our bed so that
she could push off and glide silently back and forth, her index finger perpetually in the grip of a tiny fist.

At the baptismal rehearsal, our Protestant minister looked at us
with suspicion when informed that two people named "Hank" and
"Sal" would act as godparents, and he didn't appear to be any less
perplexed when he met them. But as is often the case with religious
types, he preferred blissful ignorance to awkward enlightenment
and simply scribbled the names in his prayer book, unsure who was
who. It was just as well for the good father that one of the adults,
and not Hannah, was to hold Melinda during the actual service,
since her caterwauling helped to render the introduction of the

godparents (along with the remainder of the proceedings) virtually inaudible to the congregation, and thus obscured what might have been a few uncomfortable moments for the father.

Or was it my imagination? Could she really have been protesting so loudly that the father's lips, no more than an arm's length from me, seemed to move without words? And was it also my imagination that in that clamorous silence, my daughter turned her tiny face to me, and that her cries took on a meaning only I could discern? She seemed, to my newly enlightened way of hearing, to be asking a familiar question of me, if more vociferously than others had posed it in the past:

Do you know what's *at stake* here, Daddy?—was what she said.

And finally, I could answer and quiet her:

Yes, I do.

Acknowledgments

The author would like to express his thanks for the faith and assistance of Carolyn Carlson, Clare Ferraro and, especially, Jane Dystel and Miriam Goderich, who loved this book longer than any agents should have to before getting paid. Gratitude also to early readers Traci Beard, Laura Hilgers, Scott Gelotti and, most of all, Melinda Beard: lifelong grammar hawk, champion of understatement, slayer of cliché, and the best amateur/maternal editor ~~in this world or any other on God's Green Earth of her time~~ around.